COLD HARD TRUTH

COLD HARD TRUTH

ANNE GREENWOOD BROWN

Albert Whitman & Company
Chicago, Illinois

Library of Congress Control Number: 2017952188

Text copyright © 2018 by Anne Greenwood Brown
First published in the United States of America in 2018
by Albert Whitman & Company
ISBN 978-0-8075-8083-7 (hardcover)
ISBN 978-0-8075-8085-1 (paperback)

Printed in the United States of America
10 9 8 7 6 5 4 3 2 1 BP 22 21 20 19 18

Cover photo copyright © by Arthur Hidden—stock.adobe.com
Design by Ellen Kokontis

For more information about Albert Whitman & Company,
visit our website at www.albertwhitman.com.

For Greg (my mighty #6)

CHAPTER ONE

PIGEON

Emmie O'Brien knew she was supposed to run. But despite all of Nick's yelling to *Go! Go! Go!* her muscles locked—stuck in place. The sight of the unconscious man behind the counter of the SuperAmerica made her think of B. J., except that this one was younger. Not really a man yet. More her age. It wasn't supposed to happen like this.

"Let's go, let's go!" Nick yelled as he emptied the cash register into a plastic bag. "Why are you still standing there? Get the car started, Pigeon. We gotta get the hell out of here."

Finally, Emmie's feet started to move. Just a few tripping steps, then she broke into a run and jumped behind the wheel of the rusted-out sedan.

A few seconds behind her, Nick threw himself into the passenger seat and tossed the bulging bag into the back. Emmie's hands shook as she fumbled with the keys. She'd had her license for only a month, and it took her two tries to get out of first gear without killing the engine. She might have done better if it wasn't a stick or if Nick could have stopped screaming at her for just one damn minute.

"Hurry! Jesus, hurry!"

When she finally peeled out of the parking lot, she oversteered and jumped the curb. The undercarriage made a horrible scraping sound along the concrete before the car bounced back onto the road and leveled out.

"Watch out!" Nick yelled. "Are you trying to get us killed?"

"Stop yelling at me! You're scaring me."

They flew down Osgood, weaving in and out of traffic, headed for the highway. Up ahead, the light turned yellow, and Emmie instinctively took her foot off the gas.

"What are you doing?" Nick cried, his voice rising in panic, his body first turning to look behind them, then bracing against the dashboard. "Don't stop!"

"But the light's going to turn red." Emmie's heart pounded in her ears as the adrenaline beat a path through her body. What was she supposed to do? She couldn't calm her thoughts. She needed to calm her thoughts. She could fix this if she could just think.

By now, the light had turned. The cars ahead of her came to a stop, but she was still going too fast. Nick reached over and jerked the wheel, pulling the sedan in a careening path onto the gravel shoulder, kicking up dust. The old sedan's tires caught in a rutted groove, and Emmie slammed on the brake. The engine stuttered, then died.

"Dammit!" Nick slapped the back of her head and she shot forward, hitting her nose on the steering wheel. Bright-white stars burst in her field of vision.

"Get it started! Start the goddamn car!"

"Do you want to drive?" she yelled back. Tears pricked at the backs of Emmie's eyes, but she wouldn't let them fall. She just wanted to get the hell out of there and out of the car. In fact, she never wanted to see this car again. She wanted to go home. Wherever that was going to be.

2

"Get in back," Nick said.

"Gladly!"

That's when they heard the sirens, already close, with red lights swirling not a quarter mile behind. There was no chance for a getaway because Emmie already had her door open and one foot on the pavement. Nick was still in the passenger seat. He cursed and threw his coat over the bag of money, like that was going to do any good.

This was all Emmie's fault. None of this would be happening if she hadn't begged her dad to let her go live with her mom. All his strict rules made better sense now. Yep. This was all her fault, and Nick wasted no time in telling her how strongly he agreed.

"You'll pay for this," he said through clenched teeth. "Believe it. You'll pay."

Emmie swallowed and shook off the shivery terror that skimmed over her shoulders. She was going to jail. She, Emmie O'Brien, lawyer's daughter, was going to jail. Strangely, that knowledge brought the calm she was looking for. It would be a reprieve from her mom. An escape from Nick. "Maybe it'll be all right."

She thought she heard Nick make a scoffing sound, but what did it matter anymore?

* * *

SEVERAL MONTHS LATER

Emmie sat in a courtroom thinking about the time she'd played Betsy Ross in the second-grade play. She'd had only one line: "I've made you a flag, George." It should have been easy to get the words out. Instead, she hurled all over the Stars and Stripes, putting the entire American Revolution on indefinite hold.

She'd vowed never again to be so on display, but sometimes you weren't given much of a choice. This time, there were considerably fewer eyes on her, but the stage fright was just as real, and the weight of those eyes was no less heavy. Angie and Jimmy glared up at her from the front row. Frankie would have been there, too, but there was a warrant out for his arrest so he couldn't take the chance.

Emmie fidgeted on the witness stand, swinging her feet. Seeing her former friends' hatred for her was bad enough, but there were two people whose gaze she felt even more keenly: Nick, no longer in an orange jumpsuit but dressed in a neatly pressed suit, his eyes full of rage at her betrayal. And Tom O'Brien, her father, whose eyes flickered back and forth from fear to pain to guilt. That last look was the one that hurt her the most, and it was about to get worse.

Aunt Bridget, who Emmie'd gone to live with since being released from the juvenile detention center six months ago, smiled encouragingly. It had been a social worker who recommended Emmie live "with a supportive female presence for a while in case she needed someone to talk to about all she'd been through."

Aunt Bridget never pushed. And Emmie hadn't talked. That was about to change because she had no more choice in the matter. Testifying against Nick was part of her plea agreement, and her father knew everything already.

After today, Emmie would be moving back home with him after two years away. There would be no more hiding the truth.

The prosecutor *tap, tap, tapped* his pen against a yellow pad. "So the defendant, Nicholas Peters, had you not only delivering his product but, at the end, driving his getaway car in exchange for keeping your mother supplied with methamphetamines?"

Emmie nodded.

"I'm sorry, Miss O'Brien, but the court reporter can't take down nonverbal responses. Was that a yes?"

"Yes." Her voice came out as a rasp.

The prosecutor shifted the papers on the table in front of him. Emmie knew what questions were coming next. She'd been told. She'd prepared. Still, it wasn't something she should ever have to say in front of her father—even a father who was a lawyer himself and had to listen to this kind of shit all the time. By the look on his face, it was clearly different when your own daughter was laying out the filth.

The prosecutor cleared his throat. "How else did Mr. Peters make you pay?"

Emmie shook the images of her and Nick from her head. She sensed, rather than saw, her father lean forward, bowing his head and putting elbows to knees. He couldn't look at her. And maybe that was just as well. Even if after Nick's trial was over, they were going to try living together once more. Would they ever be able to look at each other again?

Turned out, they could. Once Emmie's testimony was done and the court recessed, Tom O'Brien put both hands on Emmie's shoulders and leaned down and in. "That was tough. I know. But you did it. It's over. And I am so proud."

Emmie kept her body taut and her mind still, but when she caught the tears welling in Aunt Bridget's eyes, Emmie dared to smile a little. If only on the inside.

CHAPTER TWO

STARTING OVER. AGAIN.

THREE DAYS LATER

Last night, when Emmie fell asleep in her father's house—the first time she'd slept in her own bed since freshman year—she'd wondered if she'd wake up thinking the last eighteen months had been one seriously nasty dream. Instead, she woke and got dressed to a healthy serving of reality, spooned up by her father yelling into the phone.

"Woman, you're daft if you think you can be at her meeting tomorrow. You've got a bloody no-contact order to contend with." Her father's Irish accent—lessened by twenty years in the States—always came on strong when he was talking to his ex-wife.

Emmie stood in her doorway, straining to listen. She hadn't heard her mom's voice in months, given the no-contact order and her mom's current residence in a rehab center. It was a strange new reality. Emmie didn't like it, but she was largely to blame for the current situation, and it could have been a whole helluva lot worse. Still, maybe her dad would let her at least say "hi."

Emmie grabbed her bag and ran down to the kitchen, where her father was still fully engaged in his rant. "She's back in my custody now. You stay away from our daughter and work your program. I'm not making any promises until that's done."

He hung up the phone like the receiver had personally offended him, turned abruptly, and—when he locked eyes with Emmie—exhaled, letting all the tension escape.

He tapped Emmie's *own* court order, which was affixed to the fridge with a magnet, and said, "The terms of your probation will be your only house rules."

She gave a quick nod of acknowledgment because there was nothing more to say about that. She'd be having no contact with her mom until a judge decided otherwise.

A car horn beeped in the driveway just as the phone rang again. Emmie's father exploded like a powder keg meeting a match as he snatched up the receiver, "Dammit, woman. Quit calling. What part of 'no contact' don't you understand? One more time, and I'm notifying the police."

"Dad?" Emmie's chest constricted.

He slammed the receiver down. "What?"

"Yeah. Um. So, Marissa's here." She pulled a pink knit hat over her head while being careful not to let her father see the nervousness that shivered down her spine. She hadn't spoken to her best friend in over a year.

Her dad's forehead furrowed.

"You know," Emmie said as if he needed reminding. "To pick me up for school?"

"Oh, right," her father said, even though he'd been the one to orchestrate this little reunion. There were few people he was willing to trust 100 percent with Emmie, so he'd called Marissa's mom last night to arrange the ride. "My daughter needs to get back into normal life as quickly as possible," Emmie'd heard him say.

Emmie's father crossed the kitchen toward her. She thought he meant to give her a hug, and as usual, the prospect of physical contact made her shoulders stiffen.

What she was bracing for here, with her own father, in her own kitchen, she didn't know. She hated her reaction, and she wished she could take it back, but there was no helping it now. Her father had seen it, and it had stopped him mid-step. The corners of his eyes tightened as if he'd been stabbed with a pin.

"Have a good first day back," he said. "And good luck."

Emmie gave him a curt nod, then gasped as she stepped outside into the subzero air. She buried her face in her scarf and hugged her coat to her chest. Another six inches had fallen overnight, and she shuffled her way across the unshoveled driveway to Marissa's pea-green station wagon. Judging by the tracks, it looked like she'd skidded to a stop, barely missing the O'Briens' garbage can.

Marissa had been Emmie's best friend since they were kids. Despite the snow, the very thought of her could bring to mind the taste of cherry popsicles and the smell of newly cut grass. Still, Emmie wasn't sure about the status of their friendship.

After she had moved out of her father's house to go live with her mom, she'd only called Marissa a few times before stopping altogether. There would be consequences. Radio silence was the death knell to the best of friendships.

Emmie took a breath and slipped inside Marissa's warm car. It smelled like the same fruity perfume Marissa had been wearing since eighth grade. At least a hundred crumpled gum wrappers filled the cup holders and littered the floor. It was weird seeing Marissa behind the wheel of a car. They'd both gotten their licenses while Emmie was away.

"Hey," Marissa said as she folded a piece of Juicy Fruit into her mouth. She seemed nervous too. "It's good to see you." She put the car

8

in reverse and turned to look over her right shoulder. Marissa looked thinner than Emmie remembered, and she had a new piercing: a tiny diamond stud in her nose.

"You too," Emmie said, ignoring the stiffness of the conversation. "Thanks for the ride. You didn't have to."

"Sure I did. I wanted to."

"Okay, thanks. And...um...I like your nose."

"I like your hair," Marissa said with a reminiscent smile.

Marissa and Emmie had done the "grass is always greener" commentary on their hair since sixth grade because Emmie would have liked nothing more than to have Marissa's long, shiny blond hair, and for whatever reason, Marissa preferred Emmie's dark brown, completely unmanageable curls.

Without warning, Nick's voice echoed in Emmie's head: *Have you ever thought about straightening your hair? You'd look way hotter if your hair was straight.*

"So," Marissa said. She pulled into the street and shifted into drive, but she kept her foot on the brake. She looked down at the steering wheel and then over at Emmie. "So this is weird, huh?"

"Yeah. Kinda." Marissa didn't know anything about Emmie's time away: her mom's addiction, Nick, the robbery, the trial. Secrets were better than lies, and sometimes secrets were the best way to keep one's friends. Or *friend*, as the case may be.

"I was worried you weren't ever going to come back." A small smile crossed Marissa's lips before disappearing again. "So are you ready for this?" She took her foot off the brake, and they started down the snow-packed road.

"Do people even know I'm back?" When Emmie said *people*, she didn't have any faces in mind. All of their middle-school friends had scattered in ninth grade, finding new cliques, new interests, and new identities. Because Emmie had missed all of her sophomore year in White Prairie, and now half of her junior year, the few new people she'd met in ninth grade were barely memorable.

"A handful do." Then Marissa raised her perfectly waxed eyebrows. "But I should warn you. I've heard a few theories about where you've been, and some people have fantastic imaginations."

Emmie recognized the attempt to rekindle the friendly banter of their past. She turned to face Marissa, and the seat belt cut across her shoulder. "Tell me."

Marissa scrunched her nose. "How do you feel about being a mother?"

"A what?"

"Some people think you left because you were pregnant."

"What?" Emmie drew her eyebrows together, disbelieving, but a second later she took a mental step back. "Well, I guess it's not a totally off-the-wall theory."

Her initial surprise had more to do with the fact that parenthood had never crossed her mind. She got a weird feeling in her gut when she thought about some kid putting her through the hell she'd put her dad through—or worse, maybe she'd turn out like her mom.

So much for slipping quietly, seamlessly back into normal life. Why did she even think it was remotely possible?

"Oh, and by the way," Marissa said, glancing over nervously, "the theory goes, you delivered an alien baby."

This time Emmie turned her head so fast she kinked a nerve in her neck. "What?"

"That last part was something I heard Kelly Winkler say. She said that the only way someone would sleep with you would be if he was an—"

Emmie groaned. "I don't want to hear it." She'd known Kelly Winkler since third grade, so she could imagine the rest. Actually, the suggestion that she'd been physically attractive to aliens might have been one of the nicest things Kelly'd ever said about her. It almost made her laugh.

But she had no right to laugh. Not when her family's life was still upside down. Not when it was all her fault.

CHAPTER THREE

JUST DESSERTS

As soon as Marissa parked in the high school parking lot, Emmie's body began to move mechanically. Undoing her seat belt. Opening her door. Grabbing her bag. She was back at White Prairie. Really doing this. Breathe, she thought. You are just your average high school junior. *Go, Jackrabbits! Rah!*

But as Emmie and Marissa marched from the parking lot to the school, their heads bent against the wind, Marissa grabbed Emmie's arm and made her stop. "Are you really okay?"

Emmie forced a smile, but she knew she wasn't fooling her friend. Marissa could read voice and body language like the rest of the world read the side of a cereal box. In a second, she could know what someone was made of. That's why Emmie had to be so careful with her. She couldn't afford to scare away her only potential ally.

"Yeah. It's just weird being back," she said.

"Listen, Em..." Marissa released a long, thin exhale through pursed lips. "I'm really trying here. I mean, you *are* my best friend." Her eyes were plaintive. "At least you *were*. And I want us to be that again, but…Can you fill me in on what the hell's been going on with you?"

A flutter ran across Emmie's stomach. Confide in her only friend, or save her from the ugly truth? Emmie shrugged. "There's really not that much to tell."

"Right," Marissa deadpanned.

When they finally reached the building, Marissa held the door open and Emmie practically leaped across the threshold, eager for the promise of heat. The faint smell of chlorine from the school's swimming pool met her nose. Physically, the place hadn't changed. The clock on the wall. The posters. The crowd of people. The din of easy conversations. The cloud of drugstore cologne. And yet, despite its familiarity, she might as well have landed on an alien planet.

Keep cool, she thought. *Be inconspicuous.* And that's when the worn heel of her wet boot hit the newly polished tile.

Emmie's ankle turned. Her foot shot out in front of her while her arms clawed at the air. *Shit!* She was airborne.

For just a second, she would have sworn she was in suspended animation—frozen cartoonlike in space, staring up at the ceiling. Mentally, she prepared for impact.

Instead, what followed was a flash of blue-and-white, the glimpse of a wristwatch with a cracked face, and finally the strange scent of cloves and…laundry soap? Then something solid caught her from behind, and the world was right side up again.

She should have said thanks. She knew she was supposed to say thanks. But the feeling of a stranger's fingers wrapped tightly around her hips made the thank-you come out as "Don't touch me!" And then a second later as "Seriously, *please*. Let go of me."

But whoever had caught her didn't let go. At least not immediately. "Steady now," a low, rich voice said just behind her ear. The breath that came with it was warm and tickled the edge of her ear.

"I got it," Emmie said as she twisted violently in the stranger's hold. *Nick is going to see. He'll make me pay.* Of course, there was no Nick. Nick was in prison.

The hands released her, and when Emmie turned, her eyes landed on a blue-and-white hockey jersey covering broad, muscled shoulders. *Oh God.* It was worse than she'd thought.

White Prairie High School had been in the hockey state tournament—both guys' *and* girls' teams—for at least a decade, and usually they won the trophy. The players were an exclusive group, and Emmie remembered people acting like there was a force field around them. They all walked around like God's gifts to the world.

The last thing any of them needed was a hero complex. This one in particular because he was tall and *ridiculously* built for a high school guy. He probably went through his day throwing his muscle around. His dark, uncombed hair fell over his eyes as he reached down and handed Emmie her backpack.

"You're welcome," he said with a playful bit of sarcasm, which sucked. Emmie'd always admired people who could pull off sarcasm without sounding like a dick. She didn't want to like anything about this guy.

He said, "Try to be more careful next time," and then he was on his way, yelling, "Jordy! Wait up!" In all likelihood, Emmie was already a distant memory.

Emmie watched him go, realizing she'd never really looked at his face. She'd been too distracted by the rest of him (not to mention her humiliation). The guy high-fived his teammate, who wore dark-rimmed glasses and had his hair shaved into a curly top fade.

The two of them wore the same blue jersey and had similar swaggers, but there was definitely something different about the guy who'd caught her. Maybe it was the way he held his body, as if he was carrying a very heavy weight. It was a posture Emmie was used to seeing. Like every time she looked in a mirror.

"Wow," Marissa said. "Max Shepherd! That was cuh-razy. You okay?"

Emmie didn't know if Marissa was commenting on her near-concussion or the fact that a hockey player had just spoken to her like they were of the same species. Before Emmie could respond, Marissa was waving at two girls who were quickly approaching.

"Sarah," Marissa said, addressing a girl with a light brown braid and circular tan lines around her eyes, "remember I told you about my friend Emmie? Emmie, this is Sarah. She just got back from Vail. She doesn't usually look like a raccoon. And this is Olivia," she said, indicating a tall black girl with natural hair and mascara smudged under her eyes.

"Looks like there's a hockey game tonight," Olivia said.

"Yeah," Sarah said. "I noticed their matching costumes."

"We should go," Marissa said. "Everyone's going. What do you think, Em? Want to go? It would be a good opportunity for you to reintroduce yourself to the fascinating world of White Prairie High."

"I don't know." Emmie didn't feel the need to support a bunch of egomaniacs. In fact, the whole thing seemed so trivial. Not like the real world. In the real world, people didn't care about sports. They cared about having enough money for their next fix, even if they didn't have cab fare to get to their probation hearing.

In the real world, B. J. Aldrich OD'd ten months ago. Right on Nick's kitchen floor. Emmie looked down at the tiles beneath her feet, shuddering, as if she could see B. J. lying there facedown. Shirtless. Faded, threadbare jeans. Track-marked arms lying awkwardly by his sides.

"You got to go, girl. Everybody goes," Olivia said.

"I'd have to check with my dad," Emmie said. With a little luck, he'd say she should stay home until she was more settled, except...*Hmmm.*

What was with the smile of victory playing across Marissa's mouth? Ah, shit. "My dad's already okay'd it, hasn't he?"

Marissa laughed. "Talked about it last night with my mom. I'll pick you up at seven."

CHAPTER FOUR

GAME FACE

THAT EVENING

Max Shepherd hauled his hockey bag out of the jeep and wheeled it through the ice-rutted parking lot toward the rink. The ground was slippery, which made him think about the girl in the hallway. Actually, a lot of things had brought her to mind today. He couldn't shake the sensation of her hip bones pressed beneath his fingertips or the fear in her eyes.

"Dude," Chris said, holding the door for him. Chris Daniels had a lion's mane of thick blond hair, and he shook it back from his face. "Did you see the sign on Jefferson's bus back there? Let's whup their asses."

Max checked the door with his hip and wheeled his bag through the entry. "No problem. We got this."

Jordy slipped his glasses into his coat pocket and gave Max a nod. When you were the White Prairie Jackrabbits, you had to put up with a lot of crap signs from opposing teams. Tonight, Jefferson boasted one of the longest signs Max had ever seen. It stretched the entire length of their bus: Awwwwwww. Look at the Cute Lil' Bunny Wabbits.

Regardless, the Jackrabbits held their chins high and swaggered their way to the home-team locker room. Their record made any teasing easier to take. These cute lil' bunnies had won the state championship seven of the last ten years, and Jefferson hadn't even made the tournament last year. Besides, what was Jefferson even talking about? They were the freakin' Mariners. *Oooo. Scary.*

Jordy held the locker room door open. Inside, it smelled like stale sweat, feet, and burned rubber. The seven juniors on the team were already there. The twins, Brock and Brady, too. While Chris and Jordy unzipped their bags, Max sat beside them on the bench and bowed his head, visualizing the game—visualizing himself pushing against the ice with his blades, trapping an opponent against the boards, definitely *not* visualizing himself in the penalty box.

He grabbed his phone and reread his dad's text from earlier that morning: Play clean. Love, Dad. *Play clean, play clean, play clean. This time, please, play clean.*

His meditation was interrupted by the arrival of their team captain, John "Tack" Tackenberg. "Boys ready? Suit up!"

Nut cup, shin pads, navy-and-white-striped socks, breezers. Max shoved his feet into his skates. He was feeling good. Better than good. Shoulder pads, elbow pads, jersey. It still smelled like his mom's laundry soap.

Some of the guys were superstitious and wore the same socks—unwashed—to every game. By this halfway point in the season, you knew exactly who those guys were. Max was of the opposite mind. Fresh clothes meant a fresh start. Forget the mistakes of the last game. Start clean. *Play clean.*

Coach Polzinski came in and looked around the room, doing a head count. "I want you to keep your heads in the game. You can beat Jefferson, but not if you think you've already beat 'em. Skate hard. Give it one hundred and ten percent. Now, Shepherd—"

"Yes, Coach!" The muscles in Max's legs bunched with anticipation for the ice.

"Find the middle, Shepherd." Max knew what he meant. It was a metaphor Coach had used with him ever since last year. Ever since...

They both knew that Max's emotions swung like a pendulum, and somewhere in the middle was the sweet spot. If Max played too hot, he'd be in the penalty box in no time. But if he played too cool, he wouldn't have an impact on the ice.

"I'll find the middle," Max said. "I promise."

"All right." Coach grabbed Max's shoulder and gave him a shake. "Finish up. Let's hit the ice."

Max grabbed his phone from his cubby and read his dad's text one more time for good measure. Play clean. Clean but hard. Clean, but not cautious. Win.

He shoved his hands into his gloves, pushed his helmet down over his head and grabbed his stick, then one by one, they hopped through the swinging door and BAM! Max hit the ice. And he was alive. So very alive.

Taking three running steps, he found his stride. He carved the ice, pushing it behind him with long, powerful strokes that made him feel a little high. The crowd roared, leaping to its feet and stomping on the metal bleachers until it sounded like they'd collapse.

The band played, and classmates hoisted at least a dozen hand-painted signs into the air: SINK THE MARINERS. BOARD THE MARINERS. SPANK THE MARINERS' BOOTY. Max grinned at that one and pointed his gloved hand at the girl holding it. She screamed and jumped up and down, waving the sign even higher.

The team skated the perimeter, twice around in warm-up laps that made Max's muscles burn, priming them for more. He breathed deeply. Rink air. Cold and heady. He spotted his parents in their usual second-row spots, and beside them...a girl in a pink beanie, the knit cap slouched over dark curly hair.

He would never have noticed her except that she looked completely bored while everyone around her was cheering. She looked like she was waiting in a dentist's office. This was his life, and she acted like it was nothing. How could anyone be so calm and unaffected?

And then he recognized her. It was the girl. The girl he'd caught in the hallway. He couldn't really see her eyes, but he remembered her hair and that hat. Her lips were set in a firm straight line. Yep. She was definitely bored. Ha, he thought. I'll get you on your feet before the end of the game.

The puck dropped, and Max was in the zone.

CHAPTER FIVE

KNOW NOTHING

Emmie knew very little about hockey. As in she knew nothing about hockey. The whole game seemed like a clumsy dance routine with bulky bodies randomly climbing over the boards to skate around in circles before trading off with the next round of clowns. A freakin' worthless circus if there ever was one.

For a second, she wished she'd brought a book, but then, sometime in the middle of the third period, she could feel the tension grow. The players were doing a lot less skating and a lot more punching, especially when the ref wasn't looking. Marissa and the other girls were leaning forward. The crowd on both sides of the ice was yelling and pointing and groaning at calls that should have been made.

"Put your glasses on, ref!"

"Can you believe that call?"

Hockey sticks spanked the ice. The plexiglass rattled as players were checked into the boards, and the players who weren't on the ice pounded their gloves against the wood. The whole place was thunderous.

That's when one of the other team's players—Number Sixteen—

came up alongside one of the White Prairie guys and slashed the back of his knees with his stick. The White Prairie player's head jerked up, and his legs crumbled. Emmie could hear him howling in agony even from where she sat. It was bad. Really bad. You didn't have to know anything about hockey to know that had been a vicious cheap shot.

Everyone in the stands was pointing and yelling in protest. The whole White Prairie bench was leaning over the boards yelling, but still the clock didn't stop.

"He's in," said the man sitting to Emmie's right. "Come on, son." He and his wife leaned forward. "Play clean," they both said softly under their breath.

Whoever their son was, he was "in" all right. He didn't go for his position or for the puck; he went for Jefferson's Number Sixteen. Emmie hoped the Jefferson player liked pain, because it was clear this couple's son wanted him to hurt.

The couple clutched each other's hands as if that could stop what was about to happen, but their son was like a cement truck at full speed hitting a concrete wall. When he slammed Sixteen's body against the boards from behind, he laid him out. Holy hell, he laid him out.

Everyone in the stands, including Emmie, jumped to their feet.

Number Sixteen's skates went out in front of him and his head snapped back, yanking his body into a backward arch. He landed faceup on the ice with a sickening thud.

The whistle blew.

"*No!*" the man next to Emmie cried out in dismay.

The Jefferson kid lay on the ice. He didn't move. Emmie couldn't even tell if he was breathing. She'd seen people lie still like that, and the image sucked all the air out of her.

The crowd slowly sank onto the bleachers in horror and disbelief.

The White Prairie coach was yelling. "Shep! You can't keep doing this! What were you thinking?"

The couple's son skated to the penalty box, ripped off his helmet, and hung his head.

The Jefferson trainers shuffled onto the ice in their shoes, crouching beside their player who was still flat on his back. A long moment passed before they slowly helped the kid to sit. The crowd started to slow clap. Only then did the kid in the penalty box lift his head.

The Jefferson player put his hands against his helmet. The trainers leaned in, talking to him. He nodded, and they pulled him up to his feet.

The White Prairie player's eyes went to his parents next to Emmie, but then they slid over and up to her. That was then Emmie realized she was the only one still on her feet, watching the circus with both hands covering her mouth.

CHAPTER SIX

RECKONING

THE NEXT DAY AT SCHOOL

After the final bell, Emmie and her father entered Mrs. Henderson's tidy counselor's office. The last time Emmie had been here was freshman year when she'd been trying to get moved into the advanced English class. Since then, Mrs. Henderson had redecorated with ceramic figures of frogs, seals, and baby bunnies.

"I made them in a summer art class," Mrs. Henderson said when she noticed Emmie looking. She closed the case file she was reading—presumably Emmie's—and pushed her multicolored reading glasses to the top of her head. "Welcome, Mr. O'Brien. You two have a seat."

Emmie wondered how much of her file's thickness had been created in the last year. And what did it say about her mom? Did it say *divorced*, or was there a special check box for addict?

Five years ago, before the divorce, her mom had been totally normal. *Clean.* She and Emmie's father had made sense as a couple. But after her mom hurt her back skiing, then gained a few pounds, things started to change.

Not that Emmie's father cared about the extra pounds, but her mom had a tendency toward addiction. First with dieting, then with exercise, then with Botox. When she lost the weight, the addictions turned darker: drinking late into the night with her girlfriends, then smoking weed as if they were still in high school or something.

It just got worse after the divorce, but she hid it well.

Emmie's chest constricted at the thought of what her mother was likely going through right now. Emmie had witnessed some of the horrible withdrawal symptoms once before, back when Nick had withheld what her mother needed. Withheld it until Emmie struck whatever bargain her mom needed her to strike.

"Dan McDonald stepped out a few minutes ago," Mrs. Henderson said, referencing Emmie's probation officer. "He should be back soon. While we wait, why don't we talk about what we can do to keep Emmie safe."

"Yes," Emmie said, turning to her father. "Let's talk about what we can do to keep Emmie safe."

Mr. O'Brien shot his daughter a stern look, and Mrs. Henderson pinched her lips together in disapproval. Emmie rolled her eyes and swiveled her chair to look at the cinder-block wall. She could take care of herself. She had been for over a year. Why did they insist on treating her like she was incompetent?

"Emmie's mother is in a residential treatment center," Mr. O'Brien said, and Emmie cringed.

She always hated it when he referred to her mother as "Emmie's mother" or as "your mum" when he was speaking to Emmie. Not that it wasn't accurate, but it felt so removed. Yes, her mom had made some bad choices, but she still had a name. She'd still been his wife. Emmie remembered, and there were pictures to prove it. She was even sure her mother loved them—both of them. She just loved meth more.

"And we have a no-contact order in place," he said. "Nick Peters is in prison. We've changed Emmie's cell phone number. I've been briefed on the school's security system. We've done everything we can to keep Emmie safe."

Mrs. Henderson turned to Emmie. "You understand that your mother's no-contact order extends to school, right? Do you also understand that you are not to initiate contact with her?"

"I haven't spoken to her," Emmie said, which was true. So far. Her father shot her a skeptical look. She deserved it. She'd come close to calling just last night. It wasn't that she wanted to talk to her mom, more like she just wanted to hear her voice. She'd stopped herself, though; she wasn't allowed to let her new cell phone number become common knowledge, and if she used the landline, her father would know.

"Good," Mrs. Henderson said. "Good. And what about Mr. Peters?"

Emmie's father visibly flinched, but Emmie kept her face blank as the blood in her arms trickled cold. *And what about Mr. Peters?* She hadn't talked to him directly since the police pulled them away from the rusty sedan and pushed them into separate squad cars.

Did she want to talk to Nick? She should. At least to apologize. He had to know that she didn't want to testify against him. He had to know that they didn't give her a choice.

Based on the way he'd glared at her in the courtroom, she doubted he'd ever believe her. Sometimes even she didn't believe herself.

"He's in prison. I haven't had any contact with him either."

"What about his friends? Have they tried to contact you?"

"I told you," her father interjected. "We've changed her number."

"But you still live in the same house," Mrs. Henderson said matter-of-factly.

"We aren't listed in the phone book or on Google or in the white pages. And we have caller ID. None of those people have ever been

26

to the house. We've done what we can, short of moving away, and O'Briens don't run."

Go, Dad, Emmie thought.

"I understand," Mrs. Henderson said, lacing her fingers and resting her hands on top of Emmie's file. "I'm thinking of all the possible scenarios."

"You won't think of anything I haven't already considered myself," Mr. O'Brien said, and only then did Emmie get a sense of how much he worried. She owed him an apology. Bigger than the one she'd already given.

"Nick's friends are all on some kind of probation or have warrants," Emmie said, trying to help out her dad. "They wouldn't risk being picked up."

The door opened, and Emmie's probation officer walked in. He was a bulky man, late twenties, with thick red hair and a goatee. He leaned against the wall. "Good afternoon, everyone. Looks like the judge ordered sixty hours of community service. I've divided that into twelve five-hour shifts to be completed over the next three months." He reached over and handed the folder to Emmie. "All the information you need is in there."

When the judge had issued his order after Emmie's plea, she'd been relieved. At the time, getting credit for her ninety days at the JDC and then only needing another sixty hours of community work service in exchange for her testimony had seemed like a gift. Now it sounded impossible to accomplish.

How was she going to get all that time in, plus her homework? There'd be no time for a job now, and she had hoped to earn back all the money she'd paid out in restitution to the victims.

Emmie groaned, and all the adults in the room looked at her as if she was ungrateful for the court's leniency. "What do I have to do?" she asked.

"Since it's winter, you won't be cleaning roadside ditches," Dan said. "Instead, we've got snow shoveling for the elderly and disabled, doing inventory at Goodwill, and shelving books at the public library."

That didn't sound too bad. "I'll do the books."

"You'll do what the crew is scheduled to do on the days you're scheduled for community service."

"I'd prefer not to shovel."

"Emmie," Mr. O'Brien said. It was a warning.

"You'll work Saturday mornings. Plan on starting at seven forty-five. Go to the sheriff's office. There will be a van there to pick you and the others up."

"Who are the others?" Emmie asked.

"Believe it or not," Dan said with an amused smile, "you aren't the only kid from White Prairie High on probation."

CHAPTER SEVEN

IT'S YOU

It was Saturday. It was early. And Emmie was in a white County Corrections Department van idling at the curb in front of the sheriff's department. These were the things she knew. The rest of the details would take a couple more hours to catch up on, like why she hadn't bothered to change out of her old SpongeBob pajama pants.

God. She'd never meant to wear them in public, and now she felt totally awkward, even surrounded by these losers.

The van was three rows deep with room for nine, plus the driver and Dan McDonald at the front. Emmie was in the first row, by the window, which meant she could rest her head against the glass. The guy sitting next to her had already fallen asleep, his head tipped back, mouth agape, gob of drool on his chin. So gross.

Every time someone new would show up to claim another seat, she'd have a flicker of fear that it would be someone she knew—*someone who knew Nick.* When it'd turn out to be just some other local loser, her sleepy eyes would gloss over with relief.

The digital clock in the dashboard flipped to 7:45, and the driver shifted out of park. But before he took his foot off the brake, someone pounded on the passenger-side door window.

Emmie jumped in her seat, then leaned forward to see who was late. She could only see his chest through the window. The kid behind her muttered, "*Fresh meat*," as if they were some hard-core prison chain gang instead of a bunch of juveniles heading off to fold clothes at Goodwill.

The door slid open, and Dan McDonald pulled his clipboard out of the center console. He put a check mark by the last name on the list. "Glad to see you made it. There's a spot for you in the back."

"Cool," the guy said, climbing in, dark, longish hair falling across his face. He was barely inside, body crouched and not yet turned for the back seat, when his eyes locked with Emmie's. It was for just a second, but she swore she saw a moment of recognition.

Panic set in as she turned her head toward the window. Did he know her? Was she supposed to know him? He wasn't one of Nick's people, was he? No. Too clean cut. Wait…Where had she seen him before?

"You okay, Emmie?" Dan asked.

"Just tired," she said, resting her head against the glass.

"Get your nap while you can, everyone. We'll be at the thrift store in about fifteen."

Emmie closed her eyes and tried to soak up whatever sleep she could get, but she couldn't relax. It wasn't only the worn-out seat or the way her head bounced against the window. It wasn't the soft snores of the guy next to her either. Her neck tingled with the sensation of someone staring at the back of her head. She doubted anyone on the work crew would choose to be awake when they had the option of sleeping, but just to be sure, she turned around.

The late guy looked right at her. No apology. Then he quirked one eyebrow.

Emmie shot him a dirty look, then whipped around to face front.

She picked at a nub on her pajama pants and tried to form an early-morning thought that ultimately took her down the rabbit hole of favorite SpongeBob lines. The mental wanderings ended up wasting her entire fifteen minutes of sleep potential, and before she knew it, they'd arrived at the Goodwill.

"Let's unload, boys," Dan said as they pulled into the thrift-store parking lot. "Oh, and Emmie. Sorry, Em."

She didn't mind, and she liked the fact that Dan called her Em. She was going to be one of his "regulars" for the next three months. Generally speaking, that wasn't a good thing, but she liked the idea of belonging to something again, even if that meant she belonged to a bunch of losers.

Snoring guy climbed out first, then Emmie, then the guys in the back two rows. Emmie followed behind Dan toward the store. Only a few cars were in the parking lot this early on a Saturday, mostly moms dropping off outgrown toys and clothes.

Emmie was halfway to the door when a hand gripped her shoulder and stopped her in her tracks. The other members of the crew walked past.

"So, it's you, huh?" asked the guy with the long, dark hair.

She gave him a brief look and shrugged roughly out from under his hand. "So I'm told." She quickened her pace.

"No," he said, catching up to her again. He laughed under his breath. It was a nice sound. Warm and rich. "What I meant was, you're the girl who fell in the school entrance this week."

"Well, no. I didn't actually fall bec—" Emmie's eyes went reflexively to the guy's hands, and she spotted the broken watch face. "Oh." *Crap.* "It's you."

"Yeah," he said on an exhale. "So I'm told."

Emmie tightened her lips as a wide grin spread across his face. "Max Shepherd," he said, sticking out his hand.

Emmie glanced down at his hand, but she didn't touch it. There was only a second of awkwardness before Max grabbed her hand and said, "You're supposed to shake it. Here. Let me show you."

Emmie jerked her hand back as if she'd been burned. "Emmie," she said. "Emmie O'Brien."

His eyebrows pulled together in surprise and maybe a little concern at her reaction. "What are you doing here?" he asked.

Emmie tilted her head. There was no way she was getting into that.

"Sorry," he said. "None of my business."

She nodded. At least he wasn't a complete idiot. "It was nice to meet you, Matt."

"Max."

Yeah. She knew that. She also knew that hockey guys could stand to come down a few pegs and join the rest of the world.

"O'Brien!" Dan yelled from the doorway. "Get your ass in here. You too, Shepherd. I'm not running some teen dating service."

Emmie felt her face flame with heat, and she hustled into the Goodwill, shooting Dan a look that should have made his hair curl, but instead he laughed and shook his head.

Inside, the large rectangular room burned bright with hundreds of fluorescent bulbs, a stark contrast to the diffused light of early morning. The left half of the room was devoted to kitchen gadgets, mismatched glassware, tools, utensils, and the odd collection of carved coconut monkeys, obscene corkscrews, and other bizarre items that served no other purpose than to be regifted from person to person until they ultimately rested here.

The back of the store held the appliances, bed frames, and furniture. The right half of the room was filled with racks (and racks and racks) of clothes for men, women, and children. Glittery used prom dresses and wool coats, gently used toddlerwear, raincoats. The smell of mothballs, cedar closets, and warm bodies lingered in the nubby fibers.

The store manager doled out work assignments as the work crew yawned or glanced around uncertainly at each other. They were each given a JPWC sticker that proclaimed them a member of the juvenile probation work crew.

"Miller, Households," Dan announced, reading from his clipboard. "Thomas, Hangers. Shepherd, Large Appliances. O'Brien, Children's clothing..."

Emmie dug a piece of gum out of her pocket and made her way toward her station at the back of the room. She had her head down, which is why she didn't immediately see the elderly volunteer driving the pallet jack.

The old man must not have seen her either. He was moving a refrigerator that he'd raised at least four feet off the ground, and he was still having trouble with the controls.

Emmie looked up just as he made two sharp jerks on the levers and put the jack in reverse. The jack lurched backward. The refrigerator wobbled forward and loomed over her.

Someone behind Emmie yelled, "Look out!"

The refrigerator tilted farther forward and seemed to stop for...just... one...second before parting ways with the pallet. Emmie stood, rooted to her spot. In the split second before she was crushed, she actually had a thought, like, Well, this is it then. It's been real.

She closed her eyes and braced for impact, but instead of being flattened, she felt large hands land between her shoulder blades and throw her forward.

Air and gum rushed out of her lungs. Her feet left the floor. One shoe fell from her foot. She was airborne, flying several feet before landing on the concrete floor, spread-eagled with her SpongeBob pajama pants pushed up above her knees. *Uff!*

There was a load explosion of sound, and Emmie flipped over. She was horrified, but not surprised, to see the refrigerator smashed to pieces on the exact spot where she had been standing.

Max was beside it, his hands still up, palms out. He looked at the broken refrigerator. Then he looked at her, his eyes wide and kind of...mad?

Emmie forced an exhale.

By this time, Dan McDonald was crouched over her. The store manager came running at them, his face red. Max broke out of his position and was on Emmie like white on rice.

The old man jumped off the pallet jack and came running over to her. "Sweetheart, are you okay?"

"You could have killed her," Max yelled, standing up. He grabbed the old man by the collar and pushed him against the cinder-block wall.

"Hey! Cool it!" Dan yelled at Max without leaving Emmie's side.

Emmie's face flushed with mortification. She didn't like to make a scene, and the old man was a volunteer. It wasn't like he meant for the refrigerator to fall.

"What's your problem?" she yelled at Max. "Let go of him."

Max released the old man and stalked toward Emmie. "What's *my* problem?" His eyes were like crazy eyes. If he were a cartoon, there would have been lightning bolts. Not much scared Emmie these days, but those eyes might have done it. "*My* problem?"

"Hey, now," Dan said with one hand on Emmie's shoulder and another raised, palm out, toward Max. "Take it easy."

Emmie wiggled out from under Dan's palm and stood up. The store manager said something under his breath to Dan, then led the shaken volunteer away.

"Yeah," Emmie said to Max. "*Your* problem. You didn't have to be so mean to that old man."

"Forgive me for not wanting to see someone get killed by falling appliances." Max was still angry, but it was directed at Emmie now instead of the old man. "And shouldn't you be freaking out a little? Christ!"

Emmie folded her arms. "I've never seen freaking out do anyone any good."

Max's eyebrows shot up; then his face went blank. He glanced quickly from Emmie to Dan, then back again.

Dan chuckled and leaned toward Max's ear. "Something for you to consider, *eh, Shepherd?*" Then he turned his attention back to Emmie. "Do you want to find a chair?"

She didn't even look at him. Just gave a little shrug. "No, I'm totally fine."

Max took a deep breath and rolled his shoulders back as if he was collecting himself. "Sorry," he mumbled. "I'm told I have what's called an 'overinflated sense of vigilance.'" A flash of self-deprecating humor washed across his features before he got serious again.

He mirrored Emmie's body language, folding his arms. "Usually it's a problem for me, but today it saved your life. No matter how *totally fine* you might be with this."

Jock, she thought, her gaze drifting over his well-muscled shoulders. Cocky-ass jock. Stupid-ass Rescue Ranger thinking she couldn't handle her own business. "If it helps your ego to believe that, go right ahead." Emmie turned and continued on her way toward her workstation.

"A simple thank-you would suffice," he called after her.

"I didn't ask for any help," she replied without turning around. Emmie clenched her teeth. She didn't like being a bitch, but she knew what it meant to need help, and she knew what kind of trouble came from people knowing your weakness.

"Doesn't mean you didn't need it!" he shot back, much too loudly to be discreet. It pained Emmie to admit he was right. But even if he did save her life, it wasn't like she was going to grant him three wishes or do his bidding for a week.

* * *

Midmorning, Dan came around with bananas and juice boxes for everyone. It reminded Emmie of preschool, but she was happy for the food since she'd skipped breakfast. She leaned her back against the wall and slid down to the floor, the legs of her flannel pajama bottoms pulling up around her calves.

She thought about closing her eyes and catching a five-minute nap, but she wasn't going to be so lucky. Max Shepherd was headed her way, and it looked like he had something more to say. She didn't know why he should want to talk to her anymore. He'd done his good deed for the day.

"Mind if I join you?" Max asked, his voice already familiar.

Emmie's eyes glanced over his body—the broad shoulders, T-shirt pulled tight across his chest, the narrow hips and muscular thighs. *Hockey thighs*, she thought. He chuckled low in his chest, as if he could read every thought in her head.

She frowned. "I was actually finished." She got up and returned to her station, tossing her banana peel into a trash bin as she passed.

He followed, and Emmie's shoulders tightened reflexively. She glanced around the room expecting to see...what exactly? It wasn't like Nick was able to stroll into Goodwill and bust her for talking to this guy. Still...she couldn't shake the feeling.

"You looking for someone?" Max asked.

Emmie shook her head.

Max leaned against her folding table. Emmie glanced down at his hands—always good to keep an eye on people's hands—and noticed his broken wristwatch again. She wanted to ask him about it, but didn't want to risk opening up more conversation. She started folding clothes.

"Yeah, okay," Max said. "Good talk. Aces. I've got stuff to do too."

Emmie exhaled with a sudden rush of relief and waited for him to turn away. Except that he didn't. Instead, he hesitated as if an idea had occurred to him.

"You were at my hockey game," he said. "Sorry you had to see all that."

Emmie blinked, then stopped folding the shirt she was working on. Slowly, she looked up as she put two and two together. Her memory flashed to that kid laid out flat on the ice. The visiting crowd booing. The dejected player in the penalty box. Whoa. That was *him*. It had been a really scary moment.

Even she, who knew nothing about hockey, knew it had been a bad thing. Bad enough to get him put on the work crew? She wondered if he was embarrassed having to spend time with actual criminals. Probably. Emmie straightened her spine and gave him a way to save face.

"I don't know what you're talking about. I haven't been to any hockey games."

"You were there. I saw you." His confidence was unnerving. So was the way he looked at her. His dark eyes stared into hers, then dipped once to her lips. The tingly sensation on the back of her neck returned, but this time it tightened the muscles in her stomach too. It wasn't altogether unpleasant, but it gave her the urge to run. And run like hell.

"You saw me," Emmie said with a deadpan tone of disbelief. She leaned her back against the wall and folded her arms. It was impossible that he could have picked her out of the crowd. The bleachers had been packed.

"Yes."

Dammit. This guy could not be shaken. She raised her eyebrows. "In the middle of all those people?"

"Yes."

"Liar."

"Well, let me put it this way," he said. A smug grin played at his lips and made Emmie want to slap it off. "If you weren't at the game, how would you know there were *all those people* there?"

Emmie muttered "dumb jock" under her breath and started to walk away.

"I'm sorry?" Max said, getting in front of her. There was a humorous sparkle in his eyes. "What did you call me?"

Emmie stopped, and her temper flared. "Let me talk slowly for you. It. Was. A. Hockey game. They draw a crowd. I made an educated guess."

"No, you were there. I remember your pink hat. I also remember because at the beginning, you were the only one sitting down, and at the end, you were the only one on your feet."

Wow. He really did see her, but he could keep his machismo to himself, thank you very much. "Maybe I don't like to cheer for a bunch of douchebag Neanderthals that nearly kill each other for the sport of it."

"So you *were* there," he said. He placed his palm on the wall beside Emmie's head, and her conflicted feelings flared—a strange combination of annoyance, flattery, and fear. It was like walking on a boat that was traveling over choppy waters. With each step, she wasn't sure where her foot would land. "Please," she said, "please, back off."

Max dropped his chin and took a step back. He shoved his hands in his pockets. "Sorry."

Emmie pushed her palms back against the wall for support and reclaimed her calm. "It was a dick move what you did to that kid."

"Agreed," he said, and if Emmie didn't know any better, the look in his eyes told her that she'd made him sad. Not offended. Not embarrassed. But legitimately sad. "That's why I'm here. It was either community work service, or I was suspended." He glanced around all the racks of used clothing. "Kind of a no-brainer, though my parents are pretty pissed. *At me*, you know. Not about the punishment.

"Anyway, I just wanted to say..." He paused, as if he didn't know how to put his thoughts to words. "Back there..." He gestured with his head toward the broken refrigerator, still lying like roadkill on the showroom floor. "It was cool how you kept it together like that. I was wondering if you were on some kind of antianxiety meds because I haven't found anything that—"

"Shepherd!" Dan called. "Help me with this bed frame."

"Oh. I guess...Well, I gotta go."

"Excellent idea," Emmie said, her words as stiff as her body. "Just, please, go."

Max didn't go. Instead he stared at her, his eyebrows pulled together in puzzlement. "I'm sorry. Did I scare you or something?"

Emmie about choked. "Hardly!" After Nick, or Jimmy, or Frankie, or really any of Nick's other junkies, Max Shepherd was comparatively benign.

"Good," he said on an exhale, "because people tell me I can come on too strong."

Emmie didn't know how to explain how he made her feel. Not afraid, but maybe...uncomfortable? She shrugged. "Don't worry about it. You're fine."

"Shepherd!" Dan called again.

Max glanced at Dan, then back to Emmie. His expression returned to his earlier cockiness. He waggled his eyebrows at her. "Damn straight I'm fine."

"Oh, for God's sake." Emmie rolled her eyes and moved away. "Do you ever quit?"

"Never. So if you're not afraid of me, is there something else wrong?"

"No." *Yes.*

"Do I smell bad?" Max made an exaggerated motion as if he was checking out his pits.

"Probably not at this moment."

He grinned. "Then why do you want to get rid of me so bad?"

She picked up a pair of tiny overalls and slipped them onto a hanger. "I'm just not interested. It happens. Apparently even to you. Get over it."

Max paused, as if considering the possibility.

Emmie rolled her eyes and made a sound of exasperation at the back of her throat. She hung the overalls on the metal rack with an emphatic *clank*.

That elicited another toothy grin from Max. "Prickly."

"What?"

"You're a prickly one, but I still think you're cool. Just thought we could be good friends. No worries. See you around."

Emmie moved over to the table she had been working at and watched Max Shepherd jog over to Dan with the typical confidence she recognized in all his hockey crowd. She didn't need him as a friend. She had Marissa, and one good friend was good enough.

Still, she couldn't help but acknowledge that Max was right. She had developed a prickly side, and she'd come to appreciate the people who were willing to put up with it. Right now, she could count those people on one hand. One hand with a few amputated fingers.

Just her luck that the one person who really seemed to get her would be someone like him. And he wanted to be her *good* friend? What the hell was that all about?

The fact that he was willing to overlook her thorns probably meant there was something seriously wrong with him. But who was she to judge? She looked down at the JPWC sticker on her T-shirt, subtly proclaiming her to be with the juvenile probation work crew, and had a sudden surge of humility. *Right*, she thought. Who was she to judge?

CHAPTER EIGHT

M&M'S

"So how's our little juvenile delinquent?" Jordy asked when Max climbed into the back seat of Chris's Subaru.

Chris glanced over his shoulder and gave Max an apologetic look. Obviously he was feeling guilty that Max had got in so much trouble seeking vengeance on his behalf, but he didn't need to feel bad. Max had been assigned to the work crew because he had no self-control. Pure and simple. It wasn't like Chris had asked him to be an idiot.

"Never better," Max said, pulling off his knit cap. His hair was practically standing up, and it snapped with electricity. He ran his hand through it to get it back into some sort of order. "Burger King?"

"Yeah," Chris said, "Brady is meeting us at the theater."

"Brock, too?" Max asked. Brock's girlfriend usually claimed him on Saturday nights.

"So whipped," Jordy said, pushing his glasses up his nose.

Max chuckled and caught Chris's eyes in the rearview mirror. They knew Jordy was as into *his* girl as Brock was into Quinn. Jordy was only out with them tonight because Lindsey was working.

A few minutes later, Chris pulled into the Burger King parking lot and found a spot away from the other cars. Not that his car was mint or anything, but he was paranoid about scratches. Outside, the perfume of salt and grease hung heavy on the air. They all went in and ordered the usual, pumping a quart of ketchup straight onto their trays.

"So how was the work crew?" Chris asked, sliding into a booth. "Anyone pull a shank?"

"I think it's called a shiv," Jordy said.

"No one's that hard core," Max said. Except for maybe one. Emmie O'Brien was seriously tough as shit. She'd never told him why she was on the crew, but from the comments he'd heard Dan make over the course of the morning, it sounded like she was going to be on it for a lot longer than he was. He wondered what the hell she'd done.

Max shoved several steaming-hot fries into his mouth, then quickly spit them out. Cursing, he took a big guzzle of Coke and swished it around in his mouth to put out the fire. "Either of you know a girl named Emmie O'Brien?"

Chris and Jordy shook their heads without looking up from their food. "She hot?" Chris asked, his typical question about any girl in any conversation.

The question gave Max pause, maybe because that word—*hot*— didn't quite fit. Toward the end of their shift at the Goodwill, this one girl had walked in. Hot in the way Chris meant: black yoga pants, T-shirt, tits out to here.

This Jerry kid who was on the crew kept making crude gestures behind the girl's back. He made sure Emmie saw him, too, like he wanted her to react—laugh or go *ewww*, or smack his arm or whatever. But Emmie never gave him any satisfaction. It made Max want to give her a fist bump for being so damn chill, which wasn't as lame as what Jerry was doing, but nearly.

But, yeah, Emmie was kind of hot. Not the kind that made him think about sex, at least not very much. She was the kind of hot that came from being totally above the plane. It didn't bother him at all when she called him a "douchebag Neanderthal" because she didn't seem to care what he thought about her either, and that was pretty damn cool, and she was cool in all these other interesting ways, like how she didn't react to Jerry's sleazy jokes, or cry when she was nearly killed by a falling refrigerator, or how, when the store manager read Emmie the riot act for putting things in the wrong place, she stared the guy down and never said a word.

Seemed to Max that the manager was an idiot. Emmie could probably sue the store for having an untrained volunteer nearly drop a refrigerator on her. Why rile her up? The man should have been buying her an apology breakfast or something instead of yelling at her. But Emmie barely acknowledged him, and not like Max had been staring at her chest or anything, but her breathing had never even fluctuated. How did she do it? Was it that she didn't care about *anything*?

Obviously, she'd been through more serious shit than any of that— shit that made her cringe when anyone got too close—but she'd still made it through alive. Maybe making it through alive was how she was now able to give the world a serious F-U.

That meant there was hope for Max, and he found that possibility very, very attractive. Hot even.

"He's not answering your question, Chris," Jordy said, jerking Max out of his head.

"She must be hot," Chris said through a mouthful of food. "Sounds like Max Shepherd is back from the dead."

Jordy kicked Chris's chair, throwing Chris's chest forward against the edge of the table. Chris looked up at Max, eyes wide. "Ah, shit. Sorry, dude. My bad." Died, dead...these were words his friends usually avoided whenever Max was around.

"What did they have you do on the crew?" Jordy asked, not so smoothly changing the subject.

Max was grateful for the veer. "Not much. It wasn't too hard."

Chris rebounded from his faux pas and tossed his mane of blond hair back. "That's what she said."

Max shook his head at Chris. "We folded clothes."

"Seriously?" Jordy asked with an edge of disappointment.

"Yeah," Chris said, "we thought you'd be breaking rocks with a hammer." He reached across his tray, dragging his sleeve through the pile of ketchup. Chris lifted his arm and checked out his sleeve. Then he drew the fabric into his mouth and sucked off the sauce.

"That's nasty," Max said, looking away.

"Nah," Chris said, smacking his lips. "You guys know what you're planning to say at the pep rally on Thursday?"

Max grimaced. He hated getting up and talking in front of the school, but this coming week it was the guys' hockey team's turn to lead the rally. He was comfortable on the ice, guarded by his pads and helmet. He could face an army like that. But standing on the gym floor in front of fifteen hundred students? Yeah, not so much.

He swallowed hard. It made him feel like those dreams where you show up at school naked. He needed to figure out some way to soldier through.

"You know," Jordy said, "since it's come up, maybe we should talk about our next game."

Max gave his cup a shake to make sure there was only ice left. "You mean, since you finally found a way to work what happened last game into the conversation?"

"Shut up," Jordy said while pushing up his glasses. He took a couple fries and folded them into his mouth. "I think it would be good to talk it through. Maybe we should have a plan, a signal, or something. If things get hot, something to say to calm you down. We can't afford any mistakes. You can't afford another major."

Max laughed, even though it wasn't funny. "You make me sound like a crazy person." And maybe that's exactly what he was. Maybe that's exactly how his two best friends saw him, and could he really blame them?

Chris and Jordy exchanged a look. "Listen," Jordy said, "we all know you've been going through a hard time, what with Jade and all. It's too much, Shep. It would be too much for anyone. No one blames you for how you're feeling. I'd be the same way. We just need to find a way for you to deal with it."

"Yeah," Chris said, which Max knew from experience was going to be Chris's most profound contribution to this conversation.

Max hadn't been prepared for Jordy to mention Jade. His stomach constricted, shriveling down to a hard, little pellet. "You talk like my shrink, Jordy."

"You got a shrink?" Chris asked.

Max nodded. He'd been seeing Dr. Linda for several months. His dad called her "the quack." The only reason his dad was still paying for Max's sessions was because his mom thought it was important.

Chris bent over his tray and finished off his fries. No one ever knew what to say when someone announced their head was so messed up they were seeking professional help.

"Okay, so brainstorm," Jordy said. "Tell me something that mellows you out. Like...I don't know...the sound of the ocean, or..."

"Getting mind-blowing head," Chris suggested.

Max smothered a smile, and for some awkwardly inappropriate reason, that girl Emmie popped into his mind.

Jordy leaned forward with a confused look on his face. "*M*?"

"What?" Max glanced up in alarm. Ah, hell, had he said her name out loud? "Oh, yeah. Um. *M&M's*. M&M's calm me down."

Chris laughed and rolled his eyes.

"Okay," Jordy said, shooting Chris a nasty look. "That's it then. Things get hot, we're going to start talking about M&M's, and that's your signal to cool your jets. You don't listen, and we're going to start pelting you with them. Right there on the ice. Red, blue, yellow—they're going to come raining down on you. Got it?"

Max laughed. Jordy always had the most elaborate plans. "Got it. Sounds like a fantastic strategy. I can feel it working already." Max shoved the remains of his chicken sandwich in his mouth. "You girls done? Let's get out of here."

CHAPTER NINE

BAD REFLECTION

Brady was waiting for them outside the movie theater. As expected, Brock was a no-show. Most of the girls' hockey team was hanging out in the lobby, too, though the guys hadn't expected to see them. The girls were monopolizing a cluster of tables by the concessions with their letter jackets draped over the backs of the chairs.

Katie Hines stood up from her chair and waved them over.

"What does she want?" Brady asked. Max's skin got this weird buzzy feeling, and not in a good way. Katie was Jade's cousin, so Max did his best to avoid her. Every time their eyes met, it was like looking in a mirror, and it doubled his pain to see hers.

When Brady and Chris went over to say hi, Max lagged behind and pretended to be interested in a cardboard cutout of Denzel Washington holding an assault rifle.

"What are you guys seeing?" Katie asked. She pulled a rubber band out of her long, red hair and picked apart the braid.

"*Night of Tigers*," Jordy said, adjusting his glasses. "How 'bout you guys?"

"The Last Walk."

"Chick flick," Chris said with an eye roll and a condescending tone.

That, Max thought, was one of the many reasons Chris was never going to get a girlfriend. Not that Chris wanted to get with Katie, but talking to girls always made Chris nervous, and his words came out in asshole-speak. Every. Single. Time.

"What? You don't like girls?" Katie asked, insinuating.

"Let's go get our seats," Jordy said, shoving the back of Chris's shoulder.

Max followed, but before he'd gone two steps, Katie reached out and touched his arm. He froze and looked down at his sleeve before looking up at her. Mirrors, he thought. Freakin' mirrors.

"I've missed talking to you," she said quietly so no one else could hear.

"Yeah."

"Maybe we could fix that?"

"Yeah," Max said, not really meaning it. "See you later, Katie."

"Yeah. See ya."

The guys found their seats toward the back of the theater. Brady sat the farthest over in the row, then Jordy, Chris, and Max on the aisle. The previews went on forever. As in forever.

Brady, Chris, and Jordy joked back and forth and gave each other shit. They threw the occasional piece of popcorn at each other, or at a group of girls from West Champlin who were sitting a few rows up.

Max sat quietly, thinking about Jade. Even Katie. And how it was all an incredible waste. It didn't take long for his thoughts to fall into their typical pattern of how it was all his fault for being a dick. These were thoughts Dr. Linda had been trying for months to get him to overcome. *Step back*, she'd say. *Look at the situation from the perspective of an outside observer. Can you see how you don't deserve to beat yourself up the way you do?*

Um, no. No, he didn't. No matter from what angle Dr. Linda wanted him to look at things, the fact remained: what happened to Jade was his fault. And everybody who knew her knew it.

Max blinked, and the movie screen blurred into blobs of colored water. What the hell? He touched the corner of his eye. Was he tearing up? Here? In the middle of some trailer for the zombie apocalypse? He blinked his eyes a few more times and cleared his throat.

There was a slight movement to his left, then someone whispered, "Shepherd."

Max looked over, trying to calm his features, thankful that the lights were down. Jordy's arm moved and something lifted into the air, coming right for him. Max snagged the vague shape out of the darkness with a crunching sound, then looked down to see what it was. It was a bag of M&M's.

Max looked up at Chris and smiled, because damn if his eyes didn't clear. Maybe Jordy was really on to something. Could something as simple as a candy-coated mind trick help him get control and back in the game? It sounded pretty stupid, but damn if he didn't feel just a little bit better.

Or maybe it was because the M&M's also made him think of Emmie?

Max ripped open the bag and settled back into his seat, letting the dark theater envelop him. The guys got quiet. The movie started. Assault rifles ratcheted up the plot when things got slow. A building blew up. Debris flew at the camera, and Max thought this flick would be a whole lot better in 3-D.

Halfway into the movie, something tickled the right side of his neck. He reached across his body to brush it away, but it was still there. He glanced to his right and about launched out of his seat, swinging his right fist backward and knocking over his Coke with his left. There was nothing but ice in it, but Chris dodged to his left to avoid getting splashed, and Katie—who was sitting in the seat directly behind Max—lurched backward to avoid getting smacked in the face.

"Shit! What are you doing in here?" Max whisper-yelled at Katie. "You about gave me a heart attack."

Her fingertips were now back on his shoulder, and he tensed under her touch.

"Sorry," she said. "Just wanted you to know that Elizabeth's having a party after the movie. I was wondering if you wanted to go."

It took Max a second to process what she was saying. "You couldn't have texted me that?"

She shrugged. "Thought you'd appreciate the personal touch." She gave his shoulder another squeeze. Max twitched away, hopefully without seeming rude. There was no way he was getting personal with Katie. "I'll let the guys know after the movie is over."

The man in the next row turned around and shushed them.

"If they don't want to go," Katie whispered, her breath hot against his neck, "you could go with me. I drove." She rose to leave without waiting for his answer. Max watched her go down the stairs, her pale hand trailing the wall. As he watched, he missed what was likely the best line of the movie, because the whole theater erupted in laughter.

"What did I miss?" he asked Chris.

Chris raked his hand through his thick hair, then leaned into Max's ear. "Apparently the fact that Katie's got it bad for you. Make a move, Max. Time to get on with life."

Max turned his face to really look at Chris, but his friend's eyes were locked on the screen. Max sat back hard in his seat. Was Chris serious? Get on with life? Wasn't that exactly what he was doing? He was going to school. He'd stuck with the team. He was paying for his mistakes. He was out at a goddamn movie!

Max was definitely getting on with life. Getting it on with Jade's cousin was out of the question.

In fact—he turned toward the stairs, but by this time Katie was gone—just the idea of spending time with her made his chest shake and his stomach churn. She'd want to talk about Jade. She still wanted to know the details, and Max couldn't do that to her. Once you had those pictures in your head, it wasn't like you could shake them. If he told her all that shit, she'd never be able to think of Jade in any other way but broken. Bloody. He had to live with that. Jade's mom had to live with that.

Max used to get along great with Jade's mom. Now she'd cross to the other side of the street if she saw him coming. That's what came from sharing a trauma. You avoided as many triggers as you could. Sometimes that included avoiding the only people who understood your nightmare. Sometimes avoidance was the only way not to shatter.

When he looked up at the screen, everybody in the movie had died. Jade, he thought. I'm so sorry. So sorry. So sorry.

The credits ran, and Max's head was suddenly filled with the high-pitched keening of metal on metal. It wouldn't stop. Like a glass-shattering note that just kept going and going and going. The M&M's weren't working anymore. His queasiness had moved well past nausea. His fingers were twitching, and he knew if he stayed where he was, he was going to lose it. Right here in front of everyone.

"I got to get some fresh air," Max said; then he bolted from the theater. He ran down the hallway and crashed his palms into the bar on the exit door before stepping onto the sidewalk. The cold air slapped him hard across the face.

He paced back and forth a couple times, his hands shoved deep into his coat pockets, trying to decide whether he should go back inside or head for Chris's car. Going inside meant talking about what they were going to do next. He didn't want to go to the party. He didn't want to talk to Katie. Hell, he didn't want to talk to anyone. He wanted to go home.

Max ran in the direction of Chris's car, punching an SUV with the side of his hand as he ran past and setting off its security alarm. The sound scared him so badly he nearly tripped. He wove through the aisles, finally finding Chris's car, but of course it was locked.

He picked up a dirty chunk of ice and launched it at a light pole. The ice shattered and rained down in little black chunks. It felt kind of good, so he chucked another. Then another.

He shouldn't be here, and he didn't mean the parking lot. Why couldn't *he* have been thrown against a light pole and smashed to pieces? Life would be so much easier for everyone if that were the case. Max hauled off with another ice chunk, letting it fly while cursing loudly at the sky.

It took the guys another five minutes to catch up to him. By the time they got to the car, Max had his cap pulled down low, his hands shoved into his coat pockets, and was feeling about as deep in the well as he could. That's what Quack Linda called it: being in the well. That dark, lonely place where nobody could reach him.

"Got enough fresh air?" Chris asked.

"Just take me home," Max said, blowing a puff of frosty breath into the cold, night air.

"Whatever you want," Jordy said, so about ten minutes later, they were dropping him off on the sidewalk outside his house. Max shoved his hands in his pockets and pulled out the crinkled M&M's wrapper. He exhaled a slow steady stream that vaporized on the air, then turned the paper over in his hands a couple times before pressing it flat against his thigh so only one *M* showed.

Emmie.

He breathed deeply. Weird how a stupid logo could give him the same feeling as taking off all his pads after a game. That feeling like he was suddenly weightless. *Tonight*, he thought, tonight might be the first night in a long time he wouldn't hope to die in his sleep.

CHAPTER TEN

CHEMISTRY

THURSDAY

Emmie was perched on a high stool at her lab table. She hadn't been in school enough last year to pass chemistry, so now that she was back at WPHS, she was taking it again. Apparently being present in class wasn't going to make the subject any more understandable. She couldn't get her mind to settle on what Mr. Beck, the student teacher, was saying. He might as well have been talking in Latin, or Elvish like the kid who sat behind her in calculus.

To be fair though, she hadn't been able to get her mind to settle on much of *anything* since Saturday. It wasn't the near-death-by-refrigerator experience that was troubling her, though that was something. Rather, it was the nagging question of why she had been so cold to Max Shepherd when he had only been trying to be friendly. The answer kept slipping away even as she grasped it—like eating soup with a fork—until a familiar voice spoke in her head.

Why would anyone want to be your friend when you betrayed the ones you had?

Nick.

Emmie blinked and tried to refocus on Mr. Beck. He was sitting on the table at the front of the classroom, swinging his legs. His khakis were pulled up around his ankles, showing off a pair of purple argyle socks. He was still talking, as evidenced by the dull buzz in the back of Emmie's head.

Two girls with flat-ironed hair sat at the lab table to Emmie's left. They were whispering about the upcoming Snow Ball. The guy behind Emmie was drum-rolling two pencils against his table like he was auditioning for a garage band.

"This works well for a simple explanation." Mr. Beck kept swinging his legs, making him look like a kindergartner waiting for his milk break. It was mesmerizing—the purple argyle, back and forth, back and forth—and it took Emmie's mind off more troublesome thoughts.

"But it doesn't really explain why the properties of certain things change under different elements, such as why metals give off a characteristic color when heated in a flame, am I right?" Mr. Beck paused, and the silence lengthened to the point of discomfort.

Emmie looked up to make sure he wasn't staring at her, and that she hadn't missed a question. Ah. He was doing her dad's trick; he was waiting them out. Someone would answer eventually.

Or not.

Mr. Beck smiled and hopped off the table. By now, the static electricity from all that swinging had caused the bottom of his khakis to stick to the top of his socks. "And it doesn't explain why lasers give off a particular wavelength. Now atoms," he said, and Emmie zoned out again until Mr. Beck's voice became small and hollow, and a million light-years away.

You and I are alike, came the memory of Nick's voice as they sat together on the couch, three movies into a Star Wars marathon. *Pea pods.*

It's two peas in *a pod*, Emmie'd said, which had earned her a pinch on the back of her arm.

She'd tried to move to the other side of the couch, but Nick had put his arm around her and pulled her close. *Why you always so tense? Is it because your momma's looking twitchy again? Maybe I need to kiss you like I did last night.*

Now safely seated in Mr. Beck's chemistry class, Emmie wondered how she might change under different elements. Could she be a different version of herself now that she was away from Nick? Could she relax? Could she be nice?

She felt steely and cold most of the time, like metal. Max was definitely more of a flame. She resolved to attempt a chemistry experiment. Next Saturday. She would try to have a normal conversation with Max.

Her father would like to see her getting back to her old self. Maybe if she did, he'd stop trying to figure out what he'd done to make her want to go live with her mom. What he didn't understand was that he'd done nothing wrong. Emmie could see that now, even if at the time she thought his house rules bordered on abuse. She had a whole different perspective on things now. Butting heads over curfew and household chores was nothing compared to putting makeup over a black eye.

The girls to her left were now hypothesizing about who would make good couples for the Snow Ball and who might end up on the winter court. Emmie turned to look at them and in the process spotted a familiar profile waiting in the hallway.

Max freaking Shepherd.

That nervous twisting sensation was back, somewhere low in her gut. She fought the urge to smooth down the frizz in her curls. So ridiculous. It was going to be hard to be nice if the mere sight of him turned her into an idiot. What was the deal? And also, how had she gone all week and never noticed that he had chemistry right after her?

Maybe he wasn't usually so early to class. The bell for next hour hadn't even rung yet.

Emmie's throat tightened at the thought of having to pass him in the doorway. It had been five days since she saw him last, but the memory of Max Shepherd, his tricep bulging as he leaned against her folding table, was fixed on her brain. *I think you're cool. I thought we could be good friends.*

At the forefront of those thoughts was how different Max was from Nick, in both body and personality. Both were tall, but Nick was thin, his belly nearly concave and his muscles long and taut. Max was broad and solid. As if someone had opened up his head and filled his entire body with concrete.

Nick was all about adrenaline and excitement, always seeking the next rush. Max was…well, not that exactly. Max seemed more like energy trying to be contained. Like an atom bomb.

"The atom," Mr. Beck said, "has a wavelength…"

Emmie sighed. When it came to chemistry, she and Max were hardly on the same wavelength. That was just the cold, hard truth.

"De Broglie's prediction of the duality of matter opened the door to a new branch of science called quantum mechanics," Mr. Beck said. "Do you know what the major difference between classical and quantum mechanics is?"

No one answered. The bell rang, and the class stood up in response. Mr. Beck kept talking. "In classical mechanics, the motions of bodies are much larger than the atoms that make it up. The energy seems to be absorbed…"

Then Mr. Beck stopped, and a look of disgust clouded his face. "Holy—! Did one of you really just fart that smell? That's not healthy. That is not the smell of a human fart."

A small group of guys laughed so hard Emmie thought they might actually turn inside out. She tried to ignore them and put her head down as she passed through the door.

As she did, something warm gently squeezed her wrist. Her head jerked up, and Max met her eyes. He didn't say a word, but when he released her, the corners of his mouth twitched.

Out of habit, Emmie stiffened and braced for Nick's retribution, but of course it never came. Still, she walked down the hall as quickly as she could, paying no mind to the people she jostled and allowing reality to settle back in.

What was Max doing, touching her like that? Was he trying to get a rise out of her, teasing her for being such a cold fish on Saturday? She felt a strange wave of sadness when she realized that was exactly what he was doing.

Emmie straightened her shoulders and cleared her throat. No matter. Why should she care? There was no reason to stress over a friendship she'd never had and never even wanted. There was no reason to fantasize…well, not *fantasize* fantasize, but, like, think about being friends with him. Not even *good* friends.

* * *

After French, Emmie met Marissa at the lunch table. Sarah was there, too, and already halfway through her salad. She was wearing her downhill-ski-team sweatshirt. The tan lines around her eyes had nearly faded. It was spaghetti day. Marissa was quick to comment on Emmie's new white blouse and how she'd never wear white on spaghetti day.

"Should I get a garbage bag from one of the lunch ladies?" Sarah asked. "I can cut armholes, and you can wear it like a smock."

"Thanks, but no thanks," Emmie said. She turned to Marissa. "How'd your sociology test go?"

"Awesome. I think it's my calling. Either that or anthropology. Or maybe archeology. Can't you see me on one of those desert digs?"

Emmie could totally see it. Marissa was just the type. She was all about science, and she didn't mind getting dirty. But before Emmie could answer her, there was an eruption of laughter from a few tables behind them.

Marissa looked past Emmie's shoulder. "And speaking of the study of man..." Marissa said under her breath.

Emmie turned on her stool. The hockey guys weren't in matching jerseys today, but there was no mistaking them. If it wasn't their hair, which most of them wore longer than any of the other guys in school, it was the swarm of gnat-girls hovering around their table. Tiny, flighty, spray-tanned things. Each one of them nearly identical and indistinguishable to Emmie's eye.

It didn't take her more than a second to spot Max in the mix. He was apparently the cause of the laughter because he was in the midst of telling a very animated story. She couldn't hear what he was saying, but judging by his hand gestures, it had something to do with his time on the work crew. Weird that he would want to advertise that.

There was something else she noticed. It was the same thing she'd noticed after he caught her in the hallway the first day, that posture that told her despite his easy smile and animated gestures, there was something raw hiding underneath it all.

Olivia arrived and plopped down on the stool next to Emmie. "Everyone going to the pep rally?" she asked.

Marissa and Sarah nodded; then a second later the girls began discussing the pep rally that was coming up next hour, as well as the winter formal. It occurred to Emmie that she needed to pay more attention to what was going on around this school because that dance was all anyone seemed to want to talk about. Had there been posters? Was this like a big thing?

"I heard Simon Godfrey might ask Joanna to Snow Ball," Olivia said.

Sarah shook her head. "No. She's already going with Chad."

Emmie wondered which one of the gnat-girls Max was going to ask to the dance. There'd been at least three of them flitting around his head last time she checked. There was no way in hell she would ever flit.

Even so, the next thing she knew, she was thinking about what it would be like to dance with Max with his head bent low and that hair falling over his eyes. And then she thought about what an idiot she was being. Again. For like the tenth time that day.

She turned around one more time to look at him just as Max—still mid-story—glanced up. Emmie sucked in a breath. Max stopped talking. Their eyes locked.

Emmie could remember certain moments when time stood still. Like when she told Nick her mom needed some "help," and he left her waiting...breathless...waiting, waiting before he finally said, "I'll see what I can do." Or the moment they all noticed B. J.'s arms laid out awkwardly against the cracked linoleum in Nick's kitchen, unmoving, and everyone waited to see who would be the first person to check his pulse.

This was one of those moments. Just as eternal, just as breathless, and just as damning.

A few of the gnat-girls noticed that Max had stopped talking and looked to see what had his attention. Emmie whipped around, bending her head over her tray. With shaking hands, she opened her milk carton. Idiot, she thought, cursing herself. Idiot.

CHAPTER ELEVEN

RALLY

The bleachers in the school gymnasium were filling quickly as Emmie, Marissa, and Sarah found seats at the end of a row near the stairs that descended to center court. Emmie sat on the edge so she could set her backpack on the stairs. She would rather have gone to the library to work ahead on some English assignments. She seriously doubted her pep needed to be rallied, but Marissa had insisted.

Down on the floor, most of the hockey team was already sitting on a row of blue metal folding chairs. At center court, there was a microphone on a stand. Emmie glanced to her left and found Marissa staring up at something over Emmie's shoulder. Marissa's mouth was in the shape of a little o.

"What's wrong?" Emmie asked with a laugh. "Are you having a stroke or something?"

"Mind if I sit here for a sec?" asked a deep voice just as a warm body dropped onto the few empty inches at the end of the bleacher. Emmie caught the spicy scent of cloves.

Marissa shifted to her left to make more room for Max, but Emmie didn't budge. "What are you doing?" she asked.

Emmie could already feel a large number of eyes on her, wondering why Max Shepherd was practically sitting in the new girl's lap instead of being down on the floor with the rest of the team. Max turned his body in to her, and their knees bumped as Emmie felt his hand, shaky on her hip. Her back stiffened. "Wha—?"

Max caught her eye, holding her gaze as he slipped her phone out of her pocket. Then, before Emmie understood what was happening, he was tapping at the keyboard with both thumbs.

"Give that back," she said. She reached for her phone but he turned toward the aisle, blocking her like she was one of his opponents on the ice. Emmie groaned. She definitely needed to put a password on that thing. "What are you doing?"

"Don't get weird. I'm just giving you my number," he said, making a few more passes with his thumbs. She heard a soft buzz from his own back pocket. "And now I've got yours."

"You can't do that," she said, then dropped her voice low. "My number is private."

"Why?" Max asked.

Why? Emmie couldn't exactly get into an explanation of that now, here. Not with him and not with Marissa sitting so close. She needed to put an end to whatever ridiculous attraction was going on between them, nip it in the bud. But when she still didn't respond in any way to Max's question, he pressed on.

"I thought we could carpool to the crew on Saturday. Call me." He slipped her phone slowly back into her pocket, sending shivers up her spine. "I gotta go sit with the team now."

Max laid his palm on Emmie's shoulder and pushed himself to standing. His hand, the pressure, the warmth, all felt the same as outside Mr. Beck's classroom, except that this time she knew it wasn't a joke.

He meant for her to notice his physicality. The heat of his body, his hand on her hip, the brush of his knees against her thigh, the toe-curling view of his jeans riding low on his hips as he walked away from her, joining his teammates on the gym floor...He meant for her to react. And boy, did she. Emmie's heart was pounding in her ears.

She might have gotten mad at herself, or at him, but she didn't. Mainly because Max didn't look nearly as confident as he was trying to act. There'd been nervousness around his eyes, and if Emmie had to guess, he looked a little sick. As he slowly descended the stairs, head bowed, the fingers on his left hand were twitching.

Marissa bumped her shoulder against Emmie's and shook her head. "The world is a weird and wonderful place, my friend."

"What's that supposed to mean?" Emmie asked, conscious of the fact that a few people were still turning their heads to look at her.

Marissa's eyes lingered on Max as he dropped onto his folding chair, then settled her gaze on Emmie. "Just when I think I've got it figured out, I run into an evolutionary wonder like the singing snail."

"The singing snail? Is that a real thing?" Sarah asked.

"It's a metaphor," Marissa said with a grin.

"A metaphor for what?" Emmie asked. Her gut was a tumble of trouble.

"For you. It's not natural for something so teeny and quiet to cause such a commotion, but you, my friend, you are definitely on the path toward causing a commotion. You are an evolutionary wonder."

Emmie groaned again. Half the time she had no idea what Marissa was talking about. "I didn't cause a commotion."

"Not yet, but it's coming," she said. "You wait. It's the year of the singing snail."

Emmie rolled her eyes, and Marissa laughed. The sound of it made Emmie happy, and that right there was a welcomed thing.

* * *

This is it, Max thought. He hated these pep rallies more than anything else on the planet. He particularly hated them when his team was the focus. Who would have thought a bruiser on the ice would suffer from such intense stage fright? It was embarrassing.

This was his school. This was nothing more than a gym full of kids. The same people who came to watch him play every Saturday night. But at least then he could wear his helmet. Shoulder pads and gloves. On the ice he was armored. Here? On the gym floor in regular clothes, he felt naked. He didn't know how the basketball team played in just shorts and a T-shirt. God help the swim team.

And now...with what Coach was having them do...Max wondered if he could will himself into an epileptic seizure. Maybe he could get wheeled out of here and miss the whole thing.

"It'll be special," Coach had said at their last practice. "It'll show the school that they are as much a part of this team as you are."

It was total bullshit, but here they were, lining up at center court. Vice Principal Zenner handed Coach the microphone, which squealed through the loudspeakers for a second before Coach tapped it two times with his index finger.

"Good afternooooooooon, White Prairie!" Coach said, and the crowd stomped its feet.

Max and the rest of the team stood shoulder to shoulder in a long line behind Coach, facing the bleachers, feet shuffling, heads raised to the crowd, mouths smirking, index fingers lifted in the air. All except one. Max thought he was going to throw up.

"The boys' varsity hockey team is close to wrapping up its regular season. Looks like we're going to be either the number one or number two seed in the tournament again this year."

More cheering. More chins lifted. Max's stomach turned. It was unreasonable to think that the whole gym was looking only at him, but he didn't dare raise his head to find out if he was wrong.

"Every game, the guys play for themselves, for their own personal goals, and certainly for the school as a whole. But I asked them to think about what that means. When we think about playing for the school, that's a big concept. A little abstract maybe. So I asked the guys to think about your actual faces. We want to think of *you* when we're playing. We're playing for *you*."

Coach paused, but there was no immediate reaction from the crowd.

"So, I asked each of the guys to pick some smaller aspect of the school that they could dedicate Saturday's game to. In a second, I'm going to call each player forward. Each player is going to announce who he's dedicating his game to: some*one* or to some *group* in particular. He will be thinking of you when he hits the ice. When that player scores, he's scoring for you. If he calls on you, I want you to come down and join us on the floor."

The band struck up the school song, and everybody was on their feet. Max kept his head down and wondered if Emmie was standing too. Somehow he doubted it. At least, standing and cheering wouldn't have been her first choice. Maybe her friends would have dragged her to her feet.

When the band stopped, Coach called out Chris's name. Max watched Chris's worn Nikes swagger forward.

"Chris Daniels. Lucky number seven. And this Saturday night I'll be playing for the Drama Club. Come on down, thespians!" He mispronounced it so it rhymed with *lesbians*. He could be such a tool.

Some clapping. Some nervous laughter from the crowd, which wasn't sure if this was for real. Was the drama club really supposed to go down onto the gym floor? Chris raised his arm and repeated, "I said, 'Come on down!'" like this was *The Price Is Right* game show or something.

Slowly a small group of kids joined Chris on the floor, looking like deer in the proverbial headlights.

Jordy stepped out of the back line next and joined Chris. "Jordy Keller. Number three. Saturday, I'll be playing for the FFA."

Cowboy boots stomped on the bleachers, and a few girls went "Woooooooo!" before running down onto the floor. Okay. So the school was getting the hang of it.

Brady was next. He was playing for his personal math tutor and Mrs. Peck in the lunch room. Only his tutor, a senior girl with spiky blond hair and hipster glasses, joined him on the floor. Tack was playing for the Mathletes. Brock dedicated his game to the Concert Choir. By now, there were about a hundred kids on the gym floor.

The juniors stepped forward and did their thing, but Max wasn't listening. And then it was his turn. If all eyes hadn't been on him before, they were now. He felt the weight of them like a concrete slab lying on his back. Coach handed Max the microphone, and he nearly dropped it.

Max cleared his throat. "Max. Um…Max Shepherd. Number eleven. I'm playing for…" He took a deep breath and let it out. "Emmie O'Brien and all of the other new students at White Prairie High School this year."

There was a moment of complete silence in the gym. Or maybe Max imagined it. When he looked up, Emmie's friend was pushing her off the bench and toward the stairs. The next thing Max knew, he was surrounded by three strangers, and then…finally…Emmie.

She looked confused, like she couldn't believe what he'd done. Well, that made two of them, but she was there. She'd come. She didn't run out the back like he was afraid she might, but none of that changed the fact Max's heart was still pounding against his sternum. Ah, hell. Was he going to throw up right here in front of Emmie and the whole damn school?

Max reached out and touched Emmie's shoulder. He didn't mean to do it—it was merely instinct, to steady himself—but the sudden wave of calm that washed over him about knocked him over nonetheless. It was the weirdest thing.

The feel of Emmie's shoulder under his fingers grounded him, stilling his heart, and the whole cacophony of the gym faded away.

He barely heard the band strike up a rousing rendition of "We Are Family," but when everyone on the floor gathered into one big huddle, index fingers raised in the air, all Max could think was *damn!* Was it possible for a single person, someone he barely knew, to be the one to pull him out of his headspace?

After all his joking around with Chris and Jordy, was she really his lucky M&M?

Emmie's side was pressed up against Max in the huddle, and when the crowd started to jump to the beat of the music, forcing Emmie to do the same, the warmth of her body flooded through him.

In that moment, Max Shepherd felt like a giant. Better, he felt like himself. Like his old self. He was ready to take on the world.

CHAPTER TWELVE

BLUNT

FRIDAY NIGHT

Max hated going to the Happy Gopher because it was where Jade used to work, and there was no escaping her memory among the ketchup bottles and red-checked curtains. The thing was, there were half-priced appetizers on Friday nights, so his friends always insisted they come. Old habits were hard to break.

As they found their regular seats, Chris sloughed off his letter jacket revealing his *I ♥ Hot Moms* T-shirt. Lindsey groaned and dragged Jordy to the opposite side of the table. Jordy was blinking hard, wearing contacts for the first time.

Lauren, Elizabeth, Brock, and Quinn piled their jackets in the corner. Max could tell Katie was waiting to see where he was going to sit before she chose her chair.

When their waitress came around, the guys got Cokes, while the girls ordered diets and raspberry lemonades, then their usual sampler platters and an extra basket of onion rings.

Besides the continued comments on the success of yesterday's pep rally, the conversation was on repeat from last Friday night: their chances in the tournament, how plastered so-and-so got the weekend before, and the new stereo equipment Chris was (six months later) still planning to buy for his Subaru.

The whole conversation was so familiar that Max could predict each joke, each laugh, each friendly shoulder punch. Sometimes he got bored, but tonight it was a good thing. His friends' predictability made it easy for his mind to wander: to falling refrigerators, to the shiver that ran down Emmie's arms when he slipped her phone into her pocket, then later to the heat of her body pressed against him in the huddle.

He still couldn't believe he'd done it. Actually called her out by name. And then the way her own natural calm split off and seeped into his body. Is that what it was between them? Like some emotional mitosis? He wasn't a big science guy, and it wasn't like he believed in magic. There was only one thing he knew for sure. Emmie O'Brien made him feel like everything was going to be all right.

Max drifted back to his friends' conversation and was gratified that he still knew what they were talking about, which had now changed to the subject of the upcoming dance and who'd be on this year's winter court. Great.

Max shifted uncomfortably. He'd taken Jade to White Prairie's winter dance the last two years. Chris and Jordy shot him a questioning glance, Jordy blinking like an owl. Max gave them a small nod. *Yeah, I got it, guys. It sucks to remember, but I can deal.*

The front door opened, and a cold wind blew in. Max hunched his shoulders, turned to look, and for a second had this crazy feeling that his thoughts were so intensely powerful that they could summon a person just by thinking about them. It wasn't a completely whacked-out idea. He'd never seen Emmie at the Happy Gopher before, but there she was with her lunch table friend, heading toward a corner booth on the other side of the room.

Max watched as she shucked off her coat and hung it on the hook beside the booth. He wondered what it would feel like to get his fingers caught in all those crazy curls, then thought about how soft her body looked in that fuzzy blue sweater. How soft it probably felt too. The idea caught him off guard.

Max wasn't sure when or why, but somewhere along the line he'd become seriously attracted. Emmie O'Brien didn't have any of Jade's polish—like he doubted Emmie ever spent over an hour on her makeup. In fact, he wasn't even sure she wore any.

No, Emmie was nothing like Jade. She was wild-haired and smart-mouthed and even a little scary. But now that he thought about it, scary-beautiful in a way he wanted to capture and keep all to himself, and it pissed him off to notice a couple guys on the other side of the restaurant turn to check her out. *Soccer players.*

As usual, Emmie held her body in a completely unaware way. Max didn't think she understood how beautiful she was, or how enticing. That was probably a good thing, because even as tiny as she was, she'd crush him if she had even the vaguest idea of her power.

Emmie set her phone on the table and leaned in toward her friend, who was already in the midst of what was apparently—judging by the wide eyes—an extremely intense story. Max pulled out his phone and texted: Hi, Emmie.

He watched, holding his breath, as she picked up her phone, looked at it, then put it down on the table without responding.

What the hell? She couldn't even say hi? He'd put his name in her phone. She knew it was him. Sorry, he texted. Just trying to be friendly.

Jordy got up and said, "I hate these things." He pulled a contacts case out of his pocket and headed for the bathroom.

Lauren tucked her glossy black hair behind her ears, then ripped the tops off a bunch of sugar packets and filled one of them with salt for the salt-and-sugar game.

"Who are you texting?" Chris asked.

"No one," Max said without taking his eyes off Emmie, who looked down at her phone, her eyebrows drawing together. She glanced around the restaurant but didn't see him.

This time, Emmie picked up her phone and texted back: Please don't bother me. You shouldn't have my number.

Max pinched back a smile so his friends wouldn't ask any more questions. He was glad she'd responded, despite the response itself. Sorry again. I didn't realize saying Hi was a bother.

There was no more response. Max watched. Waiting. Emmie's friend seemed to be wrapping up her story. She sat back against their booth, seemingly ecstatic when Emmie threw her head back and laughed. God, she looked great doing that. He'd never seen Emmie laugh before, and by Marissa's reaction, he wasn't the only one she'd been holding out on.

Around Max's table, everyone besides him had tossed back a sugar packet, and they all were holding their faces as blank as they could, their eyes darting around the table to try to detect the unfortunate person to have gulped back the mouthful of salt.

Max excused himself just as Brock yelled, "Chris!" and Chris lunged for a glass of water.

Katie turned her head when Max stood up, and he felt her eyes on his back as he crossed the restaurant to Emmie's table, slipping into her booth beside her. Emmie jumped to her left, making a little squeak, and he was pretty sure he saw her friend mouth, *Oh my God.*

"Hey," Max said.

"What are you doing here?" Emmie asked. She didn't look happy to see him.

Max shrugged. "I'm here most Fridays, but I'm *here* here in this booth because I figured you weren't into texting and liked the more direct approach. I can be direct."

"You certainly can," her friend murmured, and Emmie shot her a look that said *Judas!*

"Everyone's sitting over there," Max said, indicating the long row of tables that had been moved together for his group.

"Not everyone," Emmie said. "Believe it or not, you and your friends are not *everyone*."

"Fair enough. My friends and I are sitting over there. There's room. Do you want to join us?"

Emmie's friend's face was priceless, though Max didn't know how to interpret it. She was surprised, intrigued, or scared to death. Maybe a combination of all three. Max made a mental note that the team should really work on its social skills. Branch out. The guys were awesome. Mostly. The girls could be cool too. When they wanted to be.

"I don't think so," Emmie said.

"Oh, come on." God, was he really going to beg? Had it come to this?

"I'm here with a friend already. Do you know Marissa?"

Max reached over the table and shook Marissa's hand. She was pretty. Pale and fine featured. Her eyes were—Max guessed—even wider now than they usually were, and he regretted that he was the cause of that.

Marissa bit her lip like she was deciding whether to say something or not, and Max pulled his hand back with a jerk. Oh no. He knew the look on her face. He knew what was coming.

Jade hadn't gone to White Prairie, but somehow this girl seemed to know about their connection. Any second she was going to say the dreaded words. *I'm so sorry for your loss.*

Those words made everything worse. They brought him right

back to the receiving line at the church. Jade's mom looking ashen, drugged up on sedatives, her dad looking like he'd been hollowed out with a spoon.

The familiar shaking started somewhere below Max's heart, somewhere over his stomach. In another second, the nausea would come. Then the sweats. He balled his hands into fists and pressed them into the cushioned seat as if he were in a plane, falling to earth, and he was bracing for impact.

Max felt Emmie press her right hand against the side of his left fist. He didn't know if it was on purpose, if she was acting on instinct, or if it was some kind of miraculous accident. Didn't matter. He felt it. The heat of her. The solid assurance of her. He still didn't get it, this thing she did to him, but he wasn't complaining and he wasn't going to question it.

Emmie's hand didn't stay there for long, but it was enough. His heart rate slowed and nearly stilled. The plane leveled out. Max caught his breath.

"So how do you think you're going to do in the tournament?" Marissa asked.

Max blinked. Then he almost laughed. He'd had it all wrong. This girl knew nothing about Jade. He'd freaked for no reason. God, he was weak. What a basket case.

Katie came up to the table in that second. She laid her palms flat at the corner of the table by Marissa and leaned toward Max, squishing her boobs together. Her long, red hair fell forward in soft loops. Max noticed, but it did nothing for him.

"Sorry to interrupt, but our food's here."

"Yeah, okay. I'll be right over."

Katie stared at Max for a second longer, then bit the inside of her cheek. "Are you going to introduce me to your friends?"

"Yeah, sure," Max said, taking another deep breath. "This is Emmie O'Brien and Marissa…"

"Cooke," Marissa said.

"Oh yeah," Katie said as if she were trying to place her. "Aren't you in one of my classes?"

"We have sociology together," Marissa said. Then, when Katie's expression didn't show the slightest bit of acknowledgment, Marissa added, "I sit a couple seats behind you."

"Oh, right," Katie said slowly, then, "Right!" She turned her attention back to Max. "So are you coming?"

"I said in a minute." He didn't take his eyes off Emmie. Her head was bowed, and her jaw was set. Max sensed Katie walking away, as well as Marissa turning her head to watch her go.

"Aren't you going to go eat?" Emmie asked without looking up.

"I will."

The corner of her mouth tightened, and she swallowed what seemed to be a pretty big lump. "Marissa," she said, "you're going to have to excuse us for a second."

"Where are we going?" Max asked.

"Out."

Max slid off the bench, and Emmie led the way to the door. Max heard Chris yell from behind him, "Hey, Shep. What up?"

Max followed Emmie out into the cold. The wind flung ice crystals up off the snowbanks, and the shards bit at their faces. Emmie turned to face him.

"Are you all right?" she asked.

Max steadied himself. So the hand thing had been on purpose after all. "Yeah, of course. Totally fine."

"Great," she said, her mood changing from concern to irritation. "Then do you care to tell me what's going on with all...*this*?" She made a hand gesture back and forth between their two bodies.

Max narrowed his eyes, not sure how to answer. She acted like no one had ever shown interest in her, which was impossible. "I like you. Why are you so surprised?"

"Well, you can't. So stop it right now."

"I can't?" She was cute when she was mad, but Max wasn't going to be an idiot and point that out. Especially since he could see cute-mad slipping very quickly into scary-mad, and he didn't want to lose any ground.

"No," she said. "You can't." The wind picked up, and Max's hair snapped at his face, but he didn't go back inside.

Emmie made a sound, as if she'd about had it with him.

"Listen, Emmie," he said. "You can't *make me* not be interested in you just by stomping your foot, but if you're not into it, that's fine. No harm, no foul. Just thought you should know how I felt."

She rolled her eyes, "What's your game?"

"You mean hockey?"

She shook her head in frustration. "No, I mean your angle. What are you after? What do you want from me?"

She gritted her teeth, and Max groaned internally. He suddenly saw himself as a tail-wagging Labrador retriever trying to make friends with a rabid badger. "Come on, Emmie. We can at least be friends, right?"

Her lips tightened, and she shifted her weight. "You don't want me as a friend."

This time Max couldn't hold back a smile. "Don't I get to pick my own friends?"

"You already have. They're all inside. And let me tell you, your friends and me—*you* and me—we don't mix."

Max glanced toward the window where Jordy (back in his glasses) and Chris were laughing, warm hands reaching across the table for warm food.

"Not 'don't mix,'" Max said. "*Haven't* mixed. It's an important

75

difference. And just because they haven't been friends with you before doesn't mean they can't be now."

Emmie shivered, and Max regretted having left his coat inside. Tiny ice pellets skittered across the salted sidewalk. Emmie looked toward the restaurant windows, and Max could tell this conversation was about over.

"Listen," she said, her teeth now chattering like castanets. For a second, it sounded like she was going to cry, but that couldn't be right. This was Emmie O'Brien. Sure enough, when she looked up, her eyes were dry. "Don't you have a hockey scholarship or something that you're trying to get?"

The question surprised him. "What the hell does that have to do with *anything* we're talking about?"

"The work crew. I'm not exactly out of the woods yet," she said, looking at Max directly, perhaps for the first time since they'd come outside. Then she looked away again. "You don't want my kind of trouble interfering with any good thing that's coming your way."

Max touched her chin with his thumb and tried to turn her face back toward his, but she jerked away at his touch. "What are you doing?" she asked.

"Sorry," he said, kicking himself mentally. "It's a bad habit."

"What's a habit?"

Jesus. Hadn't Quack Linda been working with him on this very thing all last month? *You don't have to always express yourself with your hands, Max. Use your words.* It made him feel like a toddler. *Use your words. Keep your hands to yourself.*

"Emmie, please look at me."

She did. But only reluctantly.

"Can I be blunt with you?" he asked. "Do you mind if I'm blunt? 'Cause you've got to know. Right now, I think *you* might be the good thing that's come my way. I mean…" And then he heard himself. He sounded like a Hallmark card, and she was looking at him like he was an idiot.

He didn't blame her, but it wasn't nearly as bad as what he could have said—how meeting her made him feel like a drowning man whose big toe had suddenly bumped against a sand bar. Meeting her had been just as sudden, and just as surprising, and it brought with it just as much hope for rescue. But thank God he didn't say any of *that*.

Max tried again. "What I'm trying to say, Emmie…That scholarship you're talking about…If something doesn't change for me, I'm not going to get it. Hanging out with you…That would be a definite change."

"Max," she said, and once more that calm she exuded washed over him like a tidal wave. "I'll be your friend. But that's all this is going to be."

Max exhaled. It wasn't everything he wanted, but it was enough. "Good. Great."

"Now," she said, starting to move past him, "I've got to get back to Marissa."

Right at that moment, Chris stepped outside.

"Dude," he said, flipping his hair and not so subtly checking Emmie out. "Food's getting cold."

"So, I'll see you in the morning?" Max asked Emmie, and he could tell Chris's interest was piqued.

"Yeah, I'll see you tomorrow," Emmie said. "Not like I have a choice. But I want you to know, I meant what I said."

"I heard you," Max said.

Emmie looked at Chris, who was grinning like a madman, then she rolled her eyes and pushed between them to go inside. Max couldn't help but smile. They were going to be friends.

* * *

That night, Emmie thought about what Max had said about him being *interested* in her. And then she dismissed it.

The idea might have given her a warm, happy feeling deep in her belly, but she would never fit with him, or with his crowd. She didn't even think she wanted to. Sooner or later, the garbage in her life would float to the surface, and she didn't want Max anywhere near her when it did. He didn't deserve that kind of stink.

CHAPTER THIRTEEN

DRIVE-BY

THE NEXT MORNING

Max's alarm clock went off in the middle of Jack Duncan, one of the weekend radio guys saying, "Too bad it's a Saturday. Fifteen inches of fresh powder...Kids might have got a day off if there was school today."

"Doubtful," said the other guy in the booth. "Plows have been out all night."

Max opened his eyes to slits and peeked over at his window, which was whitewashed with a sheet of snow. He rolled over and groaned, covering his head with his pillow.

His door creaked open, and his mom's voice called in to him. "Your alarm's gone off twice now, honey. Time to get up. You've got the work crew. Dress warm."

Groan. Groan again. Mumble.

"Was that supposed to be an attempt at communication?" she asked with a small laugh. Max didn't have to open his eyes to know she was smiling. His mom tried so hard to act normal. To make light conversation. To make a joke. He loved her for how hard she worked at it, but the reason behind it all pinched at his gut. She kissed the top of his head. "Caveman grunts aren't going to get you anywhere with me, baby. Rise and shine."

Max nodded, then waited for her to close the door before he rolled up to sitting. M&M's on the brain. Or at least one Em, and he had the erection to prove it. He was both excited and terrified to see her today.

Last night's conversation hadn't gone nearly as well as he'd hoped, but she had at least talked to him. And she had been the one to suggest they talk alone. But then she'd put him in the friend zone. That hadn't been part of the plan, but he'd take what he could get.

The other unexpected thing was that when Max had got back to the table, Katie and Lauren told him that Emmie had gone to WPHS in ninth grade. Back then, Katie had just introduced him to Jade, and they'd started to date. He'd never even noticed Emmie. That was hard to imagine now.

Katie said there were rumors that Emmie had to leave after ninth grade because she got knocked up by some sketchy guy. She'd had the baby, given it up for adoption, and now she was back. The guys made no comment on Katie's story, just kept their heads down, eyes on their plates. The girls, however, were all over it.

"Seriously?"

"Ninth grade?"

"What a skank."

Max hadn't believed any of it, and his opinion hadn't changed by morning. Not that he'd think badly of Emmie if it was true, but it just didn't sound right. His alarm went off again, and he sent Emmie a text.

Hey, it's me. Max.

After a minute...

Yeah, I know. You put your name in my phone.

80

Right. He smiled to himself. Max pictured her sitting up in bed, sheets sliding over her shoulders, pooling around her waist. He wondered what she wore to bed. Maybe nothing.

He quickly pushed the image away. They were just friends.

So, are you going in today?

Seriously?

Can I give you a ride?

I have my own car.

Yeah, but I know all the shortcuts.

Give it up, Max.

Max laughed but didn't respond. He looked down at his phone while the screen went black. Then, for whatever reason, he smiled at his reflection.

* * *

Max got to the sheriff's department right on time, but he was not the first to arrive. He'd hoped he was going to be early enough to get a seat beside Emmie, who was in her usual first-row spot by the window. Unfortunately, there was already a guy sitting—*and sleeping*—next to her. The second row was full, too, so it was the farthest back for him again.

Max climbed in, feeling tight from all the layers of clothes he was wearing. Emmie was dressed in an oversize winter coat and her usual bright-pink hat. She kept her warm gloves on even though she was in the van. Her arms were folded over her chest. Dan McDonald arrived last and seemed pleased to see they were all there ahead of him and in their places. He didn't get in the van, but leaned into the open door to speak to them.

"We're shoveling out a halfway house today."

Emmie lifted her head from the window and looked toward Dan.

"Which halfway house?" she asked, barely concealing the note of anxiety in her voice.

Dan glanced at Emmie and held her eyes for a second, giving his head the tiniest of shakes. It seemed like he was sending her an unspoken message because she slumped back against the window as if he'd answered her question. What was her problem with halfway houses? She didn't seem like the type to judge.

"I hope everyone is dressed appropriately," Dan said. "I'll be driving separately, and I've got shovels and plenty of extra hats and gloves, so don't think you're getting out of it just because you came unprepared."

Someone in the row ahead of Max groaned.

"Ah, don't be too disappointed. I also brought a Thermos of hot chocolate. Okay, let's go. I want to see a whole lot of shoveling from all of you. If you're cold at the beginning, you won't be for long." He glanced at the driver, then slid the van door shut.

Emmie pulled off her hat, and her mass of wild curls tumbled down over her shoulders. Shit, Max thought. Good thing he got stuck in the back row. If he was sitting behind Emmie, it would have been tough to resist touching her hair, and then he'd hear about it.

It took them about twenty minutes to get to the work site. The driver pulled up to a tan brick building, three stories with about a dozen windows across, evenly spaced. All in all, the place was completely unremarkable. How many times had Max driven by it without notice? After today, he'd never drive by it again without remembering that he'd spent a day with Emmie O'Brien here.

The memory of her pressing her hand against his fist while they sat at the Happy Gopher made this snowy mess look even better. Warmer. In fact, he might actually love this place, this nasty brick building with its shitload of snow. *Seriously.* Did a disproportionate amount of snow fall here, or did all the neighbors generously share their portions just to give the juvenile delinquents something to do?

Emmie's shoulders sagged, and she made a little noise that told Max she was thinking the same thing. She pulled her hair together and gave it a twist, exposing the back of her neck. Max's stomach tightened.

"It's going to be deep, and it's going to be wet," the van driver said. Max blinked his eyes twice, then fought back a smile as Chris spoke up in his head: *That's what she said.*

"That means the snow is going to be very heavy. No macho men today, please. Bend at the knees. Take it off in layers. No macho women either, Em."

They all climbed out, and the wind bit at Max's cheeks. He zipped his coat higher and swung his arms back and forth to keep the blood moving. Emmie grabbed a shovel right away and got to work. The snow on the sidewalk was up to her knees.

All the guys on the crew grabbed shovels and spread out around the building, taking a section of sidewalk. Max purposefully started working in an area that was close to Emmie, so they could talk. He waited for her to initiate it, but she never did. She just kept her head down and her arms moving.

The driver was right; the snow was heavy. Max thought it might be too heavy for Emmie, but she seemed to be handling herself okay. Every five minutes, Max inched his way closer. Twenty minutes later, he and Emmy were shoveling in crisscross patterns, scraping up the fall-over snow that the other's shovel had left behind. Their noses were red, and their jeans and gloves completely soaked, but Max felt warm all the same.

"Hey, Emmie?" he asked.

"What?" she said without stopping her work.

"What would you think about getting something to eat afterward?" Max's question came out in huffs of breath that vaporized on the air.

"I don't think so," Emmie said. She was clearly exhausted, but she lifted her shovel and tossed the load over the snowbank at the edge of the driveway. It was so sticky that most of it stuck to her shovel. She gave an exasperated little groan and shook the shovel until the snow fell off in large, wet clumps.

"Friends do that," Max said.

She scraped her shovel along the sidewalk, lifting another load. "We're not that kind of friends."

Max stood his shovel up vertically and rested both arms over the top of the handle. "Geez, Emmie. I'm not proposing marriage. I'm proposing a sandwich." She didn't look at him, just kept on shoveling. "Will you, Emmie, take my hero sub…"

She shook her head and still refused him any kind of eye contact. The girl kept working.

"Another time then." He scooped up a thick load of snow, probably too much, but he was showing off.

"Arrogant," she muttered.

Max wasn't sure she meant for him to hear her, but he answered anyway. "Nope." He tossed the snow over the bank. "*Persistent.*"

She shook her head again, but Max noticed the tiniest of smiles. "This is ridiculous," she said.

"Well, I'll give you that. It *is* ridiculous. No one should put up such a big fight over a sandwich. If it makes you feel better, you can pay for your own."

"I'm not hungry."

"You could just get chips."

"Maybe some other time."

Max took advantage of her error. "Ah, progress. You just agreed to a future date."

She stopped and looked up into his face. He knew instantly that he'd gone too far. Without meaning to, he'd slipped into flirting, and now she was angry. The intensity in her eyes made him suck in his breath.

"Quit playing me," she said. Her voice was deadly calm, but it was not the kind of calm he craved.

"Shit, Emmie. I'm sorry. I didn't mean anything." He had to look away. Why was she perpetually on defense? If it had anything to do with the pregnancy rumors, he wanted to kill whoever'd hurt her.

Emmie walked away and leaned her shovel against the van. She grabbed a Styrofoam cup from the front seat and filled it with hot chocolate from the Thermos. She looked up just as an approaching car suddenly hit the brakes, skidding to a stop right in front of her.

It was an older-model sedan, riding low to the ground. The driver leaned out his window. He was nineteen or twenty with dark eyebrows that nearly met in the middle and a spiderweb neck tattoo. He wore an oversize puffy jacket and a baseball cap a little off center. Max could see the reflective tag under its flat bill.

Even though Emmie was bundled in a thick parka, Max noticed her back stiffen. In fact, her whole posture was rigid. Max didn't like the way this guy grinned at her, or the way everyone stopped working, or how Dan rushed in. It seemed everybody knew this guy but Max, and he instinctively moved to Emmie's side.

"Nick will be glad to know you're doing fine," the guy said, taking only a second to cast a sideways glance at Max. "And you do look *fine*, Pigeon. We're missing you at the Gold Pedal."

The guy was leering, and Emmie's face was ashen. Who was Nick? Why did this guy call her that stupid name? He was making Max's fingers twitch.

"Move on out," Dan said, stepping in front of Emmie and Max. He put his hands on the car's window frame. "We're working here."

"Just saying hi to my girl," the guy said. He gave Emmie another leering elevator look, down and up.

Max glanced at Emmie again. Nothing in her face made him think that she considered herself to be this jerk-off's "girl," but it brought Katie's gossiping back into focus. Had Emmie really had a baby last year? With this guy? With *this* guy? That couldn't be right. He looked like a disease. Max's hands balled into fists.

Dan rested his forearms on the car's open window frame and leaned into the guy's face. Dan was a big dude, and Max was glad to see that he could be scary when he wanted to be. "I said, 'Move, Jimmy.'"

"Don't get your panties in a bunch, *Danny*." The guy was all smiles. Then he peeled out, kicking up a spray of slushy snow.

Dan turned toward Emmie like he was going to put his hands on her shoulders. She stepped back abruptly, tossed the rest of her hot chocolate in the snow, and crushed her cup in her hand.

"Don't worry," Dan said, following her. "I've got this under control. I won't let that happen again."

"Yeah?" Emmie asked. "And how exactly are you going to stop them?"

Won't let what happen? Max wondered. *Stop what? What exactly was that?*

"Emmie," Max said, jogging to catch up to her and Dan. "Who was that guy?"

"It's none of your business. Leave me alone."

"I can't just leave you alone."

"Like hell you can't." Then she stormed away from him, picking up her shovel as she passed it and smacking it into the snowbank.

Max didn't bug Emmie for the rest of their shift, but he watched her. She didn't cry or give anything away on her face, but her whole body remained rigid, and her mind seemed very far away.

Apparently he wasn't the only one paying attention. As Max passed two of the other guys on the crew, one of them—Kyle, Max thought his name was—said to the other, "Did you recognize that guy who came up in the car?"

The other guy nodded. "Jimmy Krebs."

"I didn't know that girl ran with his crowd," Kyle said.

"Well, she's on probation for *something*. Jimmy didn't look too happy about it, whatever it is."

"A girl like that plays fast and loose," Kyle said. "I might have to tap that."

And that's when Max lost his shit.

His hands gave one quick twitch, and a second later, he had Kyle pinned against the brick wall of the halfway house, his fingers around Kyle's throat.

"Christ," the other kid yelled, pulling at the neck of Max's coat. Then, "Dan!"

Dan, who'd remained in the van doing paperwork, was there in an instant, his arms wrapped around Max's body, but Max wasn't backing off. Kyle's face was turning red under the pressure of Max's fingers, his eyes tense and watering. He looked so ugly that Max wanted to tear his face off.

"Let him go," Dan said.

But Max's elbow snapped backward, connecting with Dan's ribs, and Dan stepped off. Kyle tried to use the moment to get away, but Max had him back up against the wall. How dare this kid talk about Emmie that way? How dare he even *imagine* himself taking something from her? Max's fingers tightened.

Max knew he had to stop. He knew if he kept going, he'd slip into blackout mode. Either that, or he'd end up killing the kid. But Max couldn't...stop. He didn't know how...He needed help.

And that's when Max heard Emmie's voice. "Dude. Let him go."

At first, he thought she was only in his head—because the last time he saw her, she'd been on the side of the building—but then he felt her hand on his shoulder, and his body went slack. He let go of Kyle's neck and stepped back. Kyle staggered away from the wall, coughing and gagging. He bent over and spit into the snowbank.

"Emmie," Max said on an exhale. He was relieved. And he was embarrassed. What must she be thinking of him? But then he pushed away any concern he had for himself. Had she heard what Kyle said about her? Max didn't think so, but maybe she had and just didn't care.

"What the hell, Shepherd?" Dan said as Kyle and his buddy backed away. "You might have thought you were done today, but that stunt just earned you another two Saturdays on the crew."

That was fine by Max. He wasn't about to leave Emmie alone with Kyle Asswipe and his friend.

"Are you okay?" Emmie asked.

"He had it coming," Max said. He wished he knew what she was thinking about him. There was no judgment on her face or in her voice, and Max was so very, very grateful. But he still worried this new outburst gave her more reason to write him off.

"Jesus," Dan said, "why does everybody always have it coming with you?"

"Not everybody," Max said, still looking at Emmie. "Just those who don't play by the rules."

"It's you," Dan said, "who doesn't play by the rules."

This time Max managed to look away from Emmie, if only for a second. "Mine are the only rules that make sense."

"Yeah? And how's that working out for you?" Dan asked.

"I…um…" Emmie glanced toward the building. "I guess I'll get back to work." Then she walked quickly away, head down.

Back by the van, Kyle puked in the snow. Dan glanced over his shoulder and yelled, "Get in my truck, dude. I'll drive you back early." Then he turned to Max. "How are those anger management classes going?"

Max sighed. "They don't start 'til Wednesday."

Dan gave Max a withering look.

"Is Emmie in some kind of trouble?" Max asked, knowing Dan wouldn't tell him much, but hoping he'd tell him enough so he'd know how much to worry. The flickering remnants of his adrenaline rush still left a tremor in his fingers.

"Not now, but she needs to stay that way." Then Dan cocked his head to the side and looked at Max as if he was seeing him for the first time. "You want to put that energy of yours to use, put it into being a friend. The girl could use one, and someone like you wouldn't be bad to have in her corner. Just quit trying to put people through walls."

"You didn't hear what that asshole said about her." Max felt like a little kid. He knew his motivation, no matter how well intentioned, did not justify what he'd done to Kyle. So why couldn't he scramble up an apology?

"Doesn't mean I'm not adding on two more Saturdays."

"Understood."

"All right. You got yourself together?" Dan looked Max over, assessing him. "Can I trust you while I take Kyle back?"

Max gave Dan a half smile. "Yeah, I'm fine," he said. It was only a little lie.

Dan grimaced, then met Kyle at his truck, smacking the back of Kyle's head with his open hand as he unlocked the door for him. Max breathed out as the last of the tremors left his hands.

Two hours later, after Max got home, he sent Emmie an impulse text: You okay?

There was no response right away. In fact, there was no response for over an hour. But eventually—and surprisingly—his screen lit up.

Yeah. Thanks for checking. You?

Max typed out the words I'm fine, then packed up his gear for the game, still angry at Kyle and confused by what had gone down, but gratified that Emmie'd responded and that she was fine. In fact, maybe he was even a little happy.

When he got to the locker room and found that Jordy had put a family-size bag of M&M's in his cubby, well…he knew the feeling was going to last.

CHAPTER FOURTEEN

SUPERFANS

Nothing Dan McDonald could ever say would convince Emmie that he had "control" of her particular situation. She knew Nick was in prison. She knew he couldn't hurt her. But for everything that had happened, for as badly as she'd betrayed him, she didn't trust prison to be enough. Not that he would *or could* escape. Life wasn't a movie.

This morning had proven that Nick had many arms and legs, and some of them walked around free. Like Jimmy. And if Jimmy knew where to find her, then so did Frankie. And Angie too. Sometimes Angie was scarier than any of the guys. Emmie thought it was because Angie'd been with the guys so long that she'd stopped caring about anything. When you stopped caring, Emmie'd realized, you got reckless. It could even make you dangerous.

She hoped their reach wouldn't extend to school. Things were starting to fall into a comfortable pattern. It wasn't like she was popular, but at least she wasn't a freak like she'd feared. She was getting her assignments in. Teachers liked her. She had a place at the lunch table. Marissa's new friends accepted her into the group.

And then there was Max…whatever he was. She'd liked his text. She didn't need him to check up on her, but it still felt good. Especially after Jimmy's unexpected visit.

She'd been rattled. She'd tried not to let it show, but Max saw right to her heart. Without really knowing, he somehow still understood.

Suddenly, for the first time in a long time, Emmie felt that she had something to lose. It was a problem, and lord knew she had enough already. What was she supposed to do with the realization that she wanted to get to know Max better? Like, a hell of a lot better.

She shouldn't want that. More to the point, *he* shouldn't want that. But then, he didn't have the requisite information to make a sound decision, and Emmie was starting to feel selfish. Having Max around might be a good thing, particularly if she ever ran into Jimmy again.

"Whatever's bothering you, you've got to stop worrying about it," Marissa said as Emmie drove to Sarah's house on their way to the hockey game. The little hula girl mounted on Emmie's dash did a frantic hip wiggle as her car went over the washboard road of rutted snow. "It's not good for your skin."

Emmie checked traffic in the rearview mirror and caught her reflection. Marissa was right. When did she get this inside zit, right at the corner of her nose? It hurt like a mother.

But how was she supposed to stop worrying? Jimmy was going to tell Frankie. Frankie was going to tell Angie. They were all going to figure out how to find her. It didn't matter that she had a new phone number and that they didn't know her dad's address. Not if they could easily find her on the street.

Emmie shivered, thinking about what Nick and his buddies did to people who jacked them up. Usually it was junkies who didn't pay their debts. Luckily, her mom had never gotten in that much trouble with Nick, but she'd been lucky. She had other things to offer him. Emmie, for one.

"I'm just worried about my mom." It was not actually what Emmie'd been thinking about, but it was at least true. And close enough.

"Your mom? Why? What's wrong with your mom?" Marissa asked.

Emmie glanced over and decided, in that moment, that she owed Marissa at least a little explanation. Their friendship was back on track. Comfortable. Emmie trusted her. "She's…My mom's sick. That's why I came back to live with Dad." Emmie held her breath to see if that was enough of a disclosure to explain her distracted thoughts. It wasn't exactly the truth, but it wasn't a lie either.

Marissa looked over at Emmie, gap-mouthed. "What kind of sick? You mean like"—her voice dropped to a whisper—"cancer?"

Emmie swallowed. She should have known that a little information would only lead to more questions.

"Listen, Emmie. I keep telling you, you worry too much. You don't have to worry about telling me the truth. You're my friend. I love you."

"She's in rehab," Emmie said quickly, letting the last word sink like a stone. "As in drugs. Let's say, it wasn't a good idea for me to go live with her."

"I…" Marissa started. She stopped as if she didn't know how to finish, but then she figured something out. "Emmie, you don't have to walk around with so much bottled up. Whatever's going on with your mom, that's not on you. Lots of people go to rehab. Pretty much everyone in *People* magazine, and even if it got out about your mom—"

Emmie turned to her with a panicked look.

"—which it won't, but if people knew about her, they'd think she was messed up. Not *you*."

Emmie wasn't convinced. Bottling things up was the only way to stay afloat. It would take just one curious person to find out the whole story, and then they'd call her a whore. Or worse.

Emmie pulled in front of Sarah's house, and Sarah jogged down her front walk with Olivia and another one of Marissa's new friends that Emmie'd met only once. Their cheeks were all painted with blue-and-white stripes.

"Well, aren't we the superfans tonight," Marissa said when they climbed in.

"My brother and his friends were doing it," Sarah said. "I thought, Why not? Here." She reached forward and handed Emmie what looked like a waxy blue crayon. "I brought some for you. Put a couple swipes under your eyes, or a blue heart, or write #1, but don't do it looking in a mirror. That's what I did at first, and I wrote everything backward."

Emmie exchanged a glance with Marissa, then decided to give it a try. For a second, she considered writing Max's number on her cheek but luckily thought better of it because (a) she didn't remember what it was; (b) this stuff looked like it was going to be a bitch to get off; and (c) she had no business staking that kind of claim just because he'd dedicated his game to her. (Well, and to all the other new kids too.) Besides, she didn't even *want* to stake a claim.

What she did want was for him to get through the night without hurting anyone. She didn't know a lot about hockey, but she knew he had a lot riding on this game.

Emmie settled on writing *WPHS* on one cheek and a #1 on the other, making sure it wasn't backward, then handed the crayon to Marissa. The hula girl gave a little shiver when Emmie pulled away from the curb.

Once they arrived at the ice arena, Marissa and Sarah headed straight for concessions. Emmie stood at the corner of the rink where there was a gap in the plexiglass, protected by a black nylon net with two-inch mesh. The players were flying around the perimeter of the ice. So fast and strong, their legs pumping, their sticks held at waist level.

Emmie searched the ice, trying to see if she could recognize Max by his size or posture. But on skates, they all looked even bigger than in real life, and they were so covered up that she couldn't tell one from the other.

Emmie jumped when a body came flying up to the boards. She thought it was going to crash, but there was a loud scraping sound, and the mass stopped an inch from the netted gap. It was Max. Of course. And he was smiling.

He popped out his mouth guard and said, "You came to see me play."

It seemed like all the blood in Emmie's body was rushing to her face. "Not exactly."

"You can't get enough of me."

How did anyone on this planet come to have so much self-confidence? It wasn't natural. Never mind that he was right. Kind of right. A little bit, at least. Dammit. Well, there was no way Emmie was going to admit it to him.

"Hockey games are part of my punishment," she said.

Max put both gloved hands against the protective netting, and it sagged under his weight, drawing him closer to her. "What?"

"I've been court-ordered to do community work service and go to hockey games."

"You're joking. This is considered punishment?"

"Cruel and unusual."

He flashed a smile so big it reached his eyes. Emmie's stomach clenched.

"Shepherd!" the coach yelled. "No distractions."

Max ducked his head and swung away from her without another word. Her chest was still warm from his smile, but her gut twisted with her inadvertent admission. How much had the words *court-ordered* sunk in with him?

Max wasn't on Dan's crew because of the courts. Maybe he'd thought

95

the same was true for her. But she didn't worry for long. It had likely been too loud for him to hear everything she said, and by the way he glanced her way every time he crossed by her corner of the rink, she was pretty sure he hadn't heard. Or that he didn't mind.

"You and Max seem to be becoming good friends," said a feminine voice next to her. Emmie turned to look. The girl had long, raven-black hair pulled back in a blue-and-white knit headband that partially covered her ears. Emmie didn't recognize her, but she guessed she was part of Max's crowd.

"Not exactly," Emmie said.

"He dedicated his game to you, and you two were talking outside the restaurant last night."

"Oh that." She waved her hand dismissively. "Well, yeah. But I don't know him very well."

"So, Max isn't taking you to Snow Ball?" the girl asked.

Emmie sputtered and looked at her like she'd lost her mind.

The girl shrugged. "Just asking. He's a nice guy if you don't mind baggage." She gave Emmie a small smile.

Baggage? Emmie thought. What baggage? The girl acted as if Emmie should already know. She didn't. And as someone with plenty of baggage herself, Emmie wasn't going to pry into Max's personal life, even as curious as the girl's words made her. Maybe his past explained the way he acted: like a raving lunatic one minute, and a charmer the next.

When Emmie didn't say anything, the girl said, "I'm Lauren. Max and I go all the way back to kindergarten. I knew Jade. Katie was her cousin." She gestured to a tall, thin girl with long, red hair curled into loose waves. Emmie recognized her from the Happy Gopher. She'd been the one to come over to their table.

"Uh-huh," Emmie said. She didn't understand the context for the comments, but the name *Jade* struck a chord. She thought she heard someone say the name as she passed them in the hall today. *Max and Jade*, they'd said.

"Nacho?" Marissa asked, arriving suddenly and shoving a plastic tray in between Emmie and Lauren. Some of the molten gold that passed for cheese dripped off the corner, landing an inch from the tip of Emmie's shoe.

"None for me," Lauren said, "but thanks."

"Want to sit?" Marissa asked Emmie, giving Lauren a sideways glance. Marissa tilted her head in the direction of the home-side bleachers to make her meaning clearer.

"Yeah sure," Emmie said, then to Lauren, "Guess we're going."

As they walked to find their seats, Marissa leaned into Emmie's ear. "So now Lauren Schafer is seeking you out?"

"I'm not sure I'd put it that way," Emmie said.

"Mmm-hmmm," Marissa said with a wry smile. "You hear that sound?"

"What sound?" Emmie took off one of her mittens and dipped a chip into the cheese. It tasted like nothing that was natural to this planet, but it warmed her throat on the way down.

Marissa glanced up at the bleachers and nodded at Sarah who was saving them spots. Then she looked at Emmie knowingly and said, "It's the telltale sound of a singing snail."

* * *

The White Prairie Jackrabbits won 3–1. Max didn't know how he survived it because shoveling snow all morning had about wiped him out. His muscles were screaming even before he took the ice. But still, he played hard and he played clean. He didn't score, but he had three assists, and most importantly, he hadn't spent a minute in the penalty box.

Chris ripped into the bag of M&M's as soon as they got back in the locker room. "Open up, superstar. You get a treat."

"Nice game, Shepherd," Coach Polzinski said. "Sharp. Tough. All in. That's what I like to see."

Everyone pounded on one another's shoulder pads. Tack started chanting. They all followed him until they dissolved into a thunderstorm of sticks beating the floor.

Later that night, Max lay in bed and thought about what a long day it had been. He felt like he'd packed two into one. And as happy as he was that he'd made some measure of progress with Emmie, he was even happier with the progress he'd made with himself. That is, if he didn't count the Kyle incident, and Kyle wasn't worth counting.

Max rolled over and took Jade's picture in his hand. He hoped she wouldn't be mad about how good he was feeling. She probably wanted him to suffer more. Longer. Max was sure he would, but he hoped she wouldn't be mad at him for this moment of reprieve.

I'm sorry. More than you will ever know. Please don't hate me forever, he thought. And then he closed his eyes.

CHAPTER FIFTEEN

JUST A RIDE

Emmie didn't see Max after chemistry on Monday, and not at lunch either. It wasn't that she was actively looking for him, but...yeah, maybe she was. It occurred to her that she'd never had to look for him before. Max was always right there. Remembering her first morning back, how she'd slipped on the tile, she added: *Right where I needed him to be.*

It bothered her that she was bothered. Why should she be surreptitiously searching the halls for him as she and Marissa made their way from the building and out to Emmie's car? This was so very un-O'Brien of her.

She and Marissa were down the icy sidewalk and about to cross the driveway where the buses parked when Emmie heard someone behind her calling her name in a high-pitched, singsong way. *EHHH-mmie. EHHH-mmie.*

"Who is that?" she whispered to Marissa without slowing her pace. Marissa started to turn her head. "Don't look!" Emmie said, grabbing her friend's arm.

Marissa gave her a withering look. "How am I supposed to know who it is if I don't turn around?"

"Okay, look. But make it look like you're not looking."

"I used to do ballet. Should I do a pirouette? I could check to see who it is while I'm spinning."

"*EHHH-mmie,*" came the voice again.

"Oh, forget it," Emmie said as she spun around to face her taunter. "*What?*"

"Were you punished sufficiently at my game, or did you maybe have a little fun?" It was Max. Of course, it was Max. Just like him to drop out of nowhere. The two girls walking with Max scrunched their eyebrows together at Max's strange question. Emmie recognized them as Lauren (from the hockey game) and Katie (the redhead from the restaurant).

Emmie's mouth popped open, ready to deliver a sharp response, but no words came out. Maybe that was because Lauren and Katie were standing so close to Max. It gave her a strange kind of twist in her stomach to see them acting so familiar. Almost possessive.

"Where were you today?" Emmie asked Max.

Lauren gave Emmie an amused smile, but the other girl glanced up at Max as if to ask, *Who is this girl to you? Why does she care? And why are you looking so smug?*

Max didn't make any introductions. Instead, he dismissed the two girls, saying, "I'll see you two later."

Max's friends gave Emmie, then Marissa, another up-and-down look, then walked ahead.

"You noticed I was gone?" Max asked.

"I noticed." Emmie's cheeks flared hot with her confession. "Are you happy?"

"Extremely," he said, and Marissa smirked.

Emmie turned and kept walking toward the parking lot. Marissa trotted behind her as they passed between two buses and continued toward Emmie's car in the far back corner.

"You didn't answer my question," Max said, right on their heels. "Did you have fun at the game?"

"Yeah," Emmie said as she squeezed between a pickup and a station wagon. "I liked that you didn't try to kill anyone."

"I know," he said on a sigh. Like it was some huge accomplishment. "I think it was because you were there."

"Me?" Emmie asked, whipping around to face him.

Marissa choked with surprise, then tried to cover it up by acting like she had a cough. Emmie slapped her twice on the back. Maybe harder than necessary.

"Yeah, I think you're like some kind of sedative for me."

"You mean...Are you saying I'm *boring*?" It was a serious question, but also meant to give the conversation a different tone. Max sounded way too serious about what he was saying. It was bizarre enough. He didn't have to say it in front of Marissa.

"Are you kidding?" he asked. "You're like the least bor—"

"Oh shit," Marissa said. "Emmie. Your car."

"What?" Emmie asked, redirecting her focus. She barely even noticed when Max's hand clamped around her arm, and that was because her windshield was smashed in. Like, completely. Not just a spiderweb of cracks but crumpled into the car like the whole thing was made of tissue paper.

Emmie ran the rest of the way to her parking spot, practically dragging Max along with her because he wouldn't let go of her arm. She circled her car and groaned when she discovered all four tires were slashed. The word *Pigeon* was spray-painted over her back left fender— misspelled, which somehow made it worse—but what hurt the most were the five letters written across her trunk: *W-H-O-R-E*.

Max let go of Emmie's arm as her body went rigid. Her brain couldn't process what she was seeing. She knew who did it. She knew why. But she couldn't believe they'd come to her school and done this in broad daylight. The words were like scalpels, carving holes in her heart and stomach. Her limbs went numb.

Max's fist slammed down on the trunk of the car. The sudden noise made Emmie jump, as did her car on its shocks. Max's eyes were wide. Emmie thought he might have actually growled.

"Who did this?" he asked, whispering through his teeth. "I'll kill them!"

"Oh noooo," Marissa said from the front of the car, unaware of the worst of it, not to mention Max's barely controlled outrage. She leaned into the broken driver-side window. "Emmie, they took your hula girl."

Emmie rolled her eyes, and Max grabbed her shoulders. "Was it that guy from Saturday morning?" His eyes glanced to the damning word painted on the trunk, his voice raw.

The way he looked and sounded scared her. It reminded her of the way he'd looked on the ice that first time she'd seen him play. Like he was a boulder rolling downhill, crushing everything in his path. It reminded her of junkies hungry for a fix. And it reminded her of Nick.

Max must have seen the flicker of fear in her eyes because his grip relaxed and he took a step back. That simple, tender act was all Max. It reminded her of no one else.

He could let anger consume him, but she could see now—up close— how hard he fought to control it. She remembered him mocking his diagnosis: *I have what's called an overinflated sense of vigilance*, and she wondered what she'd done to be on the receiving end of his protection.

"Or one of his friends," she whispered. She didn't want Marissa to hear.

"Should we call your dad?" Marissa called back to them as she gingerly picked broken glass off the driver's seat.

"No. Not my dad." Emmie could handle this on her own, though it would be impossible to keep it from him forever. She needed time to figure out what to say. He would freak. He would probably have her on lockdown.

Marissa took a few steps away from the car, then seeing the way Max stood so close to Emmie, she said, "You know what? I think I'm going to catch a ride home with someone else."

Emmie looked at Marissa as if she'd lost her mind. *Of course* she was going to catch a ride with someone else. So was Emmie. There was no way her car was drivable. It probably wasn't even moveable.

"Oh hey, I see Justine," Marissa said, grasping her first option with overplayed enthusiasm. "Max, you've got Emmie?"

"Yeah, I got her."

"What?" Emmie asked, nearly yelling after Marissa as she walked quickly away. "Nobody's *got* me. *I've* got me."

She groaned when Marissa held up the back of her hand in dismissal. When Emmie turned back toward Max, she was glad to see the flare of his anger had faded away like a dying ember. His eyes went soft, and they searched her face for answers. There was something in his gentle expression that made her body soften and lean in to him.

"What is going on with you?" he asked.

The good feeling was replaced by a sour wave of shame. She didn't need his sympathy. She'd managed to get herself into all this crap on her own, and she didn't need someone to hold her hand now, no matter how good those hands might feel. Screw his concern. She was used to this. The words might be on her car now, but she'd never stopped hearing them in her head—*Pigeon. Narc. Whore.*

She needed Max to back off. She needed to be prickly.

"Nothing is going on with *me*," she said. "Something's going on with my *car*. Besides, it's none of your business, so no need for you to get excited about it. Just…go, okay?"

The corner of his mouth tightened. "Nice try, Emmie."

Emmie hated that she couldn't scare him off. He had twelve inches and probably seventy pounds on her. He was used to facing huge guys on the ice. How was she going to intimidate him?

"Don't lie to me," Max said softly. His eyes flashed to the car, and she saw the anger return, only to quickly evaporate when he refocused on her. "Tell me what this is all about. I can't stand back and let this go."

"What do you mean, you can't let this go? This isn't your problem. It's mine."

Max gestured emphatically at the car. "Somebody screws with you, it's my problem."

"That's bullshit," she said, folding her arms. "You're not my boyfriend."

"Not yet."

There were several beats of silence between them while Emmie let that sink in and Max—it seemed—tried to wrap his head around the fact that he'd said the words out loud. Finally, Emmie found her voice.

"Are you insane? Have you lost it? We're not playing out some rerun episode of *Degrassi High*."

A slight smile breached Max's lips. "Looking at your car? Yeah, I think I've just about lost it." His hands slipped from her shoulders, down her arms to wrap around her arm, but not like Nick used to grab her. This felt different, gentler, more pleading, like he needed her to hear him. Like his life depended on it. "Why are you mixed up with these people?"

"I'm not." Emmie pulled away from Max. There was no way she was bringing him into any of this. "It's none of your business. Thank you for your concern, but just go away. I'm sure Lauren and that Katie girl are waiting for you somewhere."

"Go away?" he said flatly. "You can't mean that."

"I do. Just leave me alone."

"With this car? Emmie, how are you going to get home?" He folded his arms. He had a point, and he knew it. Smug bastard.

"I—I don't know. I'll call a cab."

"Do you have any money?"

Dammit.

Max tilted his head like he could read the unspoken answer in Emmie's eyes. "Please. Do me a favor. Let me give you a ride."

"I can walk." Emmie adjusted her backpack and glanced toward the road.

Max rolled his eyes and tipped his head back to look at the sky. He was trying to be patient with her. "You're not walking home. Whoever did this to your car is probably still driving around. Where do you live?"

"Pioneer Drive. Behind Valley Floral." As she said it, she knew how he was going to react.

His eyebrows came together like she was the most ridiculous girl who'd ever lived. "Are you telling me you were planning to walk over five miles? It's freezing out here."

She shrugged and pulled her jacket tighter around her. "I'm tougher than I look."

Max dropped his chin and leveled her with a glance. His deep-brown eyes had nearly gone as dark as his pupils. "I have no doubt of that. You can't be a pansy ass and shovel snow like you did, or sit through cruel and unusual punishment like a hockey game. And no wimpy girl is going to be nearly crushed by falling appliances or see her car totally trashed like this and not even cry a little. You're tough as shit, Emmie. I see that. I'm just offering you a ride."

Emmie held his gaze for as long as she could, then glanced away. She bit down on her lip, then whispered, "Fine."

"Fine?" His voice went up like he was prepared for every answer except the one she gave him.

"Yeah, fine. I'll take your ride." She looked back at him and couldn't stop herself from smiling, if only just a little, at the elation on his face.

"Good." Max's shoulders dropped as if he was letting go of several pounds of pressure and finally able to relax. "That's the first rational thing you've said since you got outside."

Emmie knew he was right, and she wished she could rewind things a few minutes. She'd promised herself she was going to be nice. She was supposed to be trying harder. "Yeah, about that. I'm sorry. My first instinct is always resistance."

"Apology accepted," he said as he ushered her between the cars in the next row.

"It's not your fault I act like this," she said.

"I never thought it was." Max stopped walking and clicked the key fob in his hand. The headlights on a jeep flashed, and the doors unlocked. "Now hop in."

Emmie glanced over the jeep. It was black. It was awesome. Of course it was awesome. It was Max Shepherd's.

"Why are you always so nice?" she asked when he opened the door for her.

"I told you when we were outside the restaurant. I think you're the good thing that's come my way." He slipped her backpack off her shoulders and held it while she climbed in. Emmie marveled at how he could say something like that without it sounding completely cheesy. It was like he…like he meant it.

"You're wrong."

He handed Emmie her bag as if it were weightless, but it landed heavily in her lap.

He hadn't responded to her warning, so Emmie gestured in the direction of her car and then to herself. "You can see how big a mess I am. I'm not a 'good thing.'"

"Messes I understand," he said with a shrug. "It's the people who've got it all figured out that confuse me."

Max walked around the front of the jeep, and as he did, Emmie was thinking: What is this life I'm living? Because this moment was clearly not meant for her. He was a beautiful person—not only to look at, but in the way he cared what happened to her. She hadn't had such beauty in her life for…maybe forever.

Max unsnapped his letter jacket and started the ignition.

"It's a defense mechanism," Emmie said. "Me pushing people away."

Max made an amused sound and pushed his knit cap off his forehead so it slouched off the back of his head. "Now you sound like my therapist."

"You have a therapist?"

"You *don't?*" he asked, eyebrows raised.

The surprise in his voice got Emmie's back up, and she mustered up as much sarcasm as she could. "Should I?"

"I'd say so. Now where to? Exactly?"

Emmie groaned, then gave him directions, all the while wondering if he'd ever use them again. She couldn't imagine why he would. It wasn't like Jimmy or Frankie could trash her car *twice*. Though…if they could make her pay twice for what she did to Nick, she knew they would.

"Okay," Max said. "Let's go. Let's get the hell out of here."

Emmie sucked in a breath, startled by the unbidden memory of Nick Peters saying those same words as he jumped into the car, bulging bag of stolen money in hand.

Let's go, let's go! Why are you still standing there? Pigeon, get going. We gotta get the hell out of here.

With the heels of her hands pressed to her forehead, she forced away the memory. When her mind was clear, she glanced in Max's direction and allowed herself the luxury of looking at him while his eyes were trained on the road.

She liked the way his dark hair was always rumpled-looking on top, and the way it curled around his ears and up at the back of his neck. She doubted he ever combed it. She liked the way his eyes crinkled at the corners, and she liked the bent line of his nose. But most of all, and particularly right now, she liked how he made her feel safe and how he took her mind off the fact that her car was headed for sheet-metal heaven.

When Emmie's eyes made it to Max's mouth, she found a small smile playing at the corners of his lips. "Like what you see?" he asked.

Emmie jerked around to face front. "Shut up, Shepherd."

"You're going to call me Shepherd now?"

"Only when you look so smug."

Emmie pointed to her house, and Max pulled up along the curb. Her father wasn't home from work yet and wouldn't be for at least two hours. Two hours to figure out an explanation for why she was home without her car.

"Thanks for the ride," Emmie said as she opened the passenger door, but she froze in her seat when she spotted the tiny grass skirt, crisp as springtime against the snow-dusted sidewalk. She'd recognize it anywhere. It was the hula girl from her car. Or at least...part of her.

All the blood in Emmie's body rushed out of her head and down her arms, leaving her with a cold chill that had nothing to do with the weather. *They were here. They know where Dad lives.*

"What is it?"

Emmie's voice shook. "I think I'm in trouble."

Max reached toward her, but she was already getting out of the jeep and slamming the door behind her. A second later, Max's door opened, then closed. He caught up to Emmie just as she was picking the tattered plastic grass from the snow.

"Emmie?" he asked, snapping up his letter jacket against the cold.

"It's from the hula girl that used to be in my car." Emmie looked up at her house and hesitated. "Would you come inside with me?" Her whole body was trembling now, and she pushed one hand against her chest to steady her shallow breaths.

"No, you stay here," he said. "I'll check it out."

Max got halfway up the driveway on the side of the house before Emmie realized she couldn't let him go alone. She ran up behind him, and even though he swung his hand out to stop her, she reached the steps that led from the driveway to the kitchen first.

It was impossible to miss the arms. Two slender, plastic limbs, hands delicately posed, crisscrossed on the top step like an *X* that marks the spot. Max cursed under his breath.

Emmie scooped up the arms and put them in her pocket with the grass skirt. Tears stung at the corners of her eyes, but after what Max said to her in the school parking lot, about liking how she wasn't a wimp, she wasn't going to let him see her cry. Not now. Maybe not ever.

Emmie fumbled her key out of her bag, but it wasn't necessary. The mere pressure of her hand against the handle allowed the back door to fall open. Max pushed around to get in front of her, like he planned to be some kind of human shield. Emmie stepped into the kitchen and peered under his arm. The hula girl's severed head was sitting on a glass pie plate in the middle of the floor.

CHAPTER SIXTEEN

A LITTLE BIT OF GLUE

Before Max even had the chance to ask, Emmie said, "I can't tell you."

Her knees swayed like they were about to give way, but that was the only sign she was even remotely affected, and she had herself under control a second later. Max heard her voice in his head, right after she was nearly crushed at the Goodwill. *I've never seen freaking out do anyone any good.* How did she do it?

Max pulled her in to him, circling his arms around her. It was instinct. If he had thought about it, he would never have done it. She'd never given him any indication that this was something she wanted him to do, in fact, far from it. But this time she didn't pull away.

The unexpected intimacy shocked him. He didn't understand her obvious aversion to physical contact—even the most trivial, like a handshake—but he'd seen it often enough: the flash of fear in her eyes when nothing else seemed to scare her, the stiffening of her shoulders, the straightening of her spine. As if a hand could burn her.

The fact that she now lay so calmly against his chest was huge. *Important.* He didn't want to do anything to ruin this perfect moment.

Still, he couldn't help but tighten his hold as he puzzled out his own feelings. If he had to name them, he felt like a little boy with a broken toy. Just as sad, and looking for a bit of glue. Wondering who was going to put it back together for him.

But Emmie wasn't a toy, and deep down he knew that whatever was going on with her, it wouldn't be that easy to fix. Even though he was holding her close, he felt the familiar panic of needing to get to someone who was just out of reach. He closed his eyes and willed the memories to stay at bay. He pushed them like the ice under his skates. He pushed at the memories until they were far, far behind him.

Emmie abruptly pulled away from Max and turned her back. She picked up the pie plate and set it on the counter.

For a second, Max wondered if Emmie's hot-cold reaction had something to do with the baby rumors Katie and Lauren had told him about, but that didn't seem to line up with whatever seriously scary thing was happening to her now. Unless…maybe…the guy hadn't wanted Emmie to give the baby up? That was possible. Was all that was happening retribution for that?

"Please tell me," he said. "How do you keep yourself together like this? Any normal person would be freaking out."

"I've never seen freaking—"

"I know. You've said that before. You've never seen it do anyone any good."

She took a deep breath and bowed her head as if she was considering something. Max held his breath, afraid even the tiniest noise would change her course.

"Last year…" Emmie looked up. "Last year, this guy I knew, B. J… He was shooting up." She paused, maybe to judge his reaction. Max kept his face blank, and he tried not to think too hard about Kyle's words: *I didn't know she ran with that crowd.*

Emmie inhaled and continued. "A little bit later, he wasn't moving. When we realized what was happening, everyone started yelling that he'd OD'd. No one knew what to do. This one guy, Nick..." She swallowed hard as if his name was a jagged pill. "Nick didn't want a dead guy in his kitchen, so two of the other guys carried B. J. to a parking lot across the street. They just left him there. There was all this panic and fighting. No one was thinking straight."

"I'm sure not," Max said, urging her on, though his mind was racing. Was Emmie into drugs? She didn't seem the type. Hell, he'd somehow gotten the impression she didn't even drink, and now she was talking about shooting up? Without being obvious, he did a quick scan of her body looking for...He didn't know what. If she was into that, there would be some kind of physical sign, right?

Emmie nodded. "No one called 911 or anything. I finally did, but only when Nick wasn't paying attention, and not until it was too late. As it turned out, B. J. wasn't actually dead. At least not in Nick's kitchen. He ended up dying of hypothermia in that parking lot. If I'd called earlier, he'd probably still be alive. It's my fault."

"Emmie..." Max said her name slowly. Softly. Was this why she was on the work crew? Had she been charged with something as serious as...He couldn't even think the word.

"If I could go back and do things differently, I seriously would. Freaking out didn't help any of us. I never let myself lose control after that." She looked up then, her eyes wide and her face pale. "I've never told anyone that before."

Max stepped closer, wanting to touch her, as if that could make everything better. It was a dumb thing to think, but it was all he had. She winced, and he pulled his hand back.

"Forget I told you all of that."

"Not likely," he said. He reached toward her again and let the backs of his fingers brush against her arm. Testing her before he got any closer. "Why do you think any of that was your fault? At least, more than that kid's own fault. Or those other guys who left him?"

She swayed again, and Max wrapped his fingers around her elbow to steady her. "What do you want me to do?" he asked.

"There's nothing you can do. Except maybe stay with me until my dad gets home?" Her breath heated his cotton T-shirt, and she tentatively wrapped her arms around his waist.

Max's stomach muscles tensed, and his lungs inflated with a quick intake of breath. She turned her head to the side, pressing her ear against his chest. Max wondered if she could hear how fast his heart was beating.

"But I can't tell you anything more than that," she said. She inhaled, then released a shattering breath.

There was *more* then. Katie must have been right about the baby thing. That had to be what Emmie was referring to. Max didn't know how that would make anything she'd already told him worse, and he felt compelled to assure her of that.

"I already heard about the baby, and I don't think anything bad of you for it."

Emmie stiffened, and Max hoped it wasn't exactly the wrong thing to say. He hoped his words wouldn't break the spell, because this whole moment felt like something out of a dream. Both the good kind that left him warm and tingling and wishing he'd never woken up, and the bad kind that left him sweating and tearing at his sheets.

Emmie tipped her head back and stared into his eyes, her eyebrows pulling together in confusion.

Max kept his hands on her shoulders but stepped back so they could look at each other better. "I heard about the baby, and it's okay. It was brave of you to give it up, and I don't judge you for it. I don't understand how getting pregnant has anything to do with all the other stuff, and you don't have to explain that part if you don't want to, but tell me why that guy—"

"There's no baby," Emmie said with an exasperated eye roll.

"I know. Katie told me how—"

"I never had a baby."

"But people—"

Emmie tossed her hands up as if she didn't want to talk about it anymore and turned away. "They can think that. It's easier that way."

"You mean...What are you saying? Lying about a baby is easier than what?"

As soon as the question was out, Max wished he hadn't asked it. There was a tightness around Emmie's eyes that told him he'd taken a step too far. That was okay. He'd back off. He was glad his assumptions about that sleazy guy in the lowrider were wrong. The thought of his hands on Emmie...

"Can I sit?" he asked.

"Sure."

Max sat down in a wooden kitchen chair. Emmie walked closer. Did she miss their physical contact too? Max wanted to take her hands in his. The hug before had been spontaneous and necessary. Holding her hands now would seem too deliberately intimate. He knew Emmie well enough to know that would be more than she'd allow.

"That guy Saturday morning," Max said, already forgetting about his resolution to back off. "The one in the car," he added as if she didn't know exactly which one he was talking about.

There was a long pause. Emmie took a deep breath, then blurted out, "Jimmy and I were friends with that guy Nick I mentioned before. I had to testify against Nick in court for some other stuff. Now Nick's in prison, and there's a no-contact order. Nick's not allowed to call me, so he had Jimmy deliver a message. Hence my car."

"Hence?"

"Hence."

Max's head went blank for a couple seconds, incapable of thought. Then the image of Dan, bristling when that guy Jimmy had pulled up in his car, flashed across his mind.

"How bad a guy is Nick?" Max asked, feeling more and more separated from her, despite the closeness of their bodies. She'd lived a life he'd only seen on TV. It was a hell of a lot scarier in real life. He tried to look strong, but what Emmie was telling him made him feel weak in comparison. Like he was flattening into one of those action-hero cardboard cutouts that were propped up all over the movie theater.

"Depends on who you ask."

"And you testified against him because…"

She closed her eyes, then looked up at the ceiling before she walked past Max to the other side of the table. She sat down in a chair, facing him.

"It doesn't matter why," she said, keeping her hands under the table. Despite the fact that there was no way for Max to hold them now, he took a little satisfaction in that he was starting to understand how they worked together. He'd press, she'd hide, he'd give her some time, and she'd give a little.

"It *does* matter. Someone trashed your car and left a broken hula girl to make sure you know that they know where you live, and that they know how to get inside. Someone needs to make this right." *I need to make this right.* Max shoved his hands into the pockets of his jeans so Emmie wouldn't see his fingers trembling.

"Nick asked Jimmy to shake me up. Message received. That's all."

"That's all?" Max couldn't believe what he was hearing.

"Assuming that's all Nick asked of them, yeah, that's all. Shit. I'm going to have to tell my dad about my car."

"*Of course* you're going to have to tell your dad. Your car is trashed. You'll have to tell the police too."

She leaned forward and rested her forehead on the table's surface. Despite her earlier explanation, Max still didn't understand how she kept herself so controlled.

Emmie sat up, lips pressed together, and reached into her coat pocket. She laid the hula girl's disembodied arms and tattered skirt in the center of the table. She stared at them for a few seconds, then asked, "What do you think they did with the rest of her body?"

CHAPTER SEVENTEEN

LET ME TOUCH YOU

Max's temper flared, and his face felt hot. He was about to say that he had no effing idea what had happened to the doll's body when he heard the hitch in Emmie's voice and the subtle, unspoken meaning behind her question.

He didn't know if she was speaking about the past or worrying about the future, but someone had hurt Emmie. Hurt her body. There was no way anyone was going to touch her again. Not in *that* way, at least. Never with violence.

If Max could be a force field around her, he would. If Emmie would let him, he would be there for her like he hadn't been there for Jade. Guilt and shame had been gnawing at Max's heart for a year now, but Emmie offered the chance to banish the beast. If he could help Emmie out in the process, then this was his shot at redemption.

Emmie reached one hand across the table and gave his a squeeze. "Please don't tell anyone about any of this."

Max looked down at her small hand on his. She was in her giving mode again. He didn't know what she was specifically referring to when she told him not to tell. It didn't sound like she'd done anything wrong, nothing that would deserve community work service. And she hadn't told him that she'd been actually...hurt. As far as he was concerned, she was brave as hell for testifying against that asshole in prison. She hadn't told Max what the guy had done either, but it had to be bad.

Right now, in the midst of all this crazy, she'd chosen to open up to him, and Max was proud that she was letting him past her sharp corners. Right to the center. Was that because it was just the two of them here without the rest of the world looking in? Slowly but surely, the pieces of the Emmie jigsaw puzzle were falling into place for Max. She liked her privacy.

Max knew what that felt like. He'd give anything for *his* pain not to be up for public conversation. Maybe even Emmie had heard about Jade by now, though she'd never ventured to ask him about it. Yeah, privacy was obviously important to her. Maybe that's why she'd shut down his more public advances.

"Your secrets are yours to share," Max said. "They're safe with me, but what about you?"

"Me?" she asked, oblivious to his question.

"Yeah, are *you* safe?" Secrets were one thing, but could she keep herself safe when he wasn't around? "Do you know any self-defense?"

The corners of her mouth turned up. "I thought you were planning on taking down all the bad guys."

"Is this a joke to you?" How could she make light of this? That was exactly the attitude that would get her in trouble.

She flushed. "No. Of course not."

"Stand up."

"What?" She sat up tall and rigid in her chair.

"I said, stand up."

"Okay." She pushed her chair back slowly, letting it scrape on the floor. Then she got to her feet. So did Max.

"Now come at me," Max said.

"What?"

"Quit saying 'what' and do what I say. Come at me. Slow motion."

She moved toward him, one eyebrow arched, her curly hair framing her face.

"You're small." The corners of his mouth tipped up. "You won't overpower anyone. You need to surprise them. So as they come near you...Will you let me touch you?"

Emmie nodded, and Max wrapped his hands around her upper arms. "When they come near you, don't push away. They'll be prepared for that. Instead, let them pull you closer, and as they do, bring your knee up."

She grabbed his shirt at the shoulders and pretended, rather convincingly, to knee him in the nads. "Like this?"

Max jerked back, but she stuck close. Very close. Close enough for him to smell her shampoo and count the freckles on the bridge of her nose.

"Yeah, like that," he whispered. God, he wanted to kiss her. Her face was turned up to his. Questioning. Did she want him to? He couldn't tell, and he didn't want to make a mistake. Or lose a testicle.

He swallowed and glanced down at her lips, and he felt her tense in his arms. *Yeah, bad idea.*

"And if that doesn't work?" she whispered.

He stepped back. "Go to plan B."

"Which is?" The corner of her mouth torqued with skepticism.

"Play dirty. Bite. Scratch. Go for the eyes." Max reached out and touched the side of her arm, testing the limits of their new familiarity. "Remember that first hockey game you went to?"

"The one where you nearly killed that guy?"

Max closed his eyes for a second. "Thanks for reminding me. I was actually asking if you remembered what happened right before that."

"Um...one of your friends went down? Everyone in the stands was super pissed."

"Yeah. The other player slashed Chris behind the knees with his stick. It's a weak spot. Brought Chris right down, and he's a big guy. Plan B, I want you to go for the knees."

Emmie nodded seriously, as if she were taking her marching orders. Max could have kissed her right then. God knows, he still wanted to. He pulled off his knit cap and held it front of him so she wouldn't see just *how much* he wanted to.

That's when the back door was flung open.

Max whipped around, blocking Emmie and immediately on defense. A tall, thin man with graying hair stood inside the doorway, his panicked eyes darting from Max to Emmie and back to Max.

"Who the bloody hell are you? Whose jeep is that?" he asked in a thick accent.

"Dad, settle down." Emmie pushed past Max to position herself between him and her dad. "It's okay."

"Like hell it is," he said.

Did Emmie's dad already know about her car? Max backed up against the stove. Emmie walked across the floor toward the door and closed it. "Dad, I—"

"Did you talk to your aunt Bridget?" he asked, glancing warily at Max again. What was that accent? English? Irish? He sounded like a badass Harry Potter.

Emmie shook her head a little bit. "No."

"Someone tore open the screens on her porch and threw this inside." He held open his palm, revealing a bikini-clad plastic torso. "Is this what I think it is?"

120

"Oh," she said, her face going pale. "Someone took it out of my car."

A vein was starting to pop in the center of her dad's forehead. Emmie didn't seem scared of him.

"Does *he* have anything to do with this?" her dad asked, leveling Max with a look that Max thought was supposed to crush his balls.

"No, Dad. Don't be ridiculous. Why would he be here if he trashed my car?"

Her dad's eyebrows shot up. "Someone trashed your car? Excuse me, but I think I'm entitled to be ridiculous when your safety is at issue."

Max liked him immediately.

"This is Max Shepherd. He gave me a ride home. He's just a friend from school."

Max ignored the word *just*. She was definitely not *just* his friend from school.

"I wanted to make sure Emmie got home safely…um…*sir*. We found more doll parts here."

Her dad glanced down at the table, and the vein was officially popped. "Son…"

"Max."

"Max, thank you for bringing Emmie home, but I think it's time for you to go."

Emmie shot Max an apologetic look, but he was taking her dad's side on this. They needed to work things out. They needed to call the police. Max gave Emmie's hand what he hoped would be a reassuring squeeze and said, "See you tomorrow?"

She smiled. "Not if I see you first."

She was making a lame joke? Tough. As. Nails. Max shook his head and smothered a smile. Then, after a moment of hesitation, he let himself out the back door.

Max walked down the driveway to the road, the anger and worry still simmering at the back of his mind, and now hyperaware that someone might still be watching the house. He glanced around but didn't see anything obviously out of place. Didn't matter. If he ever caught the guy who'd messed with Emmie, there'd be something seriously out of place. Like his nose.

And that was one more promise Max Shepherd intended to keep.

CHAPTER EIGHTEEN

KIDS LIKE HER

Emmie's father watched through the kitchen window as Max made his way back to his jeep. A minute later, Emmie heard the engine start up, then the sound of Max driving away. It left her with a hollow feeling deep in her chest—a feeling she didn't have time to worry about because her father stalked past her with enough urgency that she felt compelled to follow.

He pulled his cell phone out of his back pocket and faced the living room fireplace, his back to Emmie and to the rest of the room. His free hand was on his forehead. It was a posture that expressed frustration, and Emmie knew what was coming before he ever spoke.

But then he did. "God, woman, you sound polluted."

Emmie cringed. Her mom was supposed to be in rehab, but she could already tell from her father's reaction that it wasn't going well. Her father's Irish accent flared. Emmie didn't want to be near him when he blew. Ideally, she'd wait it out in her room, but she couldn't get to the stairs without going through her father's line of sight. Maybe better to stay in the kitchen.

"Well, you've done it all arseways now, haven't you?" her father said. "You're supposed to be working your program, but no. Instead you're being the usual pain in my hole. Don't tell me you're not off your face, woman. I can hear it in your voice."

Great. It sounded like her mom had somehow figured out how to use while in a residential program. Leave it to her.

Emmie ducked back through the kitchen doorway and poured herself a glass of milk. Then she christened an unopened package of Oreos.

"Second chances? Second chances? *Well*, good for you. I'm glad you think they'll let you back in the program, but there are no more second chances, or third, or fourth with me."

Emmie searched inside herself for the stillness she so often depended on. She knew it must be there, but she couldn't find it.

"Why," her father bellowed, "in the bloody hell would you give them our address?"

Emmie sucked in her breath. Is that what had happened? Had her mom given their address to Jimmy and Frankie? Oh God, had she given it to Nick? She knew her mom would never *want* to hurt her, but her mom did lots of stuff she didn't necessarily want to do. Information could be bought and traded, and often that was the only currency her mom had to work with.

Oh God. The betrayal was a knife to the heart, and Emmie couldn't let herself believe it. She *wouldn't*.

She closed her eyes for a long moment, then she straightened her shoulders and picked up an Oreo. Her fingers trembled as she brought it to her mouth. It didn't taste as good as she'd expected. She hoped her father's rant would be over soon.

"Don't deny it. They were *here*," her father said. "Are you comprehending me? They could have been here when Emmie got home from school. And they vandalized her car *and* Bridie's house."

There was a pause as her father fell into listening mode, but it didn't last long. "You never look farther than the end of your own nose. But I swear to you—" Emmie knew her father well enough that she could picture his face getting redder and redder. He'd be hanging up soon. "Those knackers so much as touch a hair on our daughter's head—"

The conversation ended abruptly. Emmie couldn't tell who had hung up on whom. Her father walked back toward the kitchen and leaned against the doorframe, watching her calmly dunk a cookie into her milk. She didn't look up at him. She'd found her Zen groove, and she wasn't going to leave it willingly.

Her father inhaled, then let his breath out slowly. "Now," he said. "Would you like to tell me about the fella who drove you home?" He loosened his tie, pulling it down low, then slipping it over his head. He tossed it on the table and unbuttoned the top two buttons on his shirt.

Emmie guzzled the rest of her milk and set the glass on the table. "I told you. He's a friend. His name is Max Shepherd. He's on the hockey team."

"Hockey?" Her father raised his eyebrows, and Emmie cringed at the realization that he knew as well as she did that she and Max were a strange combination.

"We met on Dan's work crew."

That made him stop. "Do you really think it's a good idea to hook up with someone like that?"

"God, Dad. We're not *hooking up*."

Her father waved his hands around in the air. "I don't mean it like that. I mean, the kinds of kids on the work crew aren't exactly desirable types."

"You mean kids like me?"

He rested his shoulder against the doorframe and folded his arms. "You're twisting my words."

"I don't think I am."

Her father took off his glasses and slipped them into his shirt pocket. "I'm only saying, after all you've been through, can't you find someone of quality?"

Emmie raised her eyebrows at him. *Spit it out, Dad. This is really interesting.* Had she sunk so low in his estimation?

"I mean someone who's not in any trouble of his own," he added.

"Max isn't in the court system. He's on the work crew because of something through school...or with the team. He works hard. He's a good athlete. And he watches out for me."

That got her father's attention. "How so?"

"He brought me home today, didn't he? After what happened to my car, he wanted to check out the house before I came inside. That's saying something, isn't it? I thought you'd be happy to have someone like him in my corner."

"He's a big guy..." Her father considered what she was saying; then his eyebrows pulled together. "You're sure he doesn't want anything more from you?"

Despite her attempt to control the blood flow to her face, Emmie couldn't help the heat in her cheeks, particularly remembering the look on Max's face when they'd stood so close. She could still smell the laundry soap in the fibers of his shirt. She wasn't sure what he wanted from her, only the flickering, lusty thoughts of what she wanted from *him.*

"Max is a good guy, Dad. I can handle it."

He gave one short laugh. "You thought you could handle your mum's situation."

Emmie knew what he was doing, and she knew why. He was worried. She couldn't fault him for that.

"I'm not wrong this time," Emmie said, her expression calm. Her

126

father studied her face as if measuring it for any flicker of doubt. But Emmie was certain. Not about much. But about Max.

"You're quite sure, love?"

"I'm sure."

"Then I'll drop it. About him, at least." Her father turned to walk into the living room, saying, "But we need to call the police. I want a paper trail on what's happening. If we have to go to a hotel..."

"Dad, no..." Emmie followed him into the living room. He sat down on the couch and pulled his cell phone from his pocket. His hands went to his hair, and his fingers curled against the roots. It was such an emphatic attitude of agitation that Emmie felt bad for him.

"I don't like thinking this, but even though she denied it, I have to suspect that your mum told them where to find you. How else would they have found Bridget's house too? We're going to a hotel for a while."

"Dad, don't rush into anything. I'm fine. They're only getting back at me for testifying, but it won't go any further than this. They made their point." A not-so-little part of her thought she might have even deserved it. "Now we can all get on with things."

"You don't really believe that," he said, making it clear that *he* certainly didn't.

Emmie hated how easily her father saw through her. She wished Max was still there, with his arms around her, shielding her from the world with his body and his overinflated sense of vigilance, fixing all the broken pieces. She wondered at what a strange feeling that was to have—to want to be the comforted, instead of the comfort*er*. She couldn't remember the last time she'd felt that way. About anyone. Maybe she never had.

"Your suitcase is in the basement," her father said, bringing their conversation to an end. "I'll go get it. You pull some things together. We're going to a hotel."

Her father's feet clomped down the basement steps, and he returned with her smallest bag. Emmie looked up at him with submission, then back down at the table. She pushed the cookies aside and absentmindedly tried to fit the mangled hula girl back together. A little glue, she thought. Just a little glue.

CHAPTER NINETEEN

ANGER MANAGEMENT CLASS

Max sat in a classroom at the offices of John Livingston PsyD, LICSW in downtown Minneapolis. There were nine other guys in the semicircle of chairs, all facing a podium and whiteboard. Everyone was dressed in jeans and old T-shirts. No one looked like they'd showered. That included Max. He'd overslept. Nightmares.

John Livingston was dressed in a cardigan, a checked shirt, khakis, and loafers, but he wore his hair in dreads pulled back in a thick ponytail. Max imagined that he lit a blunt when he got home at night and probably had an old saxophone stashed in his closet.

Max's dad thought this whole thing was overkill, given Max was already seeing Quack Linda, but there was no way around it. Anger management classes were part of the conditions to Max staying on the team, and he couldn't deny that they sounded like they were designed with him especially in mind.

Still, he was nervous. Despite all his therapy, he could never get used to the touchy-feely crap. *How does that make you feel?* Relieved.

Do you see now that you have choices on how to move forward? Only two.

The same two? The same two.

They hadn't made much progress.

Fifteen minutes into class, Cardigan John was in full swing. "Anger is a perfectly natural reaction, but when it turns into full-blown rage, judgment and thinking become impaired and we are more likely to do things—destructive things—that we would not otherwise do. Uncontrolled anger can lead to serious problems with personal relationships and ruin the quality of your life."

Max raised his hand, and John looked like student participation might just give him an orgasm. "Yes! Yes! Please. Join in...?"

"Max."

"Yes, of course!"

"I have a question."

"Ask away!"

"If anger is a natural thing, then why is it so wrong? I mean, if something makes you angry, why shouldn't you let yourself feel angry? Is it worse than...I don't know...feeling sad?"

When he was done talking, the others, who had turned their heads toward him, turned in unison to face John, who looked deep in thought. He actually stroked his chin. Max didn't know people actually did that when they were thinking, but John did.

"Anger is a type of energy. Sadness is a type of energy. When you ask if anger is wrong, I think the answer is no. But the fact of the matter is, generally speaking, no one goes to jail because they're sad. Anger, on the other hand, gets people in trouble. My job is to help you cope with energies that can land you in jail."

Fair enough.

"So, Max. What is it that makes you angry?"

"I don't know," Max lied. Then he offered a truth, but not the Big Truth. "Dirty plays. Lazy refs. Slow ice."

"That's all?"

He shrugged.

"Grief," John said, addressing the group but letting Max know that he'd read his file, "is a common factor in many people's anger. It can come from many sources. Death, certainly, but any kind of loss."

John reached under the podium and drew out a stack of paper and a fistful of pencils. He went around the circle giving them one of each. "I want you all to make a list of the physical signs you get right before you're about to lose control of your anger. Maybe you feel dizzy or out of breath. Maybe some of you feel like you're going to throw up. Or you sweat."

Everyone was scribbling stuff down. Max wrote the words: *Hands shake. Black out.*

"Maybe you're noticing the same types of things are making you angry: depression or nervousness. Maybe guilt or shame."

Max wrote down *Guilt*, but then he erased it. Too much disclosure, and too soon. He had another nine weeks to go with this guy. He got the impression John liked to see the progress he was making with people build slowly over time.

"It's important to identify your triggers. That way, you can guard yourself against an overexaggerated response before you lose control," John said.

So far, he wasn't telling Max anything he didn't already know. He knew why he was angry. He already knew what triggered it to flare, and he recognized it coming. The trouble was—and he was just really realizing it now—he didn't want to stop it. Not one hundred percent anyway.

It felt good to let it loose. It felt good to step in and be able to actually *do* something, when he hadn't been able to do anything before. Max guessed that when it came right down to it, he didn't want to manage his anger after all.

What he wanted to overcome was that torturous feeling of uselessness. Quack Linda called it feelings of "ineptitude and ineffectiveness." She could call it whatever she wanted. Max wasn't interested in feeling those things ever again. He didn't need a class called *Anger Management*, he wanted a class called *How to Make Things Right Again*.

"I'm a fixer," Max blurted out, and the whole class turned to stare at him.

John gripped the podium in both hands and leaned back a little. "That's a good observation, Max. What does that mean to you?"

Crap. What was it with his mouth today? "I get upset when something's not right, but I can handle that. What I *can't* handle is not being able to fix it."

"And why do you think it's your job to fix things?"

That seemed like a stupid question. Max almost told him so, but at the last second he held back and answered him honestly. "Because if I don't, nobody else will."

"Dude," the kid to his left said. "Some things can't be fixed."

John nodded at him. Max was going to have to hate the kid. Cocky son of a bitch acted like he had this all figured out.

"Or don't want to be fixed," another kid chimed in, his voice barely above a whisper.

Max shook his head. None of this mattered to him. He knew what life was supposed to be like. He'd lived the perfect life for his first seventeen years, and he hated how easily things could fall apart. What a shock that life wasn't a pendulum that swung left, then right again. Sometimes it swung left and stuck that way, and you just wanted to shake the crap out of that clock until it did what it was supposed to do.

Max absentmindedly stroked the cracked face of his wristwatch.

Thinking about how things were "supposed to be" made Max feel dead inside. But anger…anger over how things were now…that's what reminded him he was alive. *Fixing* made him feel like a man.

If he ever ran into that Jimmy Krebs, he'd fix *him*. He'd pay for what he did to Emmie's car and the way he made her feel. Imagining his fist connecting with that guy's jaw gave Max a jolt of adrenaline-spiked blood to his heart. *Give me a gold star, Cardigan John. It may not be the conclusion you wanted me to come to, but I just aced this self-awareness test.*

Only nine more weeks to go.

CHAPTER TWENTY

TOWER GUARD

Three days after Emmie's car had been...*redecorated*, her father finally decided things had settled down enough that they could check out of the hotel and move back home. According to the White Prairie Police Department, there'd been no more sketchy activity around their house. Or Aunt Bridget's. Or at school. Her father couldn't justify another night of room service and Emmie had run out of books to read, so they were home by Friday night.

Emmie felt like she deserved a gold star or something for making it through the week without having a complete and utter claustrophobic meltdown. If not an award, then at least a night out with Marissa. But her father was having none of it.

He might have agreed to move home, but that didn't mean he wasn't still on high alert. He'd about jumped out of his skin when she cracked an egg for dinner.

"Come on, Dad. You can't keep me locked up in my room like it's some fairy-tale tower. Believe it or not, I'm no princess."

He winced, knowing what she was getting at. He'd been there in court, listening to her testimony in Nick's trial. Her father was the one who'd pressed the county attorney to add statutory rape to the growing list of charges against Nick.

If the prosecutor hadn't biked with her father every Saturday since the late nineties, he probably would have let it go. It wasn't like there weren't enough other charges to keep Nick locked up for a good long while. The fact that he was twenty-six and screwing some teenager probably didn't seem particularly important to the prosecutor. It was to her father, though.

Her dad had gotten what he wanted then, and he planned on getting his way now too. The guilt he apparently had over letting Emmie win the argument to go live with her mom fed his need to never let her win an argument again. Emmie felt the walls closing in.

"It's not safe. School. Work crew. Home. I don't even want you sticking around for school activities anymore. No more hockey games."

"But there's a million people at the games. Nothing's going to happen to me there. And my car...my car got trashed at *school*, not at a game. If you think school's not safe, I'm glad to—"

"School. Work crew. Home," her father repeated.

Emmie stared at him long and hard. Waiting him out. Trying to read what was really behind his hyper-restrictions. "You don't really think Mom—"

"How can you even speak of her? She gave our address *and* your aunt Bridget's address to a bunch of drug addicts."

"You told me she denied it."

"There's no other explanation."

Emmie sat down on the edge of her bed and flopped back against the pillows, flinging one arm over her eyes. Her father was right. Then she thought, No. No, he wasn't. "She's still my mom. She wouldn't hurt—"

"Are you hearing yourself? She already has."

135

"She didn't know all of the stuff that was going down between me and Nick. It's not like I told her."

She could hear her father moving toward the window. He moved the curtain, and the rings scratched along the rod. Emmie assumed he was peering down onto the street below. He spent a lot of time looking out of windows these days.

After a few seconds he said, "It's her fault you were with Nick Peters in the first place. It's her fault that you now have a record that's going to keep you out of any decent job."

"I'm a juvenile. My record is sealed."

"Your court record is, but not the BCA's. Any employer doing a background check can still look you up on the Bureau of Criminal Apprehension website."

Emmie uncovered her eyes and pushed herself up onto her elbows. "You mean, until you fix that too?"

He turned to face her. "I can't fix that. And what's that supposed to mean, anyway?" His vowels always got rounder when he was cross.

"Dad." She was exhausted. She didn't know how they got into this so deep. All she wanted to do was go ice-skating for the first time in her life. Marissa had invited her. She said Emmie could borrow her mom's skates. "What if Max Shepherd went skating with us?"

"And that's another thing," her father said, raising a finger in accusation. "I've been thinking about this Mr. Shepherd. What do you really know about him?"

Emmie stared at her father blankly for several confusing seconds and tried to understand what he was asking her. "Are you...are you actually suggesting that Max might be one of Nick's friends?"

Her father looked at her with an equal degree or sarcasm. "Do you actually know that he's not?"

Emmie about choked and got off the bed. "Yeah. I pretty much do." She pretended to be searching her closet for something to wear, but really she was hiding her expression. Her father's suggestion was hilarious, and grinning wasn't going to help her cause.

"'Pretty much do' does not mean 'yes,'" her father said as if he'd caught her in a lie. It reminded Emmie of her afternoon with a sheriff's deputy not so long ago. He might as well have exclaimed, *Aha!*

"Then *yes*," Emmie said with an exasperated sigh. "I absolutely, positively know that Max Shepherd is not involved with Nick. Max was even more freaked out than I was about my car. At least *I* was expecting something like that to happen."

"Well, that's just bloody brilliant," her father said, throwing his hands up. "When were you planning to let me in on this special knowledge you have?"

Emmie turned to face him, putting her back to the open closet. "One of Nick's friends drove past us during work crew on Saturday. He stopped to...talk. I figured he'd pop up again. He did. At least I assume it was him. Now it's over."

Her father blanched. "Did Dan McDonald know this guy was one of Nick's?"

"Yeah. Dan made him leave. But the important thing is, Mom didn't know where I was going to be working on Saturday. She doesn't know I'm on the crew at all. If they know where to find me, they got the information some other way. So you can stop blaming Mom for my car."

Her father didn't seem to be hearing anything she said. His thoughts looked very far away. "Dan didn't bother to call me about the incident on Saturday. That's it. No more work crew for you."

"Dad, you can't ban community work service. It's court-ordered." She knew she had him there. Her sentence was lenient enough. Not even her father could get a judge to excuse her from the work crew.

Emmie's cell phone rang. Her father looked at it with alarm, but his level of vigilance was tiring. It was only Marissa. There was still barely anyone who knew Emmie's number. Only Sarah, Dan McDonald, and Max had been added to her contacts since her first day back. *Relax, Dad.*

Emmie answered the call and listened to Marissa while keeping her eye on her father. "I don't know," she said. "I might not be able to go after all." Marissa started protesting, and Emmie cut her off saying, "My dad's afraid some undesirables might show up."

"Like the people who trashed your car? You told me you thought it was some random prank. Ems, what aren't you telling me?"

"No, that's right. That's all." Emmie glanced up at her father as he turned over his shoulder and left her doorway. "He's just—"

"What if you told him my parents were going along?"

"Are they?" That could work. Her father could hardly complain if she had adult supervision. His bedroom door closed with a definitive click.

"Do they need to?" Marissa asked.

Emmie scratched at a worn patch in her quilt, worrying it into threads. "It might help."

"I'll ask."

While she waited for Marissa to come back to the phone, Emmie hedged her bets and called down the hall to her father. "Dad?" she yelled. "Dad! Marissa's parents are going to go skating with us."

His muffled voice called back to her. "I want to talk to them."

"You don't believe me?"

"I want to talk to them," he said, this time on his way back down the hall.

Marissa was back on the line. "My mom will take us. She's going to read a book in the car, but she'll take us."

"My dad wants to talk to her," Emmie said as he reentered her room with his hand held out.

"I assumed so. Put him on."

Happy not to have been caught in a lie, Emmie surrendered her phone to her father, and he worked out the details with Mrs. Cooke. Emmie listened as her dad chose his words judiciously, only telling Mrs. Cooke as much about his concerns as she needed to know. Lying a little, saying Emmie had been feeling a little "light-headed" lately, and he wanted someone nearby who would recognize if she was "overexerting" herself.

Emmie rolled her eyes and flopped backward onto her bed again. It was a dramatic move. It was designed to be quintessentially teenagery. What it didn't say was how good it felt to have a parent who knew how to parent, even if he was going completely overboard. It was a nice change of pace. Unlike her mom, her father never looked to her for approval. His self-esteem was not dependent on his daughter.

Emmie, honey, do I look okay? Can I go out like this? Would you explain things for me when we get to the dealership? Tell them how much I need to keep the car. They'll listen to you.

When her dad hung up with Marissa's mom, he reached out to hand Emmie her phone. She surprised them both by getting off the bed and coming in for a hug.

"Sorry I'm not always the easiest person to live with," she said.

He held his arms out at his sides for a second before hesitantly wrapping them around her shoulders. His cologne smelled nice. It reminded Emmie of when she was younger, and it pained her to realize that she couldn't remember the last time they'd done this.

"I'm glad to have you back at home, Em. You know that, right?"

She pulled out of the hug and stepped back. "I do. I'm sorry. I know this whole thing has put you through hell."

"You're the one who's been through hell, love. I want you to let me pull you out."

Emmie nodded and fought back the unexpected tingle of tears pricking at her eyes. "Deal," she said, choking out the word. "So can I go skating?"

"You can. For two hours. And you need to listen to Mrs. Cooke. When she says it's time to go, it's time to go."

"Understood."

"And I'm not going to be upset if your friend Max is there too. In fact, I think it may be a good thing. You should call him."

That deserved another hug.

CHAPTER TWENTY-ONE

NOT A DATE

Max's phone buzzed in his back pocket once, twice, three times. He ignored it. If it was someone he knew, they'd text. Chris, Jordy, and he were playing the newest version of *Call of Duty* in Jordy's basement.

Jordy's girlfriend, Lindsey, was sitting off to the side, cross-legged in an overstuffed chair with her calc homework spread over her lap. She never played video games with them, content just to be near Jordy. Max had never understood that before, even with Jade, but he had a better understanding since meeting Emmie. Weird that he should miss her.

"Look out!" Chris shouted at the television screen. "Are either of you paying attention?"

"Holy…I saw somebody," Jordy said, his elbows working. "Let's see how long it takes me to shoot him."

"Who said this new map was small?" Max asked. "This map is not *that* small."

"You're small," Chris said.

Max started to get up, just rising an inch from his seat, and hip checked Chris to the other side of the couch. Chris dropped his remote, and Max grinned.

"Head shot! Ha! I'll lie and say I did that on purpose." Max was perched on the edge of the cushion, leaning forward.

"Damn it, Max. How did I miss that?" Chris asked.

"Oh, I just got a double kill by accident." Max raised his arms, victorious.

"How do you get a double kill by accident?" Jordy asked.

"Because someone ran in front of me when I was shooting the first guy." Max's phone buzzed again, and this time he looked to see who it was. He picked up immediately.

"Emmie?" But she'd already disconnected.

It was probably a pocket dial. Max couldn't imagine she'd *meant* to call him. But then he felt a flutter of panic in his chest because he could think of only one reason why Emmie would call. She was in trouble. That guy Jimmy was back to bother her. Emmie needed him.

"Who's Emmie?" Chris asked. "That girl from the work crew?"

Max dropped his remote and stood up. His feet had fallen asleep, and they buzzed like a hive as he walked on prickles across the basement to the sliding glass door, his back to Chris, Jordy, and Lindsey. He called Emmie back.

She answered with an apology. "I'm sorry. I didn't mean to bother you."

"You're not bothering me." Was she kidding? He couldn't begin to explain the weird kind of flip-flop that his heart did, like a fish lying in the hull of a boat. *Flip-flop. Flip-flop.* Part worry. Part excitement. "Are you okay?"

"Yeah, yeah," she said. He could almost hear her eye roll, and his stomach relaxed. She was okay.

"What's going on then?" Max's breath had steamed up the glass

142

door, and he drew a tic-tac-toe grid before wiping it off with his sleeve.

"You wouldn't by chance want to go skating?"

Max laughed low in his belly. "I think I need a second to let this sink in. Are you asking me on a date? A *skating* date?"

The racket of machine guns stopped behind him. Or maybe it had stopped the moment he walked away from the couch, but he was only noticing it now. If he turned around, Max was pretty sure all three heads would be turned in his direction. Their interest was no surprise. They'd all been waiting for something to bring him out of his funk.

"No!" Emmie exclaimed. "God, no. Not a date. I just need...I mean, my dad wants you to be there. This is embarrassing. Listen. Marissa and I are going to be at the outdoor rink by St. Francis Church in an hour. If you can be there, that would be great. If you can't, that's okay too."

It took Max's brain a few seconds to process. She wanted to meet him, but she wasn't asking him out. Her dad was? Was she embarrassed because her dad thought she needed to have him there? It wasn't a bad idea. Max's chest swelled with dumb-ass pride to think that her dad wanted him to be some kind of bodyguard. "I'll see what I can do."

"Well, don't pull a muscle or anything, Shepherd."

Max smiled at his reflection in the glass door. He almost didn't recognize himself. "Bye, Emmie."

"Bye."

Max shoved his phone into his pocket and turned around. As he'd suspected, Chris and Jordy were looking at him with mouths slightly slack. Lindsey was staring down at her book, but she had a big stupid grin on her face.

"What's going on?" Chris asked.

"Nothing. I'm just going to meet Emmie O'Brien at the outdoor rinks by the church."

Lindsey closed her book and shoved it into her backpack. Jordy gathered up the controllers and dropped them into the basket by the TV.

"What are you doing?" Max asked.

"I need to meet this girl," Lindsey said.

"And I'm in the mood for a pickup game," Jordy said.

"Skates or boots?" Chris asked, while Max was thinking *No. No. No.*

He didn't want a whole bunch of people around. He just wanted to see Emmie. It might not be a date, but it was at least *something.*

No one paid any attention to Max's protests. Within a few minutes, they were all in their coats and boots, waiting expectantly in the back seat of Max's jeep.

"You guys are idiots," he said, shaking his head in exasperation, but he loved their good intentions all the same.

* * *

Forty-five minutes later, Max and his friends were at one of two outdoor rinks across the street from St. Francis Church. Chris had called Brady, Brock, Tack, and some of the juniors and told them where to meet; Lindsey had called Quinn. Soon they had a pickup game in full swing, some of them in skates, others in boots.

Brock "checked" Quinn up against the boards, letting Tack steal the puck. Quinn didn't seem to mind because the so-called checking turned into a make-out session pretty quickly. No one paid them much notice.

A second later, Tack came running down the ice, pushing a spongy puck left and right with his stick. That's when Max saw Emmie get out of an SUV parked across the street. She didn't seem to see him, but Max watched as she and Marissa walked around the far side of the lower rink and headed for the warming house. Emmie's wild curls bounced against her shoulders until she wrapped them in a knot and hid it all under her hat. She had a pair of skates, their laces tied together, draped over her shoulder.

"That her?" Lindsey asked, skating over and making a T-stop in her figure skates. She moved in close, her side bumping up against Max's.

"Who?" he asked, not taking his eyes off Emmie.

Lindsey elbowed him. Pretty hard too. "Don't be stupid."

Now he turned to look at her. "Who's being stupid?"

Lindsey sighed. "I will get to the bottom of this," she said as Quinn skated over to join them by the boards. "Quinn, you need to warm up?"

"Nah, I'm good."

Lindsey's eyebrows pulled together. "I said, 'Quinn, you really need to warm up.'"

Quinn leaned her stick against the boards and shrugged. "I guess I'm cold."

"What are you doing?" Max asked.

"Taking a break," Lindsey said. "We'll be back in a sec."

Max didn't know if he should follow them or simply hope for the best. He was desperate to talk to Emmie again, but he wasn't sure he wanted to watch Lindsey's interrogation. Emmie was the one who wanted him to be here. She'd come look for him when she was ready.

"Max!" Chris yelled as he swiped the puck in his direction. Max curled it into his body and faked out Brady before taking it down to the goal. Darren, the junior goalie, wasn't suited up with his usual goalie pads. In just sweatpants and a couple layers of sweatshirts, he didn't look nearly as hard to beat as he did on game days.

"You gonna stop me?" Max taunted Darren as he crossed in front of the goal.

"Max, over here," Jordy yelled.

"You gonna stop me?" Max asked Darren again.

"Bring it, Shepherd," Darren said.

Max shot. He scored.

A few minutes later, Emmie, Marissa, Lindsey, and Quinn walked out of the warming house. *Together.* Lindsey looked up at Max from the edge of the lower rink and waved; then she gave him the thumbs-up sign behind Emmie's back. Either she was telling him that she'd gotten the goods on whatever this was between him and Emmie, or maybe it meant that Lindsey approved of her. Or maybe Lindsey was simply glad Max was showing interest in something other than flattening everybody and everything in sight.

"I'm taking a break," Max called out to the guys. They didn't respond. Just closed ranks to fill in the gap he left behind.

Down on the lower rink, Emmie was wearing a pair of old figure skates that looked too big for her. The leather was cracked and worn to the point of looking more gray than white, and her ankles wobbled. She clung to Marissa like a reluctant toddler being dragged to the edge of a swimming pool. Or...like any of the actual toddlers out wobbling around the ice with their parents.

Quinn took one of Emmie's hands, and Lindsey took the other. They dragged her out toward center ice. Marissa skated backward in front of her saying, "There you go" and "You totally got this" and "Just bend your knees a little."

From what Max knew of Emmie, she was hating life right now. To be dependent on one person was bad enough, but to be dependent on three...This was so not her deal.

"I got her from here," Max called out as he glided across the lower rink.

All four girls looked up at him. Marissa and Quinn looked surprised; Lindsey looked validated; and Emmie—the most important one—looked relieved. Her sigh vaporized on the air. "Don't laugh. It's my first time."

"I'll get you one of those folding chairs to push around the ice. That's how all the beginners do it." Max tried not to smile as he braced for her response.

"How all the babies do it," Emmie said as a four-year-old skated backward in a circle around them, turning on her edge and making a little half-turn leap.

"Then you'll have to hold on to me," Max said.

"On second thought," she said, teasing, "I'll take the chair."

"Too bad they're all being used already," Lindsey said, and Max would have kissed her for it except that he had other lips in mind right now. In particular, the pair that was right in front of him, struggling to stay pink against the cold.

I could warm them up, he thought, and it wasn't the first time something like that had crossed his mind. He'd had a similar thought outside the Happy Gopher when her ice-pale lips were telling him to leave her the hell alone. Funny what a difference a week made.

"Marissa, is it?" Lindsey asked. "Want to play hockey up at the other rink with the guys?"

"I—I don't..." Marissa glanced at Emmie with this look that asked if they'd fallen into some parallel universe.

"Don't worry," Lindsey said. "It's just for fun. I don't know what the hell I'm doing either."

Marissa shrugged an oh-what-the-hell shrug. "Sure then. I guess."

Lindsey and Quinn led Marissa across the ice toward the walkway that connected the two rinks. At one point, Marissa looked over her shoulder with a questioning look, and Emmie cupped her hands on the sides of her mouth and yelled out a supersarcastic "YOLO!"

The effort it took to raise her voice caused Emmie to lose her balance. Her arms windmilled. Max held the front of her coat and steadied her on her blades. "Marissa was right. You need to bend your knees."

"What?" she asked. Her fingers dug into the sleeves of his jacket.

"You're all wobbly because you don't have any bend in your knees."

She loosened her grip, and their hands slid along each other's forearms until their gloved and mittened fingers met. Max pulled her forward across the ice. She kept a static position: skates reasonably straight, knees bent, waist bent, shoulders stiff, head tipped down at the ice passing under their feet. Normally not the most attractive position, but she looked so effing beautiful in this moment. Completely trusting.

It was a new side to Emmie, or maybe...maybe, he thought, it wasn't new at all. Maybe it had been there all along, and he was finally seeing the real her. Maybe she hid that sweetness because that had been what got her in trouble before.

"So are you going to tell me why your dad wanted me to be here tonight?"

Emmie didn't look up from the ice but tightened her grip on his hands. "After what happened the other day, he wants to keep me locked up. He wasn't going to...*Whoa! Whoa!*"

Her feet were doing this cartoony running-in-place thing. Max kept her from falling, but he laughed until his side pinched.

"Stop laughing at me!" she cried while she dug the back tips of her blades into the ice. Her body arched, and Max lifted her back onto her feet.

"I will if you quit being so funny." He let go of her once she found her balance, and he wiped at his eyes with the back of his glove.

She grimaced, and her cheeks turned pink. Max resumed pulling her around the rink.

After a while she went back to answering his question. "Dad wasn't going to let me come skating with Marissa unless her mom came too. Though I don't know what good she's supposed to do. She's in the car reading some romance book. She's probably forgotten all about me and Marissa by now."

"I don't know how it would be possible to forget about you," Max said softly.

She looked up at him, her eyebrows raised in surprise, but then a warm smile spread across her face.

Kiss her, he thought. Kiss her. This is your chance.

But then her face clouded. "Dad said he'd be more comfortable with me going if you were going to be here too."

Max's chest swelled again with that same sense of pride he'd felt before. He was right. Her dad did see him as some kind of bodyguard. Sounded good to him. Although Mr. O'Brien probably didn't know how closely Max wanted to guard this body.

He slipped around Emmie's side and gripped her hips from behind. She'd gained enough confidence that she needed to be able to see where she was going. He still had enough of a hold on her that she wouldn't fall.

"What are...what are you doing?" she asked. "I'm going too fast. Don't push me."

"I'm giving you a little more rein," he said. "That's it. Keep your knees bent. Now push the ice away from you with the blade on your right skate. Then your left." She got too far back on her blades and would have landed hard, but he kept her upright.

"My ankles are killing me," she said.

"That's because your skates don't fit right. Let's take a break." He put pressure on her right hip and guided her into a wide-arcing turn back toward the warming house. There were no windows, so Max didn't know how crowded it would be inside. He was relieved to find it empty.

Emmie took two staggering steps on the floor and caught herself as she pitched forward, landing her mittened hands on the bench. She stood while turning, and when she was fully upright, she and Max were face-to-face, or more like face-to-chest. She wobbled and Max's hand darted out, catching her around the waist.

"Steady. You'll get the hang of it," he said. "Soon you'll be skating circles around me." He didn't mean to push her. He had barely exerted the slightest pressure at her hip, but she was so unsteady that it caused her to back up against the wall. Max's body followed hers with the momentum.

"Sorry," he said, bracing for her usual defensive response. He took a step back, even though it was the last thing he wanted to do.

Emmie surprised him by following, closing the gap he'd created. Words left him as he stared down into her eyes, so open and surprised and as unsure as he felt. Her face tipped up to meet his, and she laid her hands on his chest.

Max tossed his gloves on the bench and curved one hand behind her neck, fingers tangling in her curls. Yeah, this was in no way what Emmie's dad had in mind when he'd suggested she invite him to the rink tonight.

"This isn't exactly how I visualized doing this," Max said. "But I'll take it."

"You've been picturing doing this?" Her voice was a whisper.

Their faces were only several inches apart. He should kiss her now. *Now.* But like an idiot, he kept on talking. "Coach says, when you want something, visualize yourself getting it. He has us practice visualizing our games before we take the ice. I've been thinking about this moment for the last week or so."

Emmie's face flushed. It was a very un-Emmie thing to do, but Max liked it and pressed his body against hers. She made a little sound, but he couldn't tell if it was in response to what he'd admitted, or because of how close they were.

"Sorry if that makes you uncomfortable, Emmie, but it's the God honest truth. I'm not taking it back." Max could hear his voice, but he wasn't sure what he was saying anymore. Or why he was still talking at all. *Like, shut up! You can't kiss her and talk at the same time.*

He blamed his idiocy on Emmie. The pressure of her body against his was making logical thought impossible.

Emmie slipped one hand behind his neck and guided his head down to hers. And holy shit, this was not actually about to happen. But it was. Thank God, it was.

"Max!" Jordy said, flinging open the door to the warming house. The door crashed against the exterior wall, then swung back toward Jordy who stopped it with his butt. Max stepped away from Emmie, and she staggered back against the wall.

"Chris is bleeding all over the ice," Jordy said. "We need to borrow your jeep."

"Shit." Max looked over at Emmie, whose face was wide-eyed with shock. Whether it was from their near-kiss or from Jordy's announcement, Max couldn't tell. "You okay?" he asked her. "I'll be right back."

"Yeah," she said. "Go."

Max sighed and followed Jordy out, up and around the edge of the lower rink and to the upper, which looked like a crime scene. A two-foot circle of ice was glazed crimson. Chris was lying inside the carnage with his head propped with Brock's jacket, blood running down his chin.

"What the hell happened?" Max asked.

"Chris was being an idiot," Brock said.

"Shocker," Tack said. Chris rolled his eyes.

"He was walking on the top of the boards and face-planted on the ice," Jordy said.

Chris tried to sit up, and Brock reclaimed his jacket.

151

"I think he broke his nose," Lindsey said. She'd already removed her skates and was now wearing boots. Behind her shoulder, Jordy was putting his on too.

"Dude," Darren said, "if you weren't ugly before, this seals the deal."

"Shut up," Chris said. His teeth were red with blood. "I'm bleeding like a stuck pig."

"Did anyone call 911?" Emmie's friend Marissa asked, glancing around at everyone.

"I don't need 911, *thweetheart*," Chris said, his nose already swelling. "Just someone get me to the clinic so they can set it before it stays like this." Chris struggled to stand up. If his face was a clock, his nose said that it was seven thirty.

Max glanced back at the warming house. Emmie appeared to still be inside. Waiting for him. Waiting to finish what they'd started. Max groaned inwardly. *Damn it, Chris. Just like you to screw tonight up for me.*

"I'm staying here," Max said, "but you can take my jeep." He handed his keys to Jordy, then helped Chris out of his skates and into boots. Max, Jordy, and Lindsey walked Chris to the edge the rink where Max had parked.

Before they opened the doors, Lindsey reached into her pocket and unwrapped something. She held it under Chris's nose.

"You came with a first aid kit?" Max asked her. That girl was so prepared. Maybe that's what came from hanging out with hockey players.

She smiled deviously. "It's a maxi-pad. Superabsorbent. Plus, it's got wings." She barely covered the laugh in her voice.

"Hell no," Chris said, swiping it away.

"Nuh-uh," Jordy said. "Keep it there. You're not going to bleed all over the inside of Shep's car."

Max laughed. It felt warm and still a little foreign. Sometimes, in moments like this, he really loved his friends. Days like this one—with Emmie waiting for their first kiss and his best friend wearing a maxi-pad on his face—made Max want to keep on going.

CHAPTER TWENTY-TWO

ASSAULT

Emmie pulled her skate up on the bench and untied it. Max was right. They were too big. Maybe tightening them would keep her from looking like a flailing wombat on the ice. The adrenaline from what almost happened—and what was sure to happen as soon as he returned—was still ripping up her bloodstream like an electrical current. Max was always taking care of things. She was starting to maybe like that about him. Maybe.

She'd just tightened her second skate when Max returned. Except that when Emmie spun around on the bench, it wasn't Max.

It was Angie. Frankie's girlfriend and—before Emmie—the only girl Nick had let into his inner circle. Angie's pupils were dilated, and there was a fresh bruise on her right cheek. She looked like she was ready to kill someone. It looked like that someone was Emmie.

Emmie got up on still-wobbly ankles. "What are you doing here?"

Angie laughed without any humor. "Oh, I think you know." Then she threw her arm out to block Emmie's path to the door.

Emmie's mind slipped into survival mode. There were plenty of people outside. Nothing bad would happen if she could get out of this warming house. She was unsteady on her feet, but the fact that Angie was obviously riding the edges of a recent high leveled their playing field.

Emmie dug her toe pick into the plywood floor and got as much traction as she could. Then, with her head down, she rammed into Angie, whose body still blocked the door. When Emmie's head made impact, Angie let out an *Uff!* then staggered backward, arms grasping, and they both pitched out the door, landing in the snowbank near the edge of the lower rink.

Emmie wasn't sure which one of them got to their feet the fastest, but Angie gripped the fabric of Emmie's coat at both shoulders and said, "Emmie, please. You got to help me."

* * *

Once Jordy and Chris were on their way to the clinic, Max put his own boots on. He was done skating; he thought Emmie probably was too. Then he started jogging back to the warming house.

He was as far as the upper rink when he spotted Emmie standing outside. She was talking to Marissa, except that...Max took a double take. Marissa was still skating with Quinn and the other guys.

He jerked his head back toward the warming house. Whoever the girl was, she was wearing a torn green army jacket. No hat. No gloves. No skates.

She reminded him of the guy in the lowrider. Jimmy Krebs. And then it clicked. She wasn't here for the ice. She was here for Emmie. She was one of the people Emmie was trying to avoid, and this girl was right up in Emmie's face. Her hands were on Emmie's shoulders, and she was shaking her. Max felt the first tremors in his fingers.

"Marissa," he yelled. Pissed. "Are you paying any attention?" Marissa stared at him openmouthed. Max could tell by her expression that she was completely clueless. When it came to Emmie's situation, Marissa knew less than he did.

Max was moving. As he ran the rest of the way, he scanned the parking lot, looking for the lowrider. He didn't see anything out of the ordinary, but he knew that guy—the guy who interrupted the work crew, the guy who trashed Emmie's car—had to be nearby.

Max looked back toward Emmie and discovered the girl seemed to be dragging her toward the parking lot.

Max ran over the hard-packed snowbank and down the side of the lower rink in a spurt of lung-burning energy. He'd never hit a girl, and he hoped he had enough control to be able to say the same thing tomorrow.

"Get away from her!" Max barreled right up on top of the girl. He didn't touch her, but he might as well have. The girl staggered backward and toppled off the edge of the shoveled walkway.

"Max!" Emmie cried.

"*Uff*," the girl grunted as she landed in the slushy snow. She picked up her bare hands and shook them clean.

"Stay away from Emmie," Max snarled. He took two steps closer and loomed over the girl, who remained on the ground, crab-walking backward toward the snowdrift. "And you can tell whoever sent you the same thing."

"Stop," Emmie pleaded.

Emmie's words didn't register with Max. All that got through was the familiar sensation of the world closing in, darkness crowding his peripheral vision. His fingers twitched, and his lungs constricted until he couldn't get any air. Shit. He was going to black out.

In his moment of obvious unsteadiness, the girl got off the ground, then looked at Emmie. The dark makeup rings around her eyes were smeared, and black lines of tears tracked down her cheeks.

Under any normal circumstances, Max would have recognized that she was terrified. But he was locked in gear and couldn't shut his anger down.

Emmie grabbed his arm and yanked on it. "Max, you're being an idiot."

Max spun toward Emmie, losing focus on where his fury was supposed to go. What snapped him out of it was the expression on Emmie's face. It took him by surprise. There was no fear there.

As his mind started to comprehend that he was overreacting, Emmie's face tightened into a look of annoyance. More than annoyance. She was mad, and getting madder.

"Max," she said stiffly, "this is Angie. Angie, Max."

Angie gathered her composure. She stepped out of the snowbank and onto the walkway. She straightened her army jacket. She didn't look interested in making his acquaintance. Max couldn't say that he blamed her. He pressed his fingers to his temples, trying to focus his eyes. They were useless. His head was pounding. He staggered to the side, the world pitching.

"Thanks for the advice, Em," Angie said without looking up. She drew her thumbs under her eyes to wipe off the moisture. "But I think I'll take off now."

She turned and hunched her shoulders against the cold, her hands shoved deep into her pockets. Her hair hung in stringy ropes down her back. She hopped into a junker car with no muffler and drove off. Emmie crossed her arms, her expression stormy.

By that time, Lindsey, Quinn, and Marissa had made it down to the warming house, most likely to see what had Max so riled up. They were now standing beside Emmie, getting a front-row seat to his humiliation.

"Emmie, I—"

"Save it, Shepherd. You can't come bulldozing into my life every time you imagine a threat."

"I thought she was one of Nick's friends," he said, hoping she'd hear the apology in his voice.

Emmie glanced nervously at the other girls, then back at Max with a new darkness in her eyes. He had promised to keep Nick a secret. He was already slipping.

"And what if she was? They were my friends too. Angie came to me for help. If you hadn't noticed, she'd already taken a beating today. You made it ten times worse, scaring her like that."

"I know. I—"

"No, you don't know. You don't know me. You don't know anything about me, and I don't need some douchebag hockey player coming to my rescue every time a cloud passes over the sun. I can handle my own shit, Shepherd. I've been handling it for years. Long before I met you, and I'll be doing it long after today."

She took a deep breath. It had been a long speech. She clenched her teeth, never once taking her eyes off Max. Then she said, "Come on, Marissa. I want to go home."

"Emmie—" Max said, reaching out for her, but she was already moving away, and his fingers grasped at the air.

Marissa and Emmie went into the warming house to take off their skates. Max stood on the ice, frozen, waiting for her to come out again.

"Should I go in there, Lindsey?" he asked.

"Yeahhh, no. I don't think so. Give her some time to cool down." Lindsey turned Max around, and she and Quinn walked him back to the upper rink. And that's what they were doing too. They were *walking* him, like a blind, old man, because God knew he couldn't see well enough to know how to get there on his own.

Max was still shaking from the rush of adrenaline, not to mention the lingering sensation of being about to lose consciousness. He still didn't know exactly where he was. Each foot placement was purposefully negotiated.

He glanced up, and the guys were leaning on the boards, watching the show from afar. From their body language Max could tell that—although they hadn't heard a word—they'd seen this show often enough in the last year to know what was going on. He'd totally screwed up, and this time no amount of M&M's was going to fix it.

CHAPTER TWENTY-THREE

THE GOOD WAY

The wind blew a spray of ice crystals against Emmie's bedroom window, creating a high-pitched rattle. The sound reminded her that no matter how warm she was, cocooned in her blankets, the day was not going to be so obliging. Flat out, she did not want to go to the work crew this morning.

For a second, she thought about calling in sick. Going meant seeing Max, and the idea of seeing him actually made her feel a little queasy, so it wasn't a total lie. But then, this *was* supposed to be punishment. Spending time with him would add to her misery. Maybe if she explained that to Dan, it would even knock a day or two off her sentence. A two-for-one deal. Or double credit for time served.

She considered this possibility all through her shower, her drive to the sheriff's office, and then the incredibly awkward van ride to the library where they were scheduled to shelve books. She did her best to ignore the weight of Max's stares from the back seat of the van, the uneasy stiffness of her spine, and then the painfully silent walk from the van into the beautiful building.

By the openmouthed reactions of most of her crew mates, she was one of the few who'd ever set foot in a library before. Her mom used to take her to this very one when she was little. There was a librarian who did story hour with a Clifford the Big Red Dog puppet.

The place was the same now as it had been then. Stained-glass windows flanking the front door. Dark wood. Wrought-iron railing gracing the wide, spiraling stairway. Worn marble steps. It always seemed like a castle to Emmie. It smelled like burned dust and felt like home. The good kind of home. Before all the mess.

Dan McDonald made the assignments, and Emmie wondered if he intentionally assigned her to the first floor and Max to the third. Dan could be pretty perceptive. Or maybe Max had even confessed to Dan what had happened at the skating rink. Or maybe Max had asked Dan to assign him to a different area because he didn't want to be near her any more than she wanted to be near him. Had she been imagining him staring at her before?

The more Emmie thought about it, the more she thought that was it. She'd imagined the whole staring thing because she wanted him to still care, even when she was mad at him, even when she was at her prickliest. She didn't recognize this version of herself. *God, was she turning into* that *girl?* She didn't like it.

Most of the guys, including Max, followed a librarian onto the upper floors, while Emmie and a guy who was new to the crew were assigned to the first. An older woman with a wary expression led them to a rolling cart stacked high with books of various shapes and sizes, all worn with loose threads hanging from their hard covers. They were haphazardly stacked on the cart and on the verge of tumbling to the floor. It seemed very unlibrarian of the woman to treat the books like that, and Emmie worried for their fragile spines.

She took several books from the cart and looked at their labels, organizing them in her arms, first numerically and then by the authors alphabetically.

"What are you doing?" the new kid asked. He was short, his face pushed in like a bulldog. He obviously had never heard of the Dewey Decimal System. A biblio-neophyte.

"Organizing them so I don't have to make so many trips to the stacks." It seemed obvious to her, but she didn't want to make him feel bad by saying so.

He shrugged. "I'm taking the cart by the windows so I can sit in those chairs."

"You are not. Keep it in the middle so it's between both our areas."

He shrugged. "Try to stop me." And Emmie knew she wouldn't. She didn't have the energy for this. She let him go. He wouldn't get far. The cart was heavy, and the wheels were sure to get caught up in the loose carpet.

The stacks were comprised of metal shelves with open backs. She started shelving her armful of books, moving from aisle to aisle in a numerical, then alphabetical choreography: Religion to Literature to History. Dan found her a few minutes later.

"How we doing here?" he asked with a too-casual lean against the end of the stacks. He rolled up the cuff on the sleeve of his flannel shirt and gave it a few turns. He did the same to the other, then checked to make sure they were even. Nick used to do that.

"Good."

She went up on her tiptoes to slip a book into its spot on the top shelf, but she couldn't quite reach. Dan took the book out of her hands and slipped it into place for her.

Emmie shifted irritably. "I don't need help."

Dan gave a weak little smile. He looked tireder than usual, with pale-gray circles under his eyes. Emmie'd heard Dan mention to the driver that he'd taken on some extra work crews, and she thought about giving him one of her father's favorite warnings about not burning the candle at both ends, but she didn't.

"Everybody needs help," he said. "That's what this work crew is about: helping the community."

"Fine. I'll try harder."

He gave her a small smile. "Just try a *little*. That would be a start."

"So," she said on an exhale, "I suppose you got a call from my dad? He said he was going to talk to you about Jimmy showing up the other day."

"Yeah. We talked." Dan shifted his weight to his other foot, then turned, leaving Emmie to her work. She put her nose against the edge of the book she was holding and inhaled the quintessentially bookish scent of it, a combination of warm wood pulp and mildew.

It was something she used to do as a kid, and it had the desired effect. The tightness in her chest loosened. Strange, that. It wasn't just the smell that brought back feelings of being young and loved. She liked the feel of the books in her hands, too, and the cover art. The work didn't feel like work today. It felt like a vacation from everything she didn't want to deal with.

Maybe Max was enjoying his vacation from her, too, and that, she thought, might be good for both of them.

So it was odd that she somehow convinced herself that he was nearby. She felt him. Possibly. She didn't know if it was because she'd been thinking about him, or if it was a change in the temperature, or maybe a movement of air, but the back of her neck prickled with the sensation that he was close. Had he been reassigned to her floor? She stopped what she was doing to listen for his voice, but there was no sound. She looked up and down her aisle, but it was empty.

Embarrassed by her overactive imagination, she went back to work, returning to the cart and reloading her arms, this time with fiction. She'd imagined it. She didn't know why she bothered. It wasn't like she wanted to see him. What would be the purpose of conjuring him up now?

Emmie was about to shelve a book when she noticed that the books surrounding the spot were completely out of order. She set her armload on the floor and pulled the four offending books off the shelf. On the other side of the stack, visible through the hole she'd created, was Max. His head was bent down like he was studying something. Or possibly reading. Why was he down here? He was supposed to be upstairs.

Max didn't look at her. Maybe he didn't know she was there. Thank God, because this could get all kinds of awkward.

Emmie sucked in her breath and quietly slipped the books back the way they'd been, out of order, but filling the space. Forget the Dewey Decimal System. It was supremely overrated.

Her heart pounded as she turned for the nearest bathroom. Before she could move, he spoke. "I'm sorry for overreacting toward your friend, Emmie."

She sighed and closed her eyes. He shouldn't be sorry. He'd only done what came naturally for him. Was it fair to ask him to be someone he wasn't?

"I thought she was going to hurt you," he said. "I couldn't help myself."

Emmie nodded, even though he couldn't see her.

"But you were right," he said. "I need to stop rushing in, making all kinds of assumptions, overreacting like a...a..."

"Jackass," she said.

"Good choice. It doesn't excuse what I did, but I don't like it when people touch you."

A beat of silence pulled out between them like taffy, growing long and thin while Emmie considered her response. Max's words sounded like Nick's. Nick didn't like it when other people touched her either. It didn't matter how innocent the touch might have been. Either they or she, or both, paid the price for the indiscretion.

"You don't get a say in who touches me," she said. "I'm the only one who decides that."

"You're right. Of course, you're right. I just panicked. Like I said, I thought she was going to hurt you."

Emmie tried to imagine what the scene last night must have looked like to him. She hadn't let herself look at it from his point of view. That was a concession she hadn't been ready to make. But now…if she took Dan's advice and opened herself up to what others were offering, especially considering the last year, it was kind of nice for Max to feel so protective of her. It was over the top, definitely. But still nice.

Max remained on the other side of the stacks. She could hear his weight shift on the old floorboards, but she couldn't see him. Emmie imagined him running his hands through his hair in that way he did.

"Work a little harder on that overinflated sense of vigilance," she said, hoping he could tell that she was trying to be kind, "and maybe we can still be friends."

The air stilled, and she heard nothing more from him. For a second, she thought he'd walked away, but given how she hadn't heard the floor creak, that was unlikely. Maybe he'd realized that he was as incapable of change as she was, and her attempt at kindness had come off as an ultimatum he knew he couldn't meet.

"I don't want to be just a friend," he said, and Emmie could hear how much the words cost him. If she rejected him now, she was sure it would be one too many times.

Emmie exhaled slowly, then picked up her books from the floor as she tried to reason out a response. She knew what he meant. She'd wanted the same thing—at least last night in the warming house she had. Now she wasn't so sure.

Emmie slipped a book on the shelf, moved to the back of her aisle by the far wall and shelved another. She wouldn't ask Max to be someone he wasn't, but after everything with Nick, did she really want to be with someone so prone to violence? Except that Max hadn't actually touched Angie. And he was trying so hard to beat whatever monster was on his back. She wished she understood it, but were *trying* and *wishing* enough to make sense of the two of them together? Like an actual couple?

Emmie shook her head. The answer was clearly no. Still...the promised heat of that kiss, that lost kiss, still lingered on the edges of her memory.

When she could tell that Max had mirrored her movements in his own aisle and that he, too, had moved to the far end by the wall, she asked, "Why are you down here? Aren't you supposed to be upstairs?"

"Dan reassigned me. We were getting through things fast, and apparently the new guy down here has trouble with the alphabet. Dan's got him cleaning bathrooms instead."

Emmie smiled, and she was glad Max was still on the other side of the stacks and couldn't see it. *I don't want to be just a friend.*

"So what did that girl want with you?" Max asked. His voice sounded throaty.

"Her name's Angie. She's trying to get out. Frankie beat her up pretty bad. Things are all messed up with Nick gone. I gave her Dan's number."

Max cursed softly and quietly under his breath, as if he didn't mean for Emmie to hear.

"You didn't know," she said, trying to reassure him. "You thought you were helping."

Neither of them said anything after that. For the next several minutes, all Emmie heard were the librarian's fingers clicking on a keyboard, the front door opening and closing, and the thump and shuffle of books finding their homes.

She and Max moved in slow motion as they slid other people's stories into place, buying time for themselves and something more to say. Or were there no more words? Had they come to that inevitable place where there was nothing more to say? Had they made too many mistakes?

Then Max said, "Do you have a book in your hand right now?"

The sound of his voice, breaking through the silence made Emmie's heart do a little leap in her chest. She looked down at the cover. *A Tale of Two Cities*. "Yes."

"Open your book to a random page, and read the first line you see. That describes what your life is like."

"What?" she asked.

"I saw this online. It's like a game. Just do it."

"I already know what my life is like." Even though she refused to play, Emmie couldn't help but open the book and take a peek. *There is prodigious strength in sorrow and despair.* Did Dickens have that right? She'd certainly had her share of both sorrow and despair in the past year or so. But did she have strength?

"Okay," Max said, "try this. Read the very first line of the book. That summarizes your relationships."

This time Emmie played along, in part because she knew what the line would say before she even looked. "'It was the best of times, it was the worst of times.'"

Max made a sound. A kind of unlaugh that resembled more of a snort. "If we'd been doing this a couple days ago, I would have told you that *I* am the best of times."

"If we'd been doing this a couple days ago, I might have agreed."

There was a low metal creak as Max—presumably—leaned against the opposite side of the stacks. "Okay, now open to another page. Close your eyes and point. That describes how you kiss," he said softly.

"Max..." Emmie didn't want to go there. The memories were uncomfortable and still stung too much. They didn't need any salt.

"I screwed up and missed my opportunity last night," Max said. Then his tone switched from serious to joking. "I mean, you can't blame me for wanting to know how it would have turned out."

"Fine," she said. If she had to this, she was going to make it worth it, and she was not above cheating. She didn't blindly point, rather she quoted what she knew was somewhere in Dickens's classic pages. "Here's how that kiss was going to go: 'It is a far, far better thing that I do, than I have ever done.'"

"*Damn.* I knew it," Max said dramatically. He paused, presumably not cheating like she had. Then he chuckled. "I think that kiss might have gone to second base because here's my line: 'They range the mountain crests.'"

"God, Max. You made that up."

"Did not. It's Homer. *The Odyssey.*"

His voice came from a different direction, and when Emmie looked up, he was at the head of her aisle, and his eyes were dark. "I really am sorry," he said. "I can be good."

Emmie raised her eyebrows. "You can?"

"Well...I can be better."

Max stalked toward her, his intention all too clear. There was a flicker of panic in Emmie's chest, and she stepped back. Her left shoulder hit a bookshelf, and one thin paperback slipped off the edge, landing on the floor.

Max hesitated; then when Emmie didn't put on the brakes, he moved closer.

"Shepherd," she whispered. She was on the verge of giving in. All the bricks she'd laid between the two of them were crumbling like dry plaster.

"You make me crazy when you call me that."

"In a good way or a bad way?"

"Everything about you is the good way." He pressed against her, crushing the softness of her body with his chest. Emmie wanted to touch every beautiful line of him, to inhale the now-familiar scent of him, like cloves and soap.

Why did she always feel so light-headed when he was near her? It wasn't like her to be so affected by another person. She hated it. And she loved it.

Her eyes widened as his head came closer. Slowly, as if he was giving her the chance to say no.

When she didn't, Max lowered his head and pressed his lips to the place where her neck met her shoulder. He inhaled, skimming his nose up her neck to right below her ear. She was completely turned on by him, and that was very, very inconvenient because the library was quiet and hardly private. Any minute, someone could find them here. But that very possibility made Emmie hope he wouldn't stop.

By now, her chest was rising and falling, rising and falling. Max's hands gripped the dip of her waist.

"Max," she said, and her heartbeat stuttered in her chest. He touched his lips to her neck again, and she felt the snap of energy between them. She wasn't sure if she imagined it, but he pressed on, kissing along her jaw. She wasn't imagining it.

Max pulled back to look at her, and Emmie bit down on her bottom lip. Max hesitated, whispering a curse, then brushed his thumb across her bottom lip. Emmie's lips parted, and Max did not waste the invitation. He kissed her as if he were laying his soul at her feet.

Damn. He wasn't kidding last night when he told her he'd been visualizing this moment. His kiss was probably the most well-practiced first kiss in the history of the world—*no exaggeration*—and it was blowing her mind. It was blinding. She was drowning in him, and she feared that when they were done—*and she might never be done*—there would be nothing left of her.

Her hands came up against his chest. "Oh my God, Max," she said breathlessly, "you're *killing* me."

Max sucked in a breath, and his muscles stiffened under her fingertips. He recoiled from her, snapping backward as if attached to a bungee cord, then staggered sideways against the stacks. Emmie watched as the flush faded from his cheeks, leaving his face so pale that it was nearly gray.

"What is it?" she said. "What's wrong?"

Max's eyes were wide. Not exactly with surprise, but with something more hollow. To look at him felt like hearing a confession, and it sickened her. She felt sick. Sick. Sick.

Max's mouth opened, then closed. "I'm sorry," he said finally. "My God, Emmie, I'm so sorry. I thought I could, but…I can't. I can't do this."

Then after all that, he ran. Leaving Emmie to stand there. Stupidly. Her hands held in front of her, palms up. And empty.

Max's rejection hit Emmie harder than Nick's fist, the fist that told her she was more trouble than she was worth, that told her he should cut her mom off because Renee O'Brien was a meth-head loser and she and Emmie deserved each other. It hurt more than the look of hatred in Nick's eyes when she testified, the look that said he should have known she'd go running to Daddy when things got rough.

The guilt and the shame were still raw, still tender to the touch, and Max had not only touched the emotional bruises Nick left behind, but crushed them under his thumbs. He'd left her standing in a pile of books in the stacks on a Saturday morning. She wanted to kick Charles Dickens in the nuts for being a bald-faced liar, because she wasn't feeling any kind of prodigious strength. Despite her sorrow and despair.

CHAPTER TWENTY-FOUR

A TERRIBLE PERSON

Max collapsed onto the center of the front steps of the library, taking up a lot of physical space because that's what he did. He pushed himself into places and spaces and lives that he had no business consuming. *Max, you're killing me.* Emmie's words chilled him. She couldn't have picked anything worse to say.

But still, he shouldn't have run. If only he could learn to stop his impulses before they got beyond his control. If he could do that, maybe he wouldn't have run out on her. Maybe he wouldn't be out here freezing his ass off. *Damn it.* He got up and paced angrily, hands shoved into the pocket of his hoodie.

After a few passes in front of the library steps Max sat back down, this time on the far right side of the step, and hunched his body against the cold. If he used his imagination, he could still feel Emmie's warmth in the palms of his hands. He curled his fingers into fists, trying to hold on to the feeling for a little bit longer. But like always, eventually all that was left was himself, nails dug into his skin. Alone.

The front door of the library swung open. Max didn't turn around, but he recognized the two voices behind him.

"Where do you think you're going?" Dan McDonald asked from inside the building.

"I need a break," Emmie said from the doorway. "This will only take a second."

A second, Max thought, his heart somewhere lower than his stomach. Yeah, that sounded about right. It would only take a second for Emmie to tell him to go to hell, and that she never wanted to see him again. That he had no right to kiss her like that, then walk out. That would only be right. Emmie didn't take crap from anybody, and the way he treated her inside…practically molested her…what she must be thinking…

Max shifted even farther to his right so that his shoulder was under the metal railing and Emmie could get by. Maybe she'd just keep on walking. Maybe she was so mad she wouldn't even bother to call him out on being a Class A dick.

But instead of storming past, Emmie zipped up her coat and sat on the opposite edge of the step, leaving a wide space between them. Max felt every inch of it. But even more than the distance, Max felt the familiar calm she always seemed to bring.

He glanced at her face, which was completely placid. No hard lines. No set jaw. How had he forgotten what had attracted him to her in the first place? Emmie wasn't pissed. She was completely relaxed. He was just another disaster that wasn't going to faze her.

It was probably his duty to say something first, but he didn't know what to say. After a few agonizing moments, she said, "I think I know what happened in there."

Max made a small noise in the back of his throat. He doubted that very much. He couldn't even fully understand it.

"Tell me about Jade," Emmie said.

Max turned his face away from her. That was the last thing he wanted to do, and she was crazy for even asking. "Sounds like you know about her already, and it's too hard to talk about."

"No. I don't know anything more than her name. I don't pry. And I wouldn't normally ask, but after the way you acted in there, I think it's time you tell me." Then she added, "Even if it's hard."

Max chewed on the inside of his cheek and picked at the ice that coated the railing. Anything he could say felt ridiculously inadequate. "She was my girlfriend."

"I figured that much out already. Are you still in love with her?"

Max's shoulders slumped. She really didn't know? No one had told her? "Are you thinking she broke up with me?" Max asked. He still couldn't look at Emmie and, instead, flicked his finger against the small icicles that hung off the railing.

"Are you saying *you* broke up with *her*?"

That question finally made Max look over at her. Emmie's eyebrows were nearly to her hairline. Max could see her trying to make sense of things. Like, why would Max feel badly about kissing her if he'd already moved on from Jade?

"Jade is dead," Max said. The final word looked like a puff of smoke on the frosty air. Max covered his broken watch with his right hand.

Emmie's expression went blank. "I—I'm sorry." By the look on her face, Max could see her calculating the height and depth of the emotional-bullshit mountain she was going to have to climb in order to get to him again. Was she up for the challenge? Did she have the right kind of protective gear? Because this was about to get messy.

Max shoved his hands into the pocket of his hoodie and wished he'd thought to grab his coat. He'd never expected to be out here so long.

"Max, I'm so—"

"No." Max stood and took several steps toward the sidewalk, keeping his back to her. "Just don't." A truck rumbled past, leaving a trail of smoky exhaust in its wake.

"Don't what?" Emmie asked.

Max hung his head and once more fought back the sob that was building deep within his chest. "Don't say you're sorry."

"Okay."

With dry eyes, Max turned to face her. He would not cry. He didn't let anyone see that—not his parents, not his teammates, not even Quack Linda, even though she was sworn to confidentiality, and certainly not Cardigan John. He grimaced at the sincere acceptance on Emmie's face.

"I'm not trying to be a dick," Max said. "Or, I should say, *more* of a dick. But those words...I hate them. They're too small. They don't fit. It actually makes me feel worse when people tell me how sorry they are."

Emmie reached up toward him, and when Max came closer, she took his hand. She pulled him back down on the step beside her and hooked her arm through his. She was warm. And she was here. And for the life of him, Max couldn't understand why.

The library door opened, then after a few seconds closed before either of them turned around to see who it was.

Emmie didn't say anything. She just held Max closer. He knew it was more than he deserved after how he treated her inside, but he let her work her magic, stilling his heart until he felt his shoulders relax and his lungs fill with air.

"That's not something you get over," she said. "You *shouldn't* just get over it."

Max shook his head. Emmie didn't get it.

"Was she sick?" she asked.

Max shook his head again, unable to say anything more.

"Hey, if you don't want to talk about it, I get it," Emmie said. "It's okay. I can go back inside." She placed both hands on the icy step, readying to stand.

Max put his hand on her elbow, the nubby texture of her coat warming his fingertips. He didn't want her to go. He'd talk about Jade if it meant Emmie would stay. "It was a car accident."

Max felt Emmie's body flinch, and her subtle reaction made Max feel like he was taking a corner too sharply and he needed to grab the oh-shit handle in his jeep. Without thinking, his fingers wrapped around the edge of the step.

Max took a big breath. "She was thrown from the car. They said she died instantly."

"What?" Emmie asked, her voice rising. "Oh my God, Max."

Emmie's eyes were wide with disbelief. Her reaction was right on target. It *was* too much to believe. Max had gone through the first couple weeks after the accident waiting to wake up from what he was sure was a horrible nightmare.

He swallowed hard and stood up again. He moved to the other side of the step where he'd originally been sitting and leaned back against the railing, his hands shoved deep into the pocket of his hoodie. "Jade was a really good singer," Max said, though he didn't know why it mattered. "Did you know that?"

Emmie shook her head. Of course she didn't know that.

"I should have told her that. And man, could she laugh." Max's nose was red and running, and though he still didn't cry, he sniffed loudly. His weakness didn't seem to make Emmie uncomfortable. He was supremely grateful for that.

"She was usually really serious, but then when something hit her as funny, she'd get this blank look, and then she'd start to shake, and then she'd laugh so hard she cried. I used to love to make her laugh like that. I think that's what I miss the most."

"Max…"

"When someone dies, it's the stupid stuff you miss." Then he tipped his head skyward. The only consolation in death was that at least now Jade was free of pain. His own pain, Max feared, would never go away. That was, until he met Emmie—and now he might have killed that possibility too.

"It's just so unfair," Max said. "It makes me mad. They say I've got anger management issues."

"Sounds about right," Emmie said. "Sounds well-earned too." Her teeth were chattering now, which made Max seek out his own warmth by ducking his chin inside his sweatshirt. "So is that why you're Vigilante Man on the ice? You're out to stop the injustice of the world? You know that's a fight you're never going to win, right? You can't take care of everybody."

Max took two steps forward along the step and sat down so their knees were pressed together. He cupped both Emmie's hands in his. "I know that. I don't need to take care of everybody, but I do want to take care of you, Emmie."

Emmie's jaw dropped open, and Max cut her off before she could say anything. "I know you don't need me to." He raised their hands to his mouth and blew warm air onto them. "I just *want* to. The problem is—and I didn't realize it until I was kissing you in there—you should be with someone who not only wants to care for you, but can actually pull it off. I'm not that guy. I'm actually a terrible person."

"You're not a terrible per—"

"What would you think if I told you that, other than the funeral, I've never visited Jade's grave? Not once."

Emmie didn't respond immediately. Max imagined she was trying to reason out what kind of person wouldn't visit his girlfriend's grave. Finally, she took a deep breath and let it out slowly. "What is it about hockey guys that makes them think they get to call all the shots?"

"Ha. That's cute," Max said, tipping his head to the side. "But I don't get what you mean."

"I told you before. I'm the only one who gets to choose whom I push away, and whom I let into my life."

Emmie ducked her head, and her eyebrows pulled together, causing a little wrinkle. Then she looked up at Max, and the expression on her face made his breath catch in his throat. "It's you, Shepherd. You're the guy."

A small smile slowly pulled at the corners of Max's mouth. She was a glutton for punishment, that was for sure. And patient. And perhaps a bit of a martyr. For a second he thought about warning her off.

"I'm going to be a jerk," he said.

"Yeah, well, you know I'm going to be prickly."

Max stared into Emmie's face, then he lowered his eyes and rubbed his thumb back and forth over her knuckles. A second later, Emmie pulled him closer. She hesitated there, and he reveled in the feel of her warm breath on his lips. He hoped this was the right thing. It felt right. He wanted it to be right. And he knew that it was when she crossed the divide and kissed him.

This time, it wasn't the same frantic rush of emotion. Instead it was warm and slow, highlighted by the snowflakes melting on his cheeks and her eyelashes. When the kiss ended, she did not pull away from him, but kept her forehead pressed to his. Max savored the moment for however long it would last.

Then, when she finally pulled back, a small smile on her lips, Max felt his face go hot. Hot, because there was no good way to switch from all this seriousness into the comparatively trivial thing he'd been planning to ask her in the warming house the night before. It was a question he thought he knew the answer to, but he had to ask anyway because that was the kind of masochist he was.

Emmie could apparently tell his mind had shifted. She leaned back and looked at him hard. "What?"

"So…Snow Ball is next weekend…"

Emmie narrowed her eyes, then fell sideways away from him as if he'd told the joke of the century. "Are you for real?"

Her reaction was worse than he feared. "Last time I checked, yeah."

"You can't take me to the dance, Max."

"Why not?" he asked, though there were plenty of potential reasons why. For instance, she didn't care about such cliché things as high school dances and winter courts. Or could someone else have already asked her. Like one of those soccer players who'd been eyeing her at the Happy Gopher. That possibility caused Max's jaw to clench involuntarily.

"Because this is high school," she said. "They can't even change the cafeteria menu without the whole student body going ape shit, like it's the Second Coming or something. Max Shepherd, hockey superstar, taking the girl who got knocked up to the school dance? Are you kidding me? Their world would fall off its axis."

Max stared at her for a few seconds, waiting for the punch line. It took him another two seconds to realize she was being serious. "And what? You don't want to be responsible for all their bumps and bruises?"

She snorted. "It's not that. It's just—"

"I know it's not because you're afraid," Max said. "You're not afraid of anything. And last time I checked, you didn't care what anyone thought of you either."

Emmie's lips tightened, and she banged her heel against a thin layer of ice that had crusted at the corner of the step. It shattered like a potato chip. "So, you're asking me on a date?"

"I am."

"Hmmm."

"And you're saying…?"

"I'm thinking about saying yes."

A stupid-ass grin broke out over Max's face, even though he knew that with her, it might do him more harm than good. "I've been getting more yeses than noes out of you lately. I don't deserve it, but I'm not going to lie and say I don't like it."

"Don't mess this up, Shepherd." She picked up the tiny flecks of broken ice and flicked them at his cheek. They melted on impact.

"Just give me a little time," Max said. "I'm sure I'll manage."

"If we do this, I'll have to meet you at the dance. Is that okay? I promised Marissa I'd go with her."

Max fought back the flicker of disappointment and stared at Emmie for one long moment. He could tell it wasn't exactly the truth. Maybe she and Marissa had talked about going together, but he doubted it was a promise she needed to keep. Still, he bet that school dances were not high on Emmie's things-I-love-to-do list. If she wanted to take baby steps, he could take them right alongside her.

"If that's the way it's got to be," he said, "then that's the way it's got to be."

Emmie leaned into him and laid her head on his shoulder. He thought maybe she could begin to trust him again. It felt good to be trusted, even if it was just trickling in.

The door behind them opened again, reminding them of where they were and what they were supposed to be doing. "If you two got yourselves sorted out," Dan said, "I've got some books that need shelving."

Emmie stood obediently and reached down toward Max. His hand wrapped around hers, and she pulled him up. The significance of it was not lost on Max. She was always pulling him up.

CHAPTER TWENTY-FIVE

SNOW BALL

"I still don't understand why you're going to this thing with me instead of with Max," Marissa said as she drove to the high school. "He's your *date*. He should have picked you up."

"It's not his fault. I told him I'd already promised to go with you, so don't tell him different."

Marissa jerked her head to look at Emmie. "Well, that's just great. He probably thinks I'm some needy, dateless wonder. Was he mad?"

Emmie shrugged. "Doesn't matter. I'm with you. I'll see him there."

Marissa made an exasperated sound in her throat and switched on the windshield defoggers, while Emmie checked her lipstick in the visor mirror. She didn't typically wear a lot of makeup, and she wasn't sure about the color.

She dug a napkin out of Marissa glove box to wipe half of it off, but her hand froze midair when she saw the napkin bore a Taco Bell logo. *Nick.*

Just like him to ruin her night by jumping into her head. It had been nine months since she'd helped him rob the downtown Taco Bell, but she could still feel the adrenaline pumping in her ears.

"Everything okay?" Marissa asked.

"Yeah. Great," Emmie said. She wadded up the napkin and rubbed furiously at her lips.

Marissa parked, and they made their way into the school. They were some of the late stragglers, the dance having started an hour earlier. White Prairie students apparently weren't familiar with the concept of being fashionably late.

As Emmie and Marissa handed their coats off to the coat-check girl, a freshman who looked a little too excited about being at an upperclassmen event, Emmie marveled at Marissa's sense of style. She always thought Marissa looked amazing, but tonight she was wearing a one-shouldered navy dress, with layers of pearl bracelets crawling up her left arm. Her long, blond hair lay smooth and silky against her back. It was not a look Emmie was ever going to achieve, and she sighed in envy.

Emmie's hair was in its natural state in big, loose curls that ended just below her shoulders. Marissa had loaned her an ivory lace headband that went well with the vintage dress her aunt Bridget had helped her shop for. It was strapless and robin's-egg blue. Emmie liked how the crinoline made a rustling sound when she walked, and the body-hugging top made her feel like a princess (though she'd never admit that part out loud).

She also had a matching drawstring bag that was small enough to wear on a strap around her wrist and just big enough for a phone and few essentials. But her shoes...her shoes! If Emmie could get through the whole night in them, it would be a miracle. Five inches of crippling agony, but man, were they beautiful.

When she and Marissa stepped into the gym, it took a while for Emmie's eyes and ears to adjust. The usually cavernous room was packed, and there was a heated haze of sweat and cologne. The only light filtered in from the hallway or came from the small light on the

DJ's table and the spinning disco balls that hung from the ceiling. Emmie couldn't make out any faces, only dimly outlined forms jumping in unison to the pulsing music of Gucci Mane.

As they stood in the doorway, a guy drew closer on his way out. He was tall and broad-shouldered with a thick mane of blond hair. A hockey player, no doubt. If his body didn't give it away, the splint on his nose was the deciding factor. *Chris.*

His eyes first went to Marissa, giving her a nod of recognition, then quickly darted to Emmie.

"If you're looking for Shepherd, he's sitting on the bleachers in the back corner."

Marissa elbowed Emmie and made a high-pitched whistle, which had become her signal for what she called the *singing snail.* Emmie rolled her eyes but thrilled at the idea that Max wasn't dancing without her. Maybe he was even disappointed because she was late.

The blond guy passed through the doorway, and a second later, Sarah came bouncing up to Marissa and Emmie. "You're here! You're here! Finally!" She reminded Emmie of Tigger from *Winnie-the-Pooh.*

Marissa gave Emmie a little shove. "Go find Max. Remember. You're on a date."

Emmie fumbled a smile. It felt surreal as she took her first steps into the gym, then followed the edge of the bleachers. She was walking away from her best friend to go find Max Shepherd, varsity hockey jock, with looks that rivaled anybody in a Calvin Klein ad.

Uh…no she wasn't. Emmie made an about-face. There was no way she was going to go march into Max's circle of friends. How incredibly awkward would that be? If he wanted to be with her, he'd find her…

No. Wait.

This was freaking high school. These were privileged Daddy-Has-Enough-Money-to-Put-Me-in-Hockey kids, not a bunch of knife-hiding junkies tweaking in a dark alley. She'd faced way worse than this. Well, never knife-hiding alley dwellers, but close enough.

Emmie turned around again and marched toward the back corner of the gym.

Who were these hockey players to make her feel all kinds of awkward? No one, that's who. Max Shepherd had asked her to be his date. That's what he was going to get.

"Cute dress," said a voice coming up alongside her. It was Katie. Emmie groaned internally when she remembered what Lauren Schafer had told her at the hockey rink. Katie was Jade's cousin.

Katie's red hair was pulled to one side in a smooth spiral that draped over her shoulder. She looked like she'd just walked off the runway in a skintight, black scrap of Spandex. Emmie looked around at some of the other girls on the dance floor and, for the first time, noticed that Katie's look was the one to have.

Nick's voice rang out in Emmie's head without warning. *Have you ever thought about straightening your hair? You'd look way hotter if your hair was straight. That…and if you took off a few pounds. Got to cut you off from the cheeseburgers, hey, baby?*

"Thanks," Emmie said, rubbing the fabric of her full skirt between her fingers.

"Are you looking for Max?" Katie asked. Before Emmie could respond, Katie added, "He's pretty down. Tonight's going to be a rough night for him. He brought Jade as his date the last two years. I think it's stirred up a whole lot of stuff for him. They were such a cute couple."

Katie's face flickered with pain, but Emmie didn't know how to decipher it. Was it empathy for Max, or for the loss of her cousin? Maybe both.

"Of course," Emmie said. So Max wasn't moping on the bleachers because she was late. He was in pain. He was grieving. Of course he was. Why shouldn't he be? Emmie's heart squeezed at the agony the memories must be causing him. She couldn't imagine.

"You came with some friends, right?" Katie asked.

"Yeah," Emmie said absently. "Marissa Cooke." Then her thoughts returned to Max. He needed some time alone. If their situations were reversed, she'd want the same from him.

"From the restaurant, right?" Katie asked.

"Yeah." Emmie suddenly felt very hot. The crinoline under her skirt made her legs itch.

"I think I saw her over there," Katie said, pointing into the crowd.

Emmie glanced over her shoulder and spotted Marissa by the refreshments. "Thanks."

Emmie turned around and retraced her steps, feeling mortified and about the size of that freaking singing snail Marissa kept going on and on about. Except that she didn't exactly feel like singing.

She had to push her way through the crowd that was now rushing onto the dance floor because the DJ was playing "Despacito." More than once, Emmie was knocked sideways through a cloud of Axe and body odor, as if she were in a pinball machine, ricocheting off one person or the next.

When she finally made it to the refreshments table, she grabbed Marissa's elbow and exhaled with exhaustion. "Hey."

"Hey?" Marissa asked, taking Emmie's shoulders in both hands and giving her a little shake. "What do you mean, 'Hey'? What are you doing here? You were supposed to go find your man."

"He's not my man."

"Of course he's your man. He asked you to be his date."

Emmie shrugged and glanced over her shoulder. "He needs some time to himself."

Marissa's hands dropped from Emmie's shoulders, and her eyes

185

looked in the direction from which Emmie had come, then back to Emmie. "Time to himself?"

"It's okay," Emmie said, not wanting to see her own disappointment on Marissa's face.

"I don't get it," Marissa said.

Emmie shrugged. "I'll explain later."

Olivia came back with two glasses of punch and looked surprised to see Emmie. She handed one cup to Marissa, then said, "Girl, here. You take this." She gave Emmie the one she'd intended for herself, then, after leaving Emmie with a sympathetic look, left to get another cup.

Emmie tossed back the punch, hoping it would dull her disappointment. She couldn't allow herself to feel any self-pity when Max was hurting. Unfortunately, unlike every teen movie she'd ever seen, no one had spiked the punch. She frowned down into her empty cup, then looked up when she realized Marissa was studying her—*hard*—with her head tilted to the side.

Emmie squirmed under her scrutiny.

"Okay," Marissa said. "Who got to you?"

"Huh?"

Marissa shifted her weight and folded her arms. "You were heading straight for him. If you hadn't been wearing those shoes, you would have been running. And then thirty seconds later, you turn around and end up with me. Who got to you?"

"His friend Katie said that—"

"Katie Hines?" Marissa asked with an eye roll. "The one with the permanent resting bitch face? She's been working her angle on Max for six months. Everyone knows it, even those of us who don't run in that crowd. It's pathetic."

Emmie took a second to consider what Marissa was telling her. Had Katie been playing her? Was Emmie really so naive to believe that

Katie had been genuinely worried about how Max was feeling? "You really think—?"

Marissa's expression flickered to amusement, and her eyes focused on something beyond Emmie's shoulder. Emmie never finished her sentence.

"Yeah," Marissa said. "I really think."

"Emmie?" Max's voice said, and Emmie felt the warmth of his fingers slide around the right side of her waist. "How long have you been here?"

Emmie turned around, and his eyes dipped from her face to the top of her dress. She felt her skin flush and hoped it was too dark in the gym for him to notice. "A couple minutes ago."

"I've been waiting for you. I thought you stood me up."

Emmie felt Marissa slip quietly away and wished she had another glass of punch in her hand. The room was blazing hot. Max was too, in a crisp white shirt, a black jacket, and a skinny tie. He didn't look sad. If anything, he looked relieved. And maybe a little annoyed. Emmie fidgeted under his stare.

Emmie's attention was pulled off Max, however, by the sudden appearance of his friend Lindsey from the skating rink and her date, the kid with the curly top fade Emmie had seen in the hallway with Max her first day back. They pulled up alongside Max and flashed Emmie happy smiles—all teeth. They looked beautiful together.

"Emmie, you remember Lindsey?" Max asked. "And this is Jordy."

Jordy smiled broadly and adjusted his glasses. He looked smooth in a burgundy jacket and black pants, but he was wide-eyed and excited—so much so that he reminded Emmie of a little kid riding a perpetual Christmas-morning high.

Lindsey looked like a real-life Barbie doll, except that she still had both her shoes.

"Oh, and Quinn," Max said as another couple joined them, "and my friend Brock." Brock was wearing a black shirt and red bow tie to match Quinn's red dress. Quinn looked shorter without her skates.

"Hey," they all said, practically in unison.

A flutter of unease trembled through Emmie's belly. She couldn't help noticing how well they all matched, despite their differences. She wasn't reacting to their clothes. All of them matched in the easy smoothness they had about them, a comfortable grace that had to come from years of friendship.

Emmie and Max were two jigsaw pieces that were never going to fit. Hell, they came from completely different puzzles. But Max was still looking at her with a certain sense of relief, and Quinn and Lindsey seemed genuinely happy that she was with him.

"Are we going to dance or what?" Quinn asked when a John Legend song started. "I didn't get this dressed up for nothing."

"I don't know," Max asked. "Are we going to dance, Emmie?"

Someone bumped into Emmie from behind. It was enough to push her off balance, and she fell against Max's body, his arms quickly circling her.

"Guess so," he said, and he chuckled, sending a low vibration through his chest that Emmie could feel against her own. Max led her onto the crowded dance floor. He might have even carried her, for all she knew. She had no sensation of her feet on the floor. Jordy and Lindsey, and Brock and Quinn danced nearby. The whole room swayed.

In her shoes, Emmie had gained a little height on Max. Her head now reached his shoulder, but he still had to bend his body to get his mouth level with her ear. "You," he said, "are crazy beautiful tonight. Definitely worth the wait."

A shiver of excitement ran through Emmie's body and curled her toes. She had no response.

"For a second though," Max said, "I thought you weren't coming. I was heading out when I saw you."

Emmie's head jerked back in surprise. "You were going to leave?" She took a moment to play that idea out in her mind. What would she have thought if she'd arrived and he wasn't here? Probably that he'd changed his mind about them being together. She wouldn't have blamed him for that.

"I was going to go to your house, throw you over my shoulder, and bring you here in your raggedy SpongeBob pajama pants."

"You wouldn't have dared."

"Oh, I would have dared."

He pulled Emmie closer, as if he couldn't get close enough. She felt every hard line of him against the softness of her body.

"I suppose it would be indecent to pick you up here," he said. "You could wrap yourself around me like you did at the library. I can't stop thinking about that."

"Probably not a smart idea. There's not much keeping this dress up. Best not to get too jostled."

Max's eyes glanced down to the top of her dress again. "Interesting."

Emmie pressed her face against his chest, and finally felt a wave of comfort come over her. The same one she'd felt when they'd sat together on the library steps. She could almost imagine their jigsaw snapping together. She trusted Max. She'd forgotten what it felt like to trust someone else.

With Nick, vigilance was her constant emotion because it didn't take much for Nick to overreact. Once, a convenience store clerk called her sweetheart, and Nick broke his nose.

I don't like other people dirtying up what's mine.

Nick, he didn't touch me. He was only being nice.

Nice? Are you saying you wanted that fucker to touch you?

189

No! No.

I didn't think so. Nobody touches you, but me.

Emmie could still feel the searing pain in her scalp when Nick had yanked her back by the hair. After that night, she was quiet. She tiptoed around Nick as if he were a sleeping jackal, but with Max...

With Max, her brain was full of racket. Her heart and her stomach were in constant tango step, sometimes changing places and forgetting where they originally belonged. Strange that she was feeling weightless and floaty and thinking about their next kiss, especially since a minute ago her heart had been breaking with the weight of Max's grief.

She shoved her own happy feelings down out of respect for Jade and hoped Max was doing okay. Jade had to be hard to get over.

Though Emmie hated to admit it, she'd gone online to check out Jade's picture. There was the perfectly coiffed Facebook profile picture, and even one with her and Max. Jade was smiling at the camera, while Max's head was turned, looking at her adoringly. That one had pinched a little because Emmie understood she and Jade couldn't have been more different.

In fact, Emmie understood that she was different than pretty much *everything* in Max's world. Clearly she was the perfect distraction from his grief, from everything he didn't want to think about. But was that it? Did she only serve a temporary purpose?

"What are you thinking about?" Max asked. He stroked the back of her hair gently, as if he was afraid she might break in his arms.

"Nothing," Emmie said, turning her head away.

"Liar," Max said with a tone of amusement.

"Fine," Emmie said, looking up at him. "I was actually wondering if you were thinking about last year's dance." It was a risk, but she couldn't help herself. She needed to know how he was doing. If he needed to get out of here, that was fine with her.

Max released his hold on her just enough so he could lean back and look at her face. "Where is that coming from?"

"I know you and Jade came together last year. It's got to be tough being here without her."

"Emmie," he said on an exhale. Then he looked away for a second. When Max turned back, his face was resolute. "Yes. It's tough. It's sad. It's not fair. And it makes me mad. But this. Us." He gestured with his index finger, back and forth between his and Emmie's chests. "This is separate from any of that. Right now. With you. I'm happy. Please stop thinking about everything else."

Emmie exhaled. He was okay. Things were going to be okay. Max bent down and pressed his lips to Emmie's neck, right below her ear. Then with one arm wrapped around her, he lifted her up just enough to kiss her mouth, but not so much that she had any fear of losing her dress.

Her hands moved up his chest to the sides of his neck. Her fingers clenched in his hair, and she felt a sudden jolt of enthusiasm in her chest as he held her closer, deepening the kiss.

"Get a room, Shepherd," some guy yelled. Emmie pulled away from Max and looked to see who it was. It was his friend with the nose splint. It looked like it hurt when he laughed. Jordy and Brock shook their heads, saying, "Shut up, Chris."

When Emmie turned back toward Max, she was surprised to find him still staring into her face. It was if he'd never even heard his friend calling his name. Max's hand moved from her waist to the nape of her neck, and his fingers brushed gently through her curls. "Have I ever told you how much I love your hair?"

Emmie choked, hearing Nick in her head. *You'd look way hotter if your hair was straight.* "No. You haven't told me that."

He bent his head and spoke into her ear so she could hear him better over the music. "It's awesome. You would have made the perfect eighties rocker chick. Like that girl in that Whitesnake video." He pulled back and looked at her with a wry smile. "Have you ever seen it?"

"Are you serious?" she asked.

"I can't be the first person to tell you that."

At that point, Emmie's jaw literally dropped. Then she shook her head. "Would you please stop talking now?"

"Okay. But only because you know I'm right."

The song ended, and Emmie hated to pull away. Max must have felt the same way because he still held her, even through the long pause while the DJ figured out what song would keep everyone on the floor.

Emmie didn't know if Max was really doing as well as he said, or if he was just as good at hiding his wounds as she was with hers. Either way, she was glad to be whatever comfort she could be for him. She wondered if he knew that he gave her back just as much.

"Bathroom break," Lindsey said, grabbing Emmie's elbow and pulling her out of Max's arms.

Emmie glanced back at him with alarm, and Max yelled, "Hey!"

"Relax, Shepherd," Quinn said. "We'll have her back to you in no time."

Lindsey dragged Emmie off the dance floor, and Quinn trotted behind, saying, "We want the scoop now. The real scoop. Max won't tell the guys anything."

As Emmie tripped along the hallway—dragged by Lindsey and followed closely by Quinn—she didn't know if Max's secrecy was a good thing or a bad thing. If he was as into her as she thought he was, as much as she was into him, he would have talked. Right? But then, how much had she really told Marissa?

Quinn laughed and gave Emmie and Lindsey a friendly shove into the bathroom. The door swung shut behind them. Lindsey pulled lipstick out of her bag and leaned into the mirror.

Emmie's eyebrows shot up, and she looked at Lindsey while Quinn ran into one of the stalls. What was she supposed to say now?

"First question. Was that the first time he's kissed you?" Lindsey asked.

"No?" Emmie said, as if her answer was a question. And there was a question in it. Presumably these girls had met Jade. How would they feel about Max kissing someone new? Would they think it was too soon?

"Holy wow," Quinn said from the stall.

Lindsey squealed with excitement. "I knew it!"

Emmie smiled despite herself.

"Thank *God*, that's all I can say about that," Quinn called out. "Max has been making himself miserable for too long."

"Absolutely," Lindsey added, dropping her lipstick into her bag. She turned around and checked the back of her dress in the full-length mirror.

"That's not fair," Emmie said. "He's been through hell."

"True," Quinn added. She flushed, exited the stall, and went to the sink. "Doesn't mean we're not glad someone's finally snapped him out of his funk."

"Maybe he'll even remember to comb his hair one of these days," Lindsey said. She gave Emmie a little eyebrow raise that made her think Max's hair was some kind of inside joke with his friends.

"I thought he made it look like that on purpose," Emmie said. She always liked his tousled, I-just-rolled-out-of-bed look.

Quinn and Lindsey exchanged a look, then laughed.

"I don't know," Quinn said. "Jade kept him pretty much on point. If she could see that mop now, she'd just…" Quinn's voice trailed off, and no one wanted to finish that sentence.

"Don't listen to us," Lindsey said. "It's good that he's with you. Don't let anyone tell you different."

"Especially that stupid bastard himself," Quinn added, opening the bathroom door and holding it open for the other two to exit.

When they were halfway back to where they'd left the guys, Lindsey and Quinn ran off in one direction to catch up with their boyfriends. Emmie spotted Max in the opposite direction...talking to Katie.

He looked a little distracted as he glanced around, but Katie claimed his focus by wrapping her hand around his upper arm. Emmie watched. Wondering. Should she walk up to him? Should she watch?

Whatever Katie said made Max bow his head and laugh a little. Katie laughed too then, more animated than Max, even throwing her head back. Her hand was still on him.

It was so painfully obvious that Katie was flirting, but what was more annoying to Emmie was that Max seemed oblivious. What was with that whole speech he gave her only a moment ago? *But this. Us. This is separate from any of that. Right now. With you. I'm happy.*

Emmie was not going to let herself feel special one minute and pathetic the next. She was not going to be *that* girl. And she refused to believe that Max was *that* guy who would do anything to make her feel that way. Yes, he was obviously dense as a rock if he couldn't see how hard-core Katie was in flirting with him, but she decided that was a consequence of having a Y chromosome. She couldn't fault him for that.

When the first few beats of Rihanna's "Work" started playing, Emmie marched up to Max. She insinuated herself between him and Katie, whom she put her back to. Then she arched one eyebrow at Max. "Let's dance," she said.

"Ah," Max said, instantly focusing all his attention on Emmie. "I like it when you boss me around."

"Cut the shit, Shepherd," she said, grabbing his tie and leading him like a dog back onto the dance floor. Internally, she sighed and thought, Quinn might be right. You may be a stupid bastard, but you're my stupid bastard for now.

CHAPTER TWENTY-SIX

MIXED MESSAGES

When the dance wound down, Emmie caught up with Marissa, Sarah, and Olivia as they were heading to the parking lot. "Hey! You guys! Wait up!"

"Hey, yourself," Marissa said, looking down the hall behind Emmie. "Where's Max?"

Emmie couldn't help but smile at hearing his name. "He went out to warm up his car, but I wanted to catch you guys. Elizabeth Wannamaker invited us over for an after-party, and I want you to come too."

Marissa and Olivia exchanged a look, then Marissa sighed dramatically. "I'm like the shell, being dragged around by the singing snail."

Emmie had about enough with the whole singing-snail thing. "Would you please stop it? If you don't want to go to the party, we don't have to. I don't care either way." Which was a bit of a lie. Emmie was riding a new emotional high. In fact, she couldn't remember the last time she'd felt so happy. She wanted the evening to stretch as long as she could stretch it. But.

If Marissa didn't want to go, they wouldn't go. They'd come to-gether, and she wasn't going to bail on her at the end.

"*We?*" Marissa asked.

"Yeah. In fact," Emmie continued, "I'll tell Max that we're going to go get something to eat. I feel ready to kill whoever designed these shoes anyway. I wish it were summer so I could go barefoot."

"Are you kidding?" Sarah asked, eyebrows raised in near heartbreak. Sarah was always a little slow on the uptake, and her expression sug-gested she thought this was one of those times.

"Yeah," Marissa said, looking equally stricken. "*Geez*, Em. I was only joking. When else would I ever get invited to Elizabeth Wannamaker's house?"

Emmie blinked twice. "I thought...I mean...Since when would you *care?*"

"Well," Marissa said, a small smile spreading across her lips, "Max's friend Chris is going to be there, right?"

Emmie stepped to her left as a herd of couples pushed past them on their way to the exits. "Yes?" Emmie said, turning the answer into a question. Marissa liked Chris? Had they ever even spoken?

"Plus, I have an idea for a research project," Marissa said. When neither Sarah nor Emmie seemed to understand what she was saying, she added, "For my sociology project. I've finally come up with a topic. I got an idea listening to a couple of Elizabeth's friends talking in the bathroom. I'm going to tally how many times one of the girls calls another girl a slut or a whore—"

"Or a ratchet," Olivia added helpfully.

"And then I'm going to correlate the data to time and the amount of alcohol consumed."

"And this is going to prove what?" Emmie asked. Marissa was brilliant, but Emmie didn't see any of this translating into academic credit.

"Thesis: Misogyny is not a natural characteristic of the human condition but is promoted—even among women—by artificial conditions."

"Crap on a cracker," Sarah said. "You can turn anything into an A."

"What can I say?" Marissa gave a little shrug. "Desperation is the mother of invention."

"Yeah, I don't think that's how the saying goes," Emmie said with a laugh.

"Yet," Marissa added.

* * *

Elizabeth Wannamaker's parties were legendary. Her parents were executives at a big downtown advertising firm, and they traveled a lot. That left Elizabeth with a three-story house plus a finished basement—so technically four levels of Pottery Barn catalog awesomeness. Emmie was afraid to touch anything.

Even Elizabeth's main-floor bathroom had a tiny chandelier and magazines that were apparently chosen because their covers color-coordinated with the paint and towels. If something in this place got broken, Emmie had to imagine there'd be hell to pay.

Out in the kitchen, there were at least ten kids sitting on the granite countertops with two cases of beer on the cherrywood floor beneath their feet. There was also a cooler full of bottled mojitos. The living room, family room, and library (the Wannamakers had a *freakin' library*), were filled with kids draped over the furniture or sitting cross-legged on the floor. It was loud, and there was already a trash can filling up in the hallway.

Two guys were leaning over the can, each taking down a beer as fast they could, the overflow running down their chins and into the plastic liner.

But not everyone was drinking. The guys' varsity hockey team, for example, didn't want to risk getting caught during the season. The overall result was a high-school-party cliché that was nothing like the so-called parties Nick threw above the Gold Pedal Bike Shop.

In contrast to those at the Wannamakers' house, Nick's parties were dimly lit affairs with a small group hunkered around a flat-topped metal steamer trunk that Nick had gotten at Walmart. Jimmy was always shooting up, and Angie and Frankie would arrive already high. Every party ended with three people passed out and Emmie crushed under Nick's sweaty body on a lumpy blue mattress.

The sudden memory sent Emmie reeling. Air caught in her throat. Her vision tunneled, and a cold trickle of dread crept up her arms. She gasped for breath and staggered backward in her high heels, catching her hand on the edge of a small table and bumping a bowl of potpourri onto the floor.

"Emmie, you okay?" Max asked. He seemed to come out of nowhere, though he'd been there all along. He wrapped an arm around her waist.

"Here," he said. "Let me help you." He bent over and lifted one of her feet off the ground. Emmie steadied herself by putting one hand on his back while he slipped off her shoe. And then the other. "Let's get rid of these things."

As Emmie's shoes came off, she lost several inches of height, and the world seemed to expand around her as she shrank in comparison. She felt small. And lost. She hadn't been at the party for more than five minutes, and she already wanted to leave.

"There," Max said, "there's the girl I know."

"I need to sit down," she said. It was disorienting to see Max's face in front of her while images of Nick were still at the forefront of her mind. She felt like she was in a fun house full of mirrors. Except, it wasn't feeling very fun.

Max led Emmie to the corner of a white leather couch. He sat next to her with his arm around her shoulders. Emmie leaned forward and tried to get the blood to flow back to her head. She needed her thoughts to clear. She didn't need her past to ruin what should be a good time. She was at a party. A normal, uninspired party with normal stupid stuff like guys shotgunning beers and girls crying in the bathroom. She was with Max. And she was safe. She needed to settle down.

Chris jumped over the back of the opposite-facing couch and landed with a hard bounce. Brock walked around the arm and sat down, throwing his black-socked feet up on the glass coffee table. "So!" Chris said as a type of conversation starter.

"So," Max said, grinning and giving Emmie's shoulders a gentle squeeze.

Emmie plastered a fake smile on her face while Max talked to Chris and Brock. Something about hockey, of course, and what seed they'd end up for the tournament. When Max glanced over at her, she pretended to check her texts. She didn't really need to (she'd already seen the two from her father; it had taken quite a bit of begging for him to let her out of the house), but the phone gave Emmie a reason not to look at Max. She was afraid that if she did, he'd see right through her. And then he'd know. And then he'd leave her.

"You want to play some pool?" Chris asked. His voice was extra nasally from the splint. Brock stood up, ready to go.

Max looked at Emmie and put his hand on her knee. "Do you want to?"

"You go ahead. I'll catch up. I want to find Marissa. And maybe get some fresh air."

"You're sure?" he asked, standing up.

Emmie nodded and reached up to him. He took her hand and pulled her to her feet. The guys headed upstairs, and Emmie padded around the first level in her bare feet. Eventually she found Marissa in a small room with a group of girls who were all drinking bottled mojitos. No one seemed to notice Marissa's small notebook filled with sociology project notes on the ottoman beside her.

Raven-haired Lauren from the hockey game and Elizabeth, the hostess, were in animated conversation with Katie. They sat cross-legged on the floor, an empty bottle in front of each of them. Katie was on the girls' hockey team, but apparently she didn't police herself during the season like the guys did.

When Lauren noticed Emmie in the room, she tipped her head toward Katie as some unspoken message. Emmie tried not to notice or to wonder what they thought of her. She didn't want to spend any time in this room with them either.

"Where's Sarah?" Emmie asked Marissa.

"I don't know," Marissa said. "She went off with some guy named Jason? Or Justin?"

"Josh," another girl said with a slur. "Who knew that Sarah was such a slut?"

Marissa made a surreptitious hash mark in her notebook and looked up at Emmie with a wink.

Emmie's little bag hung from her wrist and rested against her thigh. She felt her phone vibrate inside the bag and went to check what she supposed would be her father's third text, asking again when she would be home. Instead the text read: It's Angie.

Emmie's heart gave a little stutter, and she quickly moved out into the hallway so Marissa wouldn't notice her reaction. Angie had her new number? How did she get her number? Had she somehow jacked her phone at the rink? No. That was impossible.

Then her father's suspicions got the better of her. Emmie's mom must have found her number. Her mom must have given it out. Emmie looked around. There were only a few people in the hallway with her, two of whom were seriously focused on each other. Emmie read on.

I probably shouldn't be doing this, but Nick wanted me to get a message to you. Delete this as soon as you read it. I went to visit him.

Emmie's blood felt chilly in her arms. No. She couldn't believe her mom was behind this. If her mom had her number, then why had she never called herself? So, there was that no-contact order...Still, she couldn't believe her mom would have abided by it this long without testing the limits. That just wasn't her mom.

Another text came through:

He wanted me to tell you that he's not mad anymore. He's had time to think about how everything went down, and he understands why you testified. He doesn't blame you, and he still LOVES you. I know you can't see him, but if you want me to send him a message for you, let me know.

Love? Emmie couldn't breathe. She seriously could not find any air. He'd never shown her love before, and she didn't want it now. She *was*, however, desperate for his forgiveness, and that felt really good. Before Emmie could formulate a coherent thought, another text came through:

I worked things out with Frankie too. He was really sorry. Things are good with us now.

Then finally:

If this isn't Emmie's phone, quit reading this, you nosy bastard. It's none of your business.

Emmie clicked out of her texts and slipped her phone back into her bag. She closed her eyes and tried to get a grip on what was happening. There was nothing directly threatening in Angie's message, but her stomach turned in revolt. And then she had a terrifying thought.

If they knew where she was on the crew, and where she lived, and how to reach her, what if one of Nick's friends had followed her here?

What if Angie was here, in this house? Oh my God, what if Frankie was with her?

Emmie pushed herself off the wall and raced down the basement steps in search of Max. Her eyes quickly glanced around the crowd. The faces of strangers. Laughing. Oblivious.

For the first time since moving back home, Emmie wasn't able to lie to herself. She wasn't *fine*. This wasn't *nothing*. She couldn't handle it on her own.

Maybe it was because she wasn't in her own environment. Maybe if she could just get to her own room and under the covers, she wouldn't feel the need to start screaming. *I never saw freaking out do anybody any good.* She took a deep breath and let it out. She needed to find Max.

If he wanted to put those overprotective urges of his to good use, now was as good a time as any. She wanted to go home.

Emmie tapped the nearest girl on the shoulder. "Do you know where the pool table is?"

"Upstairs," the girl said, then turned back to her small circle of friends.

Emmie whirled and ran up the stairs, taking two at a time. Then up the next flight to the second story. She walked quickly and systematically down the hallway, opening doors, looking for Max. They all seemed to be bedrooms on this level. All immaculately clean and smelling like lavender. She climbed the stairs to the third floor. There were fewer rooms up there. A study, a bathroom, and the only other door, which had to be the game room.

Emmie turned the knob and gave the door a push. She expected to find a group of guys on the other side, but instead the room was empty, save for a pool table at its center and—

Her mind could not process what she was seeing.

Max was sitting on the edge of the pool table. His feet nearly reaching the floor. Between his legs stood a girl. Emmie's mind was working so slowly that she didn't recognize her at first. Long, wavy red hair pulled out of its earlier twist. Toned shoulders. Narrow hips. Her black dress draped off one bared shoulder, and her hands rested gently on the sides of Max's face.

Emmie needed to look away. She needed to run, and yet she stood there—rooted—with her mouth hanging open. It seemed like an eternity before Max and Katie looked her way. Max's shoulders slumped when he saw her. Emmie thought she detected a small smile play at the corners of Katie's lips.

"Emmie, wait," Max said, which was strange because she still wasn't moving.

"You asshole!" Then Emmie found her feet and bolted from the room.

Hands holding both sides of the stairwell so she wouldn't fall, Emmie stormed down the two flights of stairs and into the small room where she'd found Marissa earlier. "We got to go."

"What? We just—"

"Marissa, I need to get out of here."

"Is everything okay?" Elizabeth asked, standing up from the floor. "Did you break something?"

Marissa escorted Emmie out of the room and into a private corner of the kitchen. "What's going on, Em?"

"Please," she said, her eyes stinging. Emmie looked behind her to make sure Max hadn't followed her, but of course he hadn't. He had his hands full. "I found Max with Katie."

Marissa's face was a mixture of surprise and sympathy, and Emmie hated to see it. She didn't want it. She just wanted to get the hell out of there.

"Please, let's go." Emmie's throat was as dry and ragged as a bale of hay, and just as easy to swallow.

"Yeah, let me find my keys."

Emmie grabbed her shoes from where she'd left them by the fireplace. Her feet protested when she forced them back into position.

"Sarah's getting a ride home with Josh," Marissa said as they exited the house. She unlocked her car. Emmie jumped in the passenger seat and slammed the door shut, pressing the heels of her hands against her forehead. It took a while for Marissa's defrost to work. Emmie knew it was silly to be mad about the delay. Obviously, Marissa needed to be able to see to drive, but all Emmie wanted to do was get home.

There was a loud noise at her window, and Emmie jumped in her seat. She glanced quickly to her right, then closed her eyes. Max's palms slapped a second time against the glass, and his muffled voice yelled at her to roll down the window.

Emmie cranked up the radio so she couldn't hear him. She stared straight ahead without blinking, but all she could see was Katie. Katie's bare shoulder, her hips between Max's legs, her hands on Max's face.

Why should she be so surprised? How could she have been so stupid? Did she really think she and Max were together, as in *together* together? He was a player. Like all of them. *Don't be so clingy, Pigeon. If I'm going to kiss another girl, I'm going to kiss another girl.*

Marissa turned her head toward Emmie as if waiting for instructions. Emmie yelled, "Go! Please, let's just go." She wiped the back of her hand across her eyes and—what was this? Tears? This was not her. Emmie O'Brien did not cry. Or at least, not in front of anyone else.

"You don't have to be tough for me," Marissa said as she pulled out and Max made one last slap at the car. "What happened exactly?"

"I found him with Katie. Alone in a room on the top floor. She was standing between his legs, and she had her hands on his face."

Marissa sighed. "Damnit. You can't ever trust a jock."

She was right. She was obviously right. Emmie had seen the evidence to support that statement with her own eyes. But she still felt the urge to rise up and defend Max. The shock of the moment was fading, and reason was taking over. Yes, it hurt. It hurt like a mother. But Emmie had only been Max's date to a dance. And that dance was now over. They hadn't made each other any promises. He could make out with anyone he wanted.

Then she remembered his words from earlier in the night. *But this. Us. This is separate from any of that. Right now. With you. I'm happy.* Goddamn bastard, making her believe him. Making a fool out of her.

When Emmie didn't say anything, Marissa leaned over the steering wheel and peered through the shrinking hole of visibility as the windshield frosted over again. It took another few minutes, but they did manage to get to Emmie's house in one piece. Before they got out, Emmie took a deep breath and let it out slowly. "Do you want to spend the night?"

"Definitely," Marissa said. "I'll have to call my mom."

Emmie climbed out of Marissa's car and sucked in a breath. Max's jeep was parked on the opposite side of the street, and he was standing outside it, leaning back against the hood. His head bowed.

"How—?" Emmie started.

Max looked up. Sheepish. "I told you. I know all the shortcuts."

"Go back to the party," she said.

"We need to talk," he said, crossing the street.

"I'm pretty sure that's the last thing we need to do." Emmie started to walk up her driveway, and Marissa hurried around the back of her car to catch up.

"It wasn't what it looked like," Max said from behind them. "Don't shut me out, Emmie."

Emmie kept her body as controlled as she possibly could and turned around coolly. "You were never *in*, Shepherd. Go back to your own kind. We'll both be much happier that way."

"You mean things will be easier that way," Max said.

"Same difference," she said, turning.

Max reached out and tried to stop Emmie by putting his hand on her arm.

"Don't touch me!" she said with a jerk of her shoulder.

Max pulled back his hand as if he'd been bitten. "I'm not interested in easy. I'm interested in you. And I know enough about you to know that nothing is going to be easy."

"Yeah, well..." Emmie hated that she had no better comeback for him than that. Marissa was already at the back door. Emmie finished her trek up the driveway with Max close on her heels.

"There are plenty of charity cases out there," Emmie said, turning around one last time to face him. Her hair flew around her face, caught in the wind. "I'm sure you'll find someone else to challenge your overprotective macho urges. As for me, I'm good. And I'm done. I don't need you. Nick's not going to be a problem anymore. None of them are."

Her hands balled into fists. She wasn't sure she believed what she was saying, but that was for her to worry about. Not him.

"Nick?" Max asked, his eyes wide. "Emmie, what are you...? Please let me explain. I don't want tonight to end like this."

Marissa held the back door open, and Emmie stepped into the warmth of her house. She thought she caught Marissa giving Max a sympathetic look before she shut the door, but Emmie'd give her the benefit of the doubt. She could only handle one friend's betrayal per evening.

CHAPTER TWENTY-SEVEN

CONFESSION (OF SORTS)

Once they were in the kitchen, Emmie let out a long, ragged breath. Marissa was at the window peering through the break in the curtains.

"Is he gone?" Emmie asked.

"He's staring at the house," Marissa said. "Now he's putting his hands in his pockets. He's tur...Wait, yeah, he's turning around. Okay, he's leaving."

"Good."

"Emmie?"

"What?"

"This had to be the weirdest, most made-for-TV-miniseries-ish night of my life, and I wasn't even the main character. What the hell happened back there? And don't tell me 'nothing.' Who the hell is Nick? You've been keeping things from me, and it's not fair."

Emmie hesitated for a couple seconds, then let out a breath. "You're right. There's been...stuff...going on, and I haven't told you everything because you're going to look at me differently once I do."

"Aw, Em." Marissa walked across the kitchen toward her friend. "I love you. You're my best friend. You've seen me at my worst…"

Emmie rolled her eyes and started to walk out of the kitchen and into the living room. Marissa's worst was an ugly, crying meltdown in front of the whole class when she got an F on a science test. Second to that was the time she farted during music class in fifth grade.

"No. You don't get to walk away from me," Marissa said. "Not from me."

Emmie turned and leaned against the wall. "Your worst…your worst is like a day at Disney World compared to my past year."

"Don't patronize me," Marissa said, raising her finger like a scolding mother.

"I'm not. I—"

"Did you kill somebody?"

Emmie's mouth dropped open. "I—I…" And then, though her mind couldn't help going to B. J.'s body laid out in a cold parking lot, she said, "Don't be ridiculous."

"Well, I'd still love you even if you did. I'd call the cops, but I'd still love you. I know bad shit went down. Maybe I don't know all the details, but I know enough. If that was going to scare me off, it would have happened a long time ago."

"Am I going to be another one of your sociology studies?"

Marissa shrugged and gave Emmie one of her mischievous smiles. The kind she gave Emmie in seventh grade right before they forked Kelly Winkler's front yard. Emmie could still see the thousands of white plastic handles sticking out of the grass, glowing in the moonlight.

"You can be a test case if you want to be. Does your dad still keep a gallon of…" Marissa walked back into the kitchen and opened the freezer door. "Bingo. Some things never change."

Emmie was glad her father's fetish for mint chocolate-chip ice cream had come through for Marissa. She also hoped she could take Marissa at her word because she needed to unload a boatload of shit on someone tonight, and right now Marissa was the only one volunteering for the job.

They went up to Emmie's room. Emmie changed out of her dress and gave Marissa some sweats to wear. Then they did what they did when they were little. Emmie pulled her desk closer to her bed, and they draped a quilt over both of them, making a tent. Emmie brought sleeping bags in from the storage closet and as many pillows as she could find.

Marissa pried open the plastic tub of ice cream and drove two spoons into the still-smooth surface. Emmie pulled a little lamp into the fort with them. It cast a golden glow around their faces.

The bedroom door opened, and Tom O'Brien said, "Em? Are you in there?"

Emmie split the curtain of blankets. "It's me and Marissa." Her father's face was lined with worry. Something wasn't right. "Dad?"

"I'm glad you're home already. I didn't expect you for a couple hours still. Didn't hear you come in."

Marissa leaned forward and waved her spoon at him. "Hi, Mr. O'Brien. Thanks for the ice cream."

He glanced down at the plastic tub. "Put that back in the freezer before it melts."

"We will," she said.

"Are you sure you're all right, Dad?" Something was obviously bothering him, and it didn't have anything to do with the ice cream. The lines at the corners of his eyes were more pronounced, and his jaw was tight.

"Fine," he said grimly. "We'll talk later. I'm glad you're home safe."

Mr. O'Brien closed the door behind him, and Emmie settled back into the pillows. Was she safe? She still didn't know how to take Angie's texts.

Marissa took a big bite of ice cream, and Emmie turned on Spotify. At first they said nothing, and the only sound was that of spoons clanking together as they both dove into the ice cream at the same time. Eventually the silence needed to be addressed.

"Did I see you dancing with Max's friend tonight?" Emmie asked without looking at Marissa.

"Chris. Yeah. Only for a little bit though. He asked me to dance mid-song, so it ended pretty quick."

"I didn't know you knew him."

"Just from when we went skating. His nose looks a lot better already, doesn't it?"

Emmie nodded, even though she didn't know how Marissa could tell with the splint. The silence stretched out again.

"So are we going to talk about the elephant in the room?" Marissa asked.

"Which one?" Emmie responded with a little laugh. She loved how Marissa always cut to the chase. She loved how Marissa understood how hard it was for her to admit weakness. It was like Marissa had verbally wrapped an arm around Emmie's back and was going to help her walk barefoot across hot coals.

"We can talk about the Max elephant later. For now, tell me about the bigger one. Tell me what's really been going on with you."

With a deep breath of preparation, Emmie turned to face Marissa and unloaded. She rehashed the parts of the last couple years that Marissa already knew: how she and her father had started fighting after her mom moved out during seventh grade. How in ninth grade Emmie begged him to let her go live with her mom. How he eventually relented, even though her mom hadn't been great about exercising her visitation rights.

"Pretty much as soon as I moved in, I could see how much she'd changed. I could see why she'd been skipping out on visits." Emmie gave a humorless laugh. "She was basically a mess."

"Because of the drugs," Marissa said, and Emmie appreciated how hard Marissa was trying to make the conversation sound natural. Marissa's parents ran a dry-cleaning business. Their kind of excitement was Bingo Night at the American Legion.

"When Mom and Dad got divorced, she was already smoking weed, but she'd gotten into some nastier stuff since moving out. That's why she wasn't good at keeping a schedule. When she agreed to let me move in, I hadn't seen her in a few months, but it looked like she'd aged ten years. It made me worry about her. A lot."

Sometimes Emmie wished she could hate her mom. If Emmie could do that, she wouldn't worry about what would happen when her mom got out of the treatment facility she was in. She wouldn't have to worry about her losing her car, or if she did, who'd be picking her up. She wouldn't worry about who her mom was living with, or where she'd go if there was no one to take her in.

If she could hate her mom, she wouldn't worry about whether she had enough money for her next fix, or how the drugs were slowly killing her. She wouldn't care if her mom had food in her cupboards. She could be numb to it all, and dammit, that sounded like all kinds of wonderful.

Emmie didn't say anything more for a while. Iggy Azalea was singing "Fancy." Light and shadow bounced around the inside of their blanket fort as they moved in front of the flashlight. Emmie and Marissa talked about other things. Small things. High school things. Ultimately, Marissa pressed for more.

"What did you mean when you told Max that Nick wasn't going to be a problem anymore? Who's Nick, Emmie?"

Emmie fidgeted. Marissa didn't drink or smoke, and she still hadn't even kissed anyone. At least as far as Emmie knew. Marissa had never had to watch her mother pull meth from a spoon into a syringe and slam it hard, the weeklong binges, empty rigs rolling across a steamer trunk and toppling onto the floor... If she told Marissa the truth, what would she think of her?

"When I moved in with Mom, I saw how thin and old and shaky she was, but I was sure it would only take me a week, maybe two, to get her back on track. And we had some good moments, like..." It took Emmie a second to remember.

"On one of our first nights together, she suggested we make brownies." Even now, Emmie could conjure up the warm smell of melted chocolate, stirred together with the yellow spiral of butter in the saucepan. They turned on the oven light and sat cross-legged on the floor, watching the brownies rise, then the crust cracking open. It hadn't even mattered that Emmie had to use her own money to buy the ingredients.

"A couple times, we went to the movies, and once—about a month or two after I showed up—we had a camp-out in her car. Just us, under the stars. She told me stories about what it was like growing up, and college, and how she'd met Dad and had been taken in by his *superhot* accent."

Marissa groaned, and Emmie said with a laugh, "Yeah. She promised never to use *hot* and *dad* in the same sentence again. Like, ever."

"After the second night of camping, I realized that we'd been evicted from her apartment. She didn't want me to worry. She told me not to tell Dad. When I think back, she didn't want him to know what she really spent his alimony checks on. And that's when I met Nick."

Emmie swallowed hard and gathered her nerve. "He was her dealer, but he was also this incredibly good-looking guy. I practically swallowed my gum when I met him for the first time. He was…twenty-six and tall with these really great teeth."

"Teeth?" Marissa asked.

"His dad was a dentist, but he also owned a building in the city that Nick stayed in. There was a bike shop on the ground level but this huge space above it, and Nick offered Mom and me one of the extra rooms. It was perfect."

In fact, *everything* with Nick had to be perfect. He liked things orderly. Neat. Pure. He ate organic. Which was ironic because he was cooking meth in the shed out back. Still, Nick never sampled his own product.

Do you think Mr. Hilton stays in his own hotels? Emmie'd once heard him say. *I'm sure he's got a house anywhere he needs to go.*

As a result of Nick's obsession with perfection, their new living situation was clean and comfortable. For a while, at least. Emmie quickly learned that nothing came without a price.

"Until…until Mom started struggling again, and Nick was there holding the reins. That's when I agreed to work for him. It was Mom's idea."

Emmie can work for you for free, but in exchange for you helping me out, you know?

Emmie blinked back tears, and she was grateful for the dark. Why had she agreed? Why hadn't she called her father to come get her?

The answers to those questions made Emmie feel sicker than the questions themselves. Because *it was her mom, goddammit.* She hadn't called her father because she didn't want to admit that he'd been right. That she'd been wrong.

"What kind of jobs?"

Emmie took a big bite of ice cream and let the cold freeze hit her brain. "Odd jobs mostly." She paused to measure Marissa's reaction, waiting for the tipping point where she'd have to stop, or to lie, so Marissa wouldn't think too badly of her.

Narc. Whore. Pigeon.

Angie's text message ran through her head: *He forgives you.*

"But you knew you had me, right?" Marissa asked. "You had people who cared about you. You could have called me."

"Yeah," Emmie said quietly, adjusting a spot where a blanket had sagged over the back of her desk chair. "But being with Nick was like another life. He kept Mom supplied with what she...needed. I mean, I know she should have stopped using, but the withdrawal symptoms were scary. At the time, I thought it was better if...Anyway, Nick kept it so I could keep living with her."

Emmie stopped there. Marissa didn't need to know the rest.

"Your dad must have freaked when he found out."

Emmie fiddled with the edge of her T-shirt. "It all came out after Nick got in some trouble, and I testified against him at his trial. Now I'm not allowed to talk to him anymore." The truth was, there has been a lot of guilt and fear about testifying, but ultimately she was relieved. She was so relieved about being able to leave. About getting *out*. Then she felt guilty about that too.

"Isn't that a good thing?" Marissa asked. "Is that what happened with Max tonight? Did you tell him all this, and he freaked out and went to Katie?"

Emmie shook her head. "Max already knew about Nick." *At least a little bit.* "But that wasn't it. I got this text tonight." Emmie pulled out her phone and let Marissa read Angie's message. "I was on my way to tell Max about it when I found him with Katie."

Marissa's eyebrows hit her hairline. "Oh my God! This Nick guy is why your car got trashed, isn't he?"

Emmie nodded.

"And now all of a sudden he forgives you and...still *loves* you? Isn't he like a...*man*?"

Emmie closed her eyes. She probably shouldn't have shown Marissa that part.

Marissa clenched her teeth, then said, "I'm going to kill Max for not being there for you tonight."

"Well, if you do, I'll still love you," Emmie said, echoing Marissa's words from earlier.

Marissa finished reading, then handed the phone back to Emmie. "So do you believe this Angie girl? That could be a bunch of bullshit about him forgiving you."

Emmie nodded. She knew that. That's why she hadn't responded. Still, Angie's message helped to lift the veil of guilt that Emmie'd been wearing, and it confirmed her earlier expectation. Emmie and her mom had *lived* with Nick—and by extension Jimmy, Frankie, and Angie— for nearly a year. They'd all been Emmie's *people*. They might want to mess with her for a while, but it wasn't going to go on forever. They'd sent their message, and now life was moving on.

In fact, now that she was home, she was embarrassed by her little, internal freak-out session back when she first got the message. She chalked it up to being in a strange environment. Now that she was home, she felt a hell of a lot better about it. She wasn't a wimp. Why had she acted like one?

Emmie wouldn't hide behind her father anymore. She wouldn't hide behind Max either. She couldn't. She was on her own again, and that was fine by her.

CHAPTER TWENTY-EIGHT

FORGIVEN, NOT FORGIVEN

Max woke up sick to his stomach. He always knew today was going to suck, so he was thankful for a fourth Saturday on the work crew. If Dan hadn't extended his time, he wouldn't have had this natural opportunity to see Emmie today. More importantly, she was forced into spending time with him, and he needed her more today—of all days—than he ever had before.

He got to the sheriff's parking lot early, so early he had to actually wait for Emmie to show up. Max had guessed that it was her habit to arrive first because she always got the first-row seat, by the window. Sure enough. Shortly after the van arrived, so did Emmie. She was wearing her SpongeBob pajama bottoms again, and her curls were pulled up in a knot on top of her head. Half of it was falling out in back.

Max waited in his car until she was getting into the van, then he sprinted to catch up, making sure to get ahead of the other guys who were pulling into the parking lot. When Max slid into the seat beside her, Emmie glanced over and groaned. She laid her head against the window and closed her eyes. If she meant to discourage him, she was going to have to work harder than that.

He needed her. He didn't know how to explain it to her. He'd tried once, and it had sounded all wrong. He hoped, instead, that she would simply intuit how he was feeling—like she'd done at the Happy Gopher when she pressed her hand against his, steadying him.

He'd been about to lose it when he thought Marissa was going to offer her condolences. He'd felt the shaking in his fingers and the tightening in his chest, that panicky feeling of plummeting in a plane. But that night, just one touch from Emmie had him leveling out. He needed that steadiness to get him through this day.

"You can't ignore me forever," Max said.

"I probably could," she said. She pulled out the hair binder, and her hair fell forward, creating a curtain that hid her face. He wanted to reach over and draw it behind her ear, but he knew better than to touch her now.

Hearing her voice was a little victory. "See, you're already not ignoring me."

"Let me sleep, Max."

The first two guys were nearly to the van. If Max hoped to smooth things over between himself and Emmie, he'd need to talk faster. "Nothing happened at the party. You misinterpreted the whole thing."

She didn't answer. She was terrible at faking sleep. The two guys slid open the van door and climbed in. One of them was the guy who usually sat next to Emmie. He looked at Max with confusion before figuring out the new seating arrangement. Behind them, another three guys climbed in and found seats in the back.

Dan opened the passenger door and got in. There was frost in his goatee. He placed his travel mug in the cup holder, took off his gloves, and grabbed a pen from behind his ear. When he turned in his seat to take roll, he didn't seem nearly as surprised as the rest of the crew to see Max sitting next to Emmie. "Last week for you, Shepherd."

"Yeah," Max said. "It's been fun."

"We're headed back to Goodwill today," Dan said to the group. "I'm going to need a few of you to help move some furniture that came in."

The driver put the van in gear and pulled away from the curb. Everyone's bodies rocked as he drove over a speed bump, and Max's left arm rubbed up against Emmie's right. She pulled herself in tighter and folded her arms. Max leaned closer to her and whispered, "Emmie. *Please.* That girl, she—"

"Save it," Emmie said without opening her eyes. She reached into her pocket and put earbuds in her ears.

Max sighed and straightened up. How was he ever going to fix this?

* * *

Two hours later, Max and some of the other guys had moved three full living-room sets onto the thrift store's showroom floor. Emmie was out in front folding baby clothes. Every time Max tried to go talk to her, Dan would yell at him to come out back, or Emmie would find a reason to help a customer find "the most perfect red dress" for Valentine's Day.

The shift was nearly over by the time Emmie headed for the restroom and Max found his opportunity. He followed her into the ladies' room and held the door shut so no one else could come in. Emmie spun around in surprise when she heard his voice.

"What are you doing in here?" she asked. "Get out."

"Emmie, you need to listen to me."

She pushed her hair behind her ears and stared at a spot on the wall just beyond his shoulder. "You can't be in here."

Max didn't know what the big deal was. It was just a bathroom. "I don't care."

218

"Yeah? Well, I guess you don't care about a lot of things."

Her words caught him off balance. How could she think that? Nothing could be further from the truth. If he had a flaw, it was caring too much. "Would you stop it? That girl—"

"Katie," she said, finally looking him in the eye. "Jade's *cousin*. You're such an asshole!"

"Emmie. Would you just listen?"

"Go be with her if that's who you think you should be with."

Max threw his hands up in the air, and they landed against his legs with a slap. "Should. Could. What about who I *want* to be with? I want to be with you."

Emmie rolled her eyes. "It didn't look like you wanted to be with me when you were straddling Katie, and she had her hands all over you. What happened to playing pool with Chris and Brock? Or was that some cover story to give you a way to get alone with her?"

"Of course not. That's not what happened. Please. I need—"

"You don't need anything from me," Emmie said.

She couldn't have been more wrong, but Max could hardly blame her. She didn't know today was the day. As in, *the* day. As in, *Please, Emmie. Don't leave me alone today.* But it sounded so pathetic in his head that he didn't dare let her know what a mess he was. He wanted to protect *her*. It wasn't supposed to work the other way around.

One of the Goodwill employees opened the bathroom door, saw Max standing there, and gave him a dirty look.

"Give us one second," Max said to her. The woman closed the door, but Max bet she was going to find the manager. He didn't have much time.

"I went upstairs to play pool. Remember I asked if you wanted to come with me?" He took one step closer.

"It's okay," Emmie said, stepping back, her eyes cast sideways. They seemed shinier than before, but maybe Max was imagining that under the fluorescents. "I'm not even mad anymore. I don't need you."

"What's that supposed to mean?" Max reached toward her, but she stepped away again, her hand landing on the edge of the sinks.

"I told you. I'm not in danger anymore from Nick or his friends. There's nothing for you to protect me from anymore. Everything's fine."

"What do you...How do you know? What happened?" He couldn't tell if she was lying to him. Would she put herself at risk to keep him away from her? Had he messed things up that badly?

"Nick's forgiven me. There won't be any more trouble from his friends."

"How...? Emmie, you haven't talked to him, have you? What about the court order?" Max reached out again and this time laid his hand against her arm.

She shrugged him off. "Of course not."

"Then—"

"Go back to work, Max. This isn't any of your business."

"What isn't? What's going on?"

Emmie stormed past him and flung open the bathroom door just as Dan—followed by the interfering Goodwill employee—was about to walk in. Dan stepped to the side like a matador as Emmie charged past him. Max followed Emmie out of the bathroom but stopped beside Dan.

"What's going on with our girl?" Dan asked.

"I messed up," Max said, "and"—he sighed in defeat—"apparently Emmie can take care of herself."

But Max didn't believe that last part. In fact, Emmie looked more vulnerable to him now than she had when Jimmy Krebs had pulled up in his car. For a second, Max thought about telling Dan that she'd been in contact with Nick, but he held his tongue. There was the matter of the no-contact order. He didn't want her to get in more trouble with the courts.

"That's quite the statement coming from you," Dan said.

Max continued to watch Emmie with the most intense sense of longing he'd ever felt. He was on emotional overload today—to the point that he wondered if there was a tipping point for the male mind. He wanted to hit something. He *needed* to hit something.

There were old mattresses outside, leaning up against the building. Someone had dumped them off in the middle of the night. The health department wouldn't let them be resold, but that didn't mean they couldn't serve a purpose. Max bet he could beat the stains right off them.

"How are those anger management classes going?" Dan asked as if he could read Max's mind, or maybe out of professional obligation.

"Fine," Max said.

Emmie checked her phone and quickly dashed off a text. Then she glanced over her shoulder at Dan and Max, who were both still standing outside the door to the ladies' room. The look of guilt and embarrassment on her face triggered a gut reaction in Max that something wasn't right.

The Wednesday night classes might have taught him how to curb his predilection toward overreaction, but he still had a hard time ignoring his base instincts. He didn't know how Emmie knew Nick had forgiven her, but forgiveness was a good thing. He could get behind that. Nobody got revenge against someone they'd forgiven. So why did he feel the urge to dive in front of her and take a bullet?

* * *

After the shift was over and the crew had been dropped off at the sheriff's office, Max tried to follow Emmie to her car, but she ran, jumped in, and took off while he was still standing on the sidewalk. Max tried texting her: Please. Emmie. I need to talk to you.

But she never replied.

He tried to call, but she never picked up. *Emmie, it's Max. Can I come over? It will only take a minute.*

The afternoon drew on, and as Max sat on the edge of his bed, staring at his reflection in his mirror, his nerves grew long and tight. Time slowed. It was like sitting in the penalty box and waiting out the last few seconds of the power play.

How was he going to get through this? He had a game tonight, and he didn't trust himself. His hands were already shaking, his fingers twitching against his thighs. His heart raced, and his vision tunneled. Max was afraid for anyone who got too close to him tonight. He didn't want anyone to get hurt.

When his phone rang, Max about jumped out of his skin. Emmie!

But when he looked at the screen, it wasn't Emmie's name. It was a familiar number though, and as ridiculous it sounded, he halfway expected to hear Jade's voice on the other side.

"Hello?" he asked cautiously, gripping the edge of his mattress.

"How are you doing, Max?" It wasn't Jade, of course; it was her mother, Mrs. Howard. Max knew there was a reason he recognized the number.

Things had been tense between the Howards and Shepherds since the accident. Max didn't think she was really calling to see how he was doing. Mrs. Howard was too much of a mess herself to care.

"I'm fine. How are you?" he asked.

"Of course you're fine." Her voice was ragged, gasping, as if she couldn't get enough air to form her words. "Walking around, living your life while my baby is in the ground."

And there it was. The temperature in the room seemed to drop.

Max's heart stuttered in his chest before picking up at an alarming speed. At least Mrs. Howard was getting to her point right away.

It didn't make any difference to her that he'd lost Jade too. She was crazy if she thought Max didn't feel every jagged edge of it.

A sob hitched in her throat. "It's not fair. It's not fair that you're alive when my baby is dead."

Max closed his eyes and leaned forward, elbows resting on knees. He couldn't disagree. Life wasn't fair, and the least he could do for Jade's mother was to keep his mouth shut and let her unload. Why shouldn't he be the one to shoulder her grief? She deserved that relief, and he owed her that much. More. So much, much more.

"Jade had plans. She was going to be something special. She was special. It's your fault, and you don't take any responsibility for what happened to her."

I do, Max thought. Of course I do. But when he opened his mouth to speak, nothing came out but strangled air.

He laid his hand over his eyes as the verbal onslaught continued, words biting and slashing like shards of broken glass. And then, just as quickly and explosively as it started, it was over. The phone clicked off, and his screen went dark.

Slowly, Max reached over toward his bedside table and set down his phone. His blood ran cold in his arms. His hands felt numb. The periphery of his vision was closing in. When his mom brought in his clean jersey, she stopped in her tracks.

"What's wrong?"

Max looked up. His mother's eyes were red from crying, the lids puffy against her lashes. She looked the way he felt.

"Nothing," he said.

"Babe."

He looked away. He couldn't look at her face any more.

She laid his jersey on the back of his chair. "Is there anything I can get you?"

Max tossed his pillow toward the end of his bed and bowed his head. "No."

His mom bit the inside of her cheek and nodded. She walked toward his closet and fussed with his hangers like it was suddenly important for them to be evenly spaced. "Are you ready for the game?"

"I'm always ready," Max said.

"I mean, is your head ready? It's a big game. The last of the regular season." She finished with the hangers and turned to face him. "It couldn't have come on a worse day."

"I've got it!" Max exploded. He looked up at his mother and instantly regretted his tone. The pain he caused her—now and before—were both etched into her face. He held her gaze, unable to find an adequate apology. She wasn't telling him anything he didn't already know. He wished she hadn't said anything at all. Didn't she know that when you said things out loud, it made them more real? But still he was sorry.

"Your father and I are going to get something to eat before your game. If you want, we could drop you off at the rink."

"No," Max said. "I'll drive myself."

She chewed on the inside of her cheek. Whether it was to keep herself from crying, or to decide whether she should be worried, he didn't know. "You're sure, honey? It might be nice—"

"I think I just need a little time alone."

She gave a small nod and turned to go.

Max could smell the laundry soap in his jersey from halfway across the room. It was then that he realized how stupid he'd been. No amount of fresh laundry would ever give him a fresh start. He was stuck. This was going to be his life forever, and he might as well get used to it.

CHAPTER TWENTY-NINE

BAD MOVE

LATER THAT EVENING

Emmie and her father were sitting in the living room. Everyone she knew had gone to the hockey game. It was the last one of the regular season, and it would determine White Prairie's seed in the tournament, but Emmie couldn't bring herself to go.

The evening news was about to start when there was a knock at the back door. Tom O'Brien looked at his daughter and hesitated for a second before setting his book down in his lap. "Are you expecting someone, Emmie?"

She shook her head. Marissa would just be leaving the game, and of course Max would still be at the rink, though she doubted he'd stop by unannounced. He'd called and texted her earlier in the afternoon, and she'd since turned off her phone. He knew she didn't want to see him.

For a second, Emmie thought it might be Angie at the door, and although Emmie was eager to see her, to talk to her again and to hear what things were really like, she doubted Angie would come to the house. Frankie and Jimmy wouldn't come here either—at least while she and her father were so obviously at home. They wouldn't dare.

Her father stood up. He had a certain reserved calmness about him. Emmie wondered if that's where she got it. The more stress she was under, the quieter she became. That's why Nick trusted her. Up until that fateful getaway drive, he'd called her "unflappable." Max had noticed it too.

Emmie stayed on the couch. Her father's muffled voice floated in through the kitchen. The other voice was male but not recognizable. Mr. O'Brien returned to the living room, and Emmie looked up at him with a questioning glance.

"It's for you. It's a friend of Max's."

Emmie's eyebrows came together. So now Max was sending his friends over to try to smooth things over? Nice try. She rose from the couch and dragged herself into the kitchen with an air of impatience.

It was Chris. The nose splint was gone. His broad shoulders were slumped, and his mane of blond hair hung in his face. He shuffled his feet as he stood on the O'Briens' back step, and the light above the door cast strange shadows across his face.

"How was the game?" Emmie asked.

"We won," he said, but there was no excitement in his voice. "Barely."

"So you're first seed?" she asked, trying to puzzle out his anxious expression.

Chris gave one quick nod.

"So what's wrong?" Emmie asked as her brain did a slow shift from irritation to concern.

"We can't find Max."

"What do you mean, you can't find him?" Emmie took Chris's hand and pulled him into the kitchen and out of the cold. They didn't sit down.

"He didn't show up for the game. His parents went home right after the anthem. They called Coach after first period and said he wasn't at home. He's not answering his phone. They called the police. I would have called you, but I didn't know your number. Max pointed out your house once when we drove by. Has he called you?"

Emmie pulled her phone out of her pocket. She turned it on and groaned at the long list of messages that had piled up. "Yes. A lot. I didn't want to talk to him."

"Why the hell not?" Chris's voice was rising.

"It's complicated."

"Is this about Katie?" he asked.

"Of course it's about Katie."

Chris's hands went into his hair. "There's nothing going on between Max and Katie."

"Ha. You didn't see them together."

"Emmie, come on. We started to play pool, but then Katie walked in. She'd been crying. She said she needed to talk to Max, so Brock and I left to give her some privacy."

"That was nice of you," Emmie said. Chris ignored the sarcasm.

"She's been having a hard time since Jade…I thought Max could help her out."

"This isn't helping, Chris."

"Listen, Emmie. The way Max told me, one minute she was telling him it was a betrayal for him to be with anyone so soon after Jade died, and the next minute she had her hands all over him…So I guess she meant he shouldn't be with anyone except for her. But nothing happened."

"How do you know?"

"Because Max isn't interested in Katie. He never has been. And I've never seen him so whipped over anyone like he is about you. And that includes Jade. Katie was super-pissed when he took off after you."

Emmie didn't want to admit she'd been wrong, but everything Chris was saying sounded so sincere.

"Please call him, Emmie. Everyone's worried. He'll pick up for you. He's not picking up for anyone else, and we need to find him before he does something stupid. Tonight is the anniversary of…This is the night Jade died."

Emmie inhaled quickly, then let the breath out. She'd had no idea. Is that what he wanted to talk about this morning?

"I wish I understood why he has to make himself feel so guilty about what happened. It's terrible, but—"

"Emmie," Chris said, his eyebrows raised. "Didn't Max tell you? He was the one driving the car."

Without another word, Emmie pulled out her phone and called Max's number. He picked up before the second ring.

"Emmie," Max said on an exhale. She could hear the tears in his voice and the sound of the wind behind him.

"Where are you?"

"Franklin. By the bridge."

Emmie covered the phone and whispered the address back to Chris.

"The accident scene," Chris said, spinning around, his hands in his hair. "I've driven by there twice already."

"Max. Max, are you okay?"

"I'm okay. I don't know why though."

"Stay there. I'm coming. I'll be right there."

"Who's with you? I don't want to see anyone. Anyone else, I mean."

"Just stay there. I'll be there as fast as I can." Emmie hung up and ran into the other room. "Dad, Max needs my help."

Tom O'Brien set down his book and looked over the top of his glasses at her. "You're not going out this late alone."

"I'm not going to be alone." Emmie indicated Chris.

"I don't like this, Emmie."

"Nothing bad will happen, but Max is…Dad, I really need to do this. And then I'll be home right away."

Tom O'Brien glanced at Chris, then back at his daughter. "One hour."

"One hour. Okay." The clock on the cable box said ten fifty-five. Could she be back in only an hour?

Emmie followed Chris outside but not to his car. Instead she went to her father's Outback. Chris stopped her before she got in the driver's seat. "You're not riding with me?"

"Max wanted me to come alone."

"Emmie, you told your dad—"

"I told him I wouldn't be alone. I'm going to be with Max. I'll call you in a bit. I promise." Emmie felt a momentary pang of guilt for defying her father, but she knew he'd be okay with it after the fact. She didn't have time to convince him of that now.

It started to snow as Emmie pulled out of the neighborhood. First just a few random flakes, and then a steady fall. Big, fat, wet flakes that melted on impact with her windshield but clung to the trees and mailboxes. By the time she got to the bridge twelve minutes later, the scene looked like a picture postcard, except without any of the wish-you-were-here's.

Emmie parked her car and ran toward the bridge. Max was standing against the wrought-iron guardrail, his hands wrapped around the railing. He was leaning over, looking down onto the frozen surface of the small river. The sign just beyond him read: Scenic Overlook. It would have been a pretty scene with the snow clinging to the tree branches, but Emmie couldn't appreciate any of that now.

As she got closer, she noted a viewing bench and that falling snow had gathered on only half of the seat. There was a large melted spot on the other side where she presumed Max had been sitting for hours. She didn't want to be here, and more importantly, she didn't want Max to be here, at the place where his life had changed forever. Max picked up a chunk of ice and threw it hard against a light pole.

It was bad enough to suffer through the first anniversary of losing someone you loved, but to sit at the same spot and relive it so agonizingly...She didn't know why Max was putting himself through it again like this.

Emmie's boots made a crunching sound in the snow, and Max whirled around, his face going from terror to relief. "You came."

Emmie balled her hands into fists and shoved them under her arms, but it was fear, not the weather, that was making her cold. What had he been planning? What would have happened if no one had found him?

"The question is," she said, trying to keep her voice controlled, "why hasn't anyone else? Seems like a pretty obvious spot."

Max smiled just a little, seemingly glad that she understood where they were. "Mom and Dad and a few others drove past, but I parked my car somewhere else, and I've been sitting back there in the trees." He indicated toward the pine grove with a turn of his head.

"Why weren't you at the game?"

Max looked up, chagrinned. "Did they win?"

Emmie gave one nod, and Max let out a long exhale. "Thank God."

"So why weren't you there?" She sat down on the bench, tensing at the coldness of the metal seat.

"I didn't trust myself. I was scared of what might happen. One false move, Emmie. I make one false move on the ice, act with my heart instead of my head, and my whole future is over. Or worse, somebody else's."

"Is that what you really think?"

He shrugged as if it should be obvious.

"What happened last year?" Emmie asked.

Max diverted his eyes and clenched his teeth. The muscle in his jaw popped. There was a second when Emmie thought he wouldn't tell her, but then the words exploded out of him. "Jade and I went to a party last winter. I drove."

Emmie pinched her lips together as the cold wind snapped at her face. She understood what he was saying. "So you were drinking."

"*No!*" Max exclaimed, his eyes wide. "No! Not me."

Emmie looked at him with a mixture of surprise, relief, and... confusion.

"I would have been cut from the team if I'd been caught drinking. God, no. I've never risked it during hockey season."

"Then I don't understand."

Max raised his hands in supplication. "I was having a good time at the party. I was playing cards with Chris and some other guys. Jade didn't know many people. She thought the party was kind of lame. She wanted to leave right away, but I wouldn't go."

"If you didn't leave, then how—?" Emmie started, but Max kept on talking through her as if he had to get it out. Once and for all.

"By ten o'clock, she was really pissed at me because she'd been sitting there, bored, for like two hours by that point. I told her I just wanted to finish that one card game, and then we could go...But then I started another one.

"It didn't feel like a lot of time was going by to me, but it got late. Jade was yelling at me. I think she even hit me. By the time we left, it was eleven thirty, and she wasn't talking to me anymore. I remember being glad about that because the silent treatment was better than being yelled at.

"But as soon as we got in the car, she let me have it. It was a pretty bad fight."

Emmie reached out and touched Max's arm. He inhaled and let it out slowly. His face tensed as the story came to an end.

"A few minutes after we left the party, we got hit on the passenger side by a lady who ran a red light. *She'd* been drinking."

"Max. I don't—"

"Jade wasn't wearing her seat belt. She was thrown through the windshield. I should have told her to put it on. Maybe…" He broke off, and a sob caught in his throat. Then he uttered a sarcastic-sounding laugh. "I, unfortunately, was totally fine—just cuts and bruises. But I was trapped. The way her head was, the angle it was…There was blood coming out of her ear. "

"Max, I'm sure you did what you could to—"

"I should have left the party when she asked me to leave. If I had, we wouldn't have been fighting, and we wouldn't have been at that intersection when that lady came through. But I didn't care what Jade wanted to do. I wasn't thinking about her. I was doing what I wanted, and she's dead because of it."

Emmie tightened her fingers around his arm. "You didn't know. It's not like you could predict the future."

Max acted like he didn't hear her. "That's why I didn't trust myself on the ice tonight. I made one false move with Jade, and her future is over. I didn't want to risk that with somebody else. I couldn't."

"You didn't make a bad move. That lady did. She made the bad choice. You didn't. You have no guilt in this, Max."

He nodded, and Emmie recognized the gesture. It was the way she reacted when her dad told her not to feel guilty about testifying against Nick. Her dad would say that Nick had made his own choices. It wasn't Emmie's fault he made the wrong ones. But as much as her father said it, it never felt true.

But it was true for Max. She meant what she'd told him, and she knew that her words were true. So could that mean they were true for her too? If Angie's text was to believed, even Nick was convinced it wasn't her fault. He was owning his mistakes. He didn't put the blame on her.

Max pulled out his phone and checked the time. "This time last year, we were just leaving the party. Jade was pissy. She still had a curfew, and we were cutting it close.

"She'd been grounded two weeks earlier because I got her home late. That had sucked for both of us. I didn't like her dad thinking I was irresponsible. So I was going kind of fast, not so fast that I'd get a ticket, but sometimes I think…if I'd only driven slower, we might not have been in this intersection at the same time as that lady."

Max checked the time again. It was eleven thirty-nine.

"Jade had Beyoncé blasting on the radio so she wouldn't have to talk to me anymore. By this time we were still three blocks away…two…"

"Max," Emmie said. Why was he torturing himself like this? "Don't do this."

"One…"

A horn blasted, and their heads jerked up as a pair of headlights swerved into the intersection. Emmie's shoulders stiffened, and Max threw his body across hers, even though they weren't near the street. The lights illuminated their bodies for a second before the car fishtailed through the wet snow. Emmie sat rigidly on the bench, watching the car right itself and continue on down the road.

She knew the moment Max's mind switched from fear to despair. Like a child, he curled his head into her chest, and the arm that he'd thrust out to protect her softened and wrapped around her waist. She held him while his whole body shook, shoulders heaving with silent tears that seemed to go on forever as Max slowly, and very surely, fell to pieces.

"I'm sorry." The words broke into pieces, too, like shattered glass. The sleeve on his jacket pulled up, revealing the busted wristwatch, the hands permanently stopped at eleven forty. "I'm so sorry I hurt you. I ruined everything."

"You didn't ruin anything," Emmie said. "Chris told me what happened with Katie. You were trying to take care of her, like you're always trying to take care of everyone. I misunderstood."

Slowly, Max gathered himself. He sat up and stared straight ahead. He made a big sniff and wiped the back of his hand under his nose.

"I've tried to beat the memories into the ground," he said with a short, humorless laugh. "For the longest time, that was the only way to keep from losing my mind."

"Max—"

"You're the only thing keeping me sane, Emmie. Do you understand what I'm saying?"

The air punched out of Emmie's lungs. As much as her heart swelled at his acknowledgment of their—well, whatever this was between them—she was terrified. Max had bared his soul to her. She wasn't ready to do the same. And if she couldn't…What if she never could?

Emmie had tried to tell Marissa, but she hadn't been ready to handle it all. How would Max react? She could tell he was waiting for her to say something. Varying expressions of gratitude, hope, and curiosity played across his face. The possibilities between them flickered like a candle struggling against the wind.

"We're all dabbling in insanity," Emmie said, trying to lighten the mood. It was a self-defense mechanism of the highest order. "And trust me when I say that I'm a bigger mess than you."

Max sighed dramatically. He seemed to understand the play she was making. He'd probably mastered the game himself over the last year. So he followed suit. "I don't know about bigger, but I've always known you were messy."

Emmie rolled her eyes and started to move away. "Shut up, Shepherd."

"Make me," he said, grabbing her hand. She looked down at their fingers, woven together, then up to his mouth. There were still a few tears at the corners of his eyes. He smiled and started to say something more, but Emmie silenced him with a kiss.

CHAPTER THIRTY

HOW LONG NORMAL

MONDAY

"Good morning, Dad."

Emmie's father looked up at her from his laptop, and his eyebrows came together with a lack of recognition, as if she were some exotic animal he'd never seen before. Maybe it was the unfamiliar bounce in her step.

With the new intimacy between her and Max, Emmie felt tall for the first time in her life. Weightless. A little swimmy in the head, even. She liked it.

"Who are *yeh*, and what have you done with my daughter?"

Emmie liked it when her father joked around, but she couldn't help but notice the same nervousness at the corners of his eyes that she'd seen on Friday night. He was wearing a suit, which meant it was a court day for him, but she hadn't seen him buried in paperwork like he normally was when he was in trial. "Is everything okay?"

"Of course, love. Everything's fine." He picked up the gallon of milk from the counter and turned his back on his daughter.

"Why don't I believe you?" she asked, following behind him.

He shrugged. "Either because you're not trusting, or I haven't proven myself to be trustworthy." Her father was sometimes very literal about things.

"Or because you put the milk in the pantry," Emmie suggested, grabbing the carton off the cereal shelf. She returned it to the fridge.

"Wow," he said, slipping his hand behind his neck.

"Something's on your mind," Emmie said with confidence. She and her father had finally found their groove. They understood each other, and they had figured out how to live together too.

He gave her a weak smile. "Yes, but it's nothing you need to worry about, Ems."

Emmie narrowed her eyes. "Which makes me worry even more."

Her father worked harder, stretching his mouth into a grin. "Seriously, love. Don't you have a boy band to fawn over or something? Be a normal kid for five minutes, and leave the adult stuff to the adults."

"Now that you mention it, I was thinking about getting Harry Styles tattooed on my butt."

"Who?"

Emmie sighed and glanced out the window. Max's jeep was pulling into the driveway. "Never mind. Max is here."

"I like that kid."

"Yeah, me too," she said.

"Why don't you get *his* face tattooed on your arse?"

"*God*, Dad."

"Okay, fine, but you should invite him over for dinner sometime soon. I'd like to get to know him."

Emmie thought that sounded like torture, and she told him so.

"Torture for you?" her dad asked.

Emmie slung her backpack over her shoulder and started for the door. "For everyone involved."

"We could do fondue," he said. "It's a meal *and* an activity. Keeps everyone's hands busy so we don't have to talk as much."

Emmie wrapped her arms around her father's neck and kissed his cheek. "Love you, Dad. Thanks for everything."

"Anything for you, love. Anything."

"Have a good day in court." With those words, the tension returned to his face, but he managed a *thanks*, then she was out the door.

Emmie felt Max's eyes on her as she skipped down the back steps and walked quickly to his jeep. She hopped up into the passenger seat and knocked the snow off her shoes before closing the door. "Wow, it's cold out today."

He leaned over and kissed her, slipping one hand behind her neck. Be still my heart, Emmie thought, suddenly feeling plenty warm. When he pulled away, she glanced up toward the kitchen window to see if her father was watching. She couldn't tell. All she saw was the reflection of trees.

"My dad wants to have you over for dinner."

"Sounds good."

"It does?"

Max looked over at her as if he'd missed some critical part of the conversation. "Doesn't it?"

"I don't know," Emmie said with a shrug.

"I told my parents about you last night," Max said.

"You did?" Emmie hoped he'd found something good to tell them and that he'd been smart enough to keep the work crew details to himself. Juvenile records didn't exactly make parents all warm and fuzzy.

"They were freaking out by the time I got home. I think they thought I'd gone and offed myself."

Emmie didn't mention that the thought had crossed her and Chris's minds as well.

"I told them what happened, and how you'd found me. My mom thinks you're some kind of angel."

Emmie made a scoffing noise and turned her head to watch the little kids playing in the snow at their bus stops.

"I didn't do anything to correct her," Max said. "I think she pretty much nailed it."

* * *

That morning, and for the very first time, Max and Emmie walked into the school together. Holding hands. A few people turned to look, but mostly people seemed worried about themselves—what they had to do, and where they needed to be. It all felt so normal, and Emmie wondered how long normal would last. Could last.

Max talked in terms of needing her, but was that just to get himself through the hockey season? A part of her knew that it was unfair of her to think so poorly of him, but no matter how often Max told her that he cared about her, it wasn't like he loved her or anything. Not that she needed him to say it. In fact, the words meant nothing.

Come on, don't you love me, Pigeon? You know how much I love you.

I don't love that you call me that.

What? Pigeon? Aw, baby, it's cute. You're cute. I notice your mom's looking kinda strung out. What you planning to do about that? 'Cause I got some ideas if you want to get creative.

When Max and Emmie reached her locker, Emmie spotted Katie talking to Lauren Schafer and Elizabeth Wannamaker. Lauren touched Katie's arm and indicated with her head in Max's direction. Katie came right for them. *Oh crap. What now?*

"Can I talk to you for a second?" Katie asked Max.

"Anything you need to say to me you can say in front of Emmie."

Katie glanced at Emmie and bit her lip. "Okay, I probably should say this to both of you anyway. I'm sorry about the other night. I wasn't thinking. Clearly." She bowed her head, and color washed into her cheeks. "Anyway. I'm super-embarrassed about it, and I'm sorry if I made any trouble between you. I'm glad to see you together."

Clearly this was more bullshit. Emmie could buy Katie's apology, but the part about her being glad to see them together? Doubtful. Emmie didn't have the patience for such blatant lies. She would have respected Katie a lot more if she'd just said, "I hate that Max is into you, but whatever." Emmie glanced up at Max, ready to take his lead.

Max—whose apparent ability to forgive was what eye rolls were designed for—put his hand on Katie's shoulder and gave it a quick squeeze. Then he let go. "It was a rough weekend. You okay?"

"Yeah, I'm okay."

Katie gave Emmie another look of apology, then turned to go back to her friends.

"She's not all bad," Max said.

"I never said she was." Emmie turned and worked her locker combination. "I was pissed at you, not her."

"None of the hockey girls are that bad. They're only a little—"

"Exclusive? Territorial?"

"Yeah. That. But if you spent that much time on the ice for so many years with the same people, it kind of happens naturally. It's not a conscious choice."

Emmie shrugged. Some prejudices were harder to shake than others. She was as guilty of that as anyone else.

She squirmed all through history and chemistry without Max, though he sent her a few texts and pictures of himself in his classes: Max feigning sleep. Max with pencil-walrus fangs. A picture of a detention slip for texting in class. Emmie slapped her hand over her mouth before she laughed out loud.

As they passed each other in Mr. Beck's doorway, Max let his body brush against hers in such an intentional way that it sent shock waves through her veins and brought a rush of heat to her chest.

"You've got a problem with personal space," she said, teasing.

"Big guy," he said, "tight doorway."

At lunch, Max sat at Emmie's table, earning a smug smile from Marissa. Before they were done eating, Emmie got a text from her father: I want you to come home after school. Immediately. She showed it to Max.

"Are you in trouble?" he asked.

"Sounds like it, but I have no idea what for."

Max's forehead furrowed. "Is it about Friday night? Did you leave to find me without telling him?"

"No," Emmie said, shaking her head. She had no basis for understanding the message. "I told him I was going, and I was home when I said I'd be." She texted back a quick Why?

"I can't give you a ride," Max said. "I've got a thirty-minute detention to do for those texts I sent you during class."

"Yeah. Hey, Marissa?" Emmie asked. "Can you give me a ride home today?"

Marissa shook her head while she swallowed a mouthful of tater tot hot dish. "Can't. I got science club."

"Sorry," Sarah added. "I've got a dentist appointment after school."

"I can give you a ride," said an unexpected female voice.

Emmie looked up at Katie, who'd stopped behind Emmie's seat on her way to return her tray.

"You can?" Emmie asked.

Katie gave a little one-shouldered shrug. "Sure. Why not?"

Emmie glanced at Max, then back up at Katie, whose eyes were trained on Max. "Okay, sure. I'll meet you by the front doors."

"'Kay," Katie said without any more fanfare, and then she walked away.

"Weird," Marissa said.

"Totally," Emmie said with a groan. "This is going to be all kinds of awkward. Why didn't I say 'no thank you'?"

Max stabbed a tot with his fork and made a swirling gesture at Emmie with it. "Have you ever wondered if you're just an extremely bad judge of character?"

"Are you serious?" Had he completely forgotten about Elizabeth's party?

"Yeah, I'm serious. Katie might be…"

"Delusional?" Sarah offered.

"Pushy?" Olivia added.

"Man stealing?" Marissa suggested.

Max shook his head and fought back a grin. "Yeah. All that. But she's not the Antichrist. At first, you thought hockey guys were total douche canoes, and now look at me."

"You *can* be a total douche canoe," Emmie said. He really did have short-term memory loss. Maybe he'd been slammed up against the boards one too many times.

"I'm just saying, it was nice of her to offer you a ride. It's her way of following through on her apology. Give her a chance."

Marissa raised her eyebrows in a way that said, *We'll see about that.* They were probably both right.

As it turned out, Katie was a no-show after school. Emmie didn't take time to find out whether it was intentional or if Katie had innocently forgotten. Instead, she ended up bumming a ride from Jerry Moffet, whom she'd probably said fewer than ten words to in the past, but he lived on her street. When she got home, her father was in the driveway waiting for her.

"Who was that?" he asked as if she'd just gotten out of Charles Manson's car.

"Jerry. He lives down the street."

"What happened to Max?" Her father pulled her inside the house and closed the door, locking it. The kitchen smelled like butter and onions. "I thought he was giving you a ride home."

"He stayed after school to do some...extra credit," Emmie said, thinking that a little white lie never killed anyone. She kicked off her boots, and the snow immediately started to melt on the kitchen floor.

"Well, next time, call me. I don't want you getting rides home from strangers."

"*Dad.* Jerry's not exactly a stranger, but what's with all the high alert?"

"Nothing. I rented a movie for us tonight." He walked to the stove and gave whatever concoction was on the stove a couple brisk stirs. "You like John Hughes movies, right?"

"But I was going to do homework with Marissa."

"We're staying in tonight."

"But—"

Her father looked up from the soup pot to his daughter. For a second, she thought he was going to give in, but then he said, "That's the end of this conversation."

"Because I got a ride with Jerry Moffet?" Emmie hated how whiny she sounded, but come on. Really?

"No," her father said with a sad smile. "Not because of Jerry. Because I love you."

It didn't make any sense, but Emmie couldn't argue when he put it like that.

"So I'm not grounded?"

"Should you be?"

"No."

"Can I still go out with Max tomorrow night? We were going to hang out after school, then go out to dinner. It's kind of our first official date."

"You went to the dance with him."

"I went to the dance with Marissa. I just met him there. Tomorrow was going to be kind of special."

Emmie's father considered her for a second. "You'll be with Max?"

"Yeah."

"All the time?"

"Of course. That's okay, right?"

Emmie's father nodded, but only reluctantly. He leaned against the counter and picked an apple out of the bowl.

"Nothing bad is going to happen, Dad." She thought for a second she'd tell him about Angie's text and how Nick had forgiven her, and how everything was going to be okay. But thankfully, she caught her tongue before she had to explain how she knew.

"I know. I'm a dad. I like to worry." Then, after a second, he added, "So, does this mean you're dating Max? You feel...close"—he adjusted his collar—"to him?"

Emmie looked down and slowly nodded. She did feel close to Max. She didn't like being separated from him.

Her father twisted the apple's stem until it broke off, but he didn't take a bite. "You're still raw from all that happened last year."

Emmie's head popped up, and he put his hand out to stop her protest before she got started. "Don't be upset. Everyone has their own raw spot, love. Somewhere deep inside us that hurts to touch. If you're going to let someone get close to yours, you have to know that you can trust them with it."

Emmie swallowed hard. She had a raw spot. Could she trust Max?

"I think you can trust that boy, and it's good that you two have each other. That's why I'm letting you go out tomorrow. And because I trust you too."

Emmie smiled and closed the gap between her and her father. She wrapped her arms around him, pressing the words *thanks* and then *I love you* into the fabric of his shirt.

CHAPTER THIRTY-ONE

DINNER DATES

Max glanced over at Emmie in the passenger seat of his jeep. She was riding along with him to his anger management class with Cardigan John because Max thought it was about time they have a real date, and there was a Thai restaurant right around the corner from John's office that he wanted to try. He'd never had Thai food before, but he liked how it made him sound when he suggested it to Emmie. Like he was worldly and sophisticated about food he couldn't pronounce.

Maybe it would suck, but as long as he was with Emmie, it would be the best dinner ever. Max rolled his eyes at how cheesy his thoughts had become. Lately, he barely recognized himself.

After a few moments, Max looked over at Emmie again. She was worrying her lip between her teeth, and it looked like she was going to mangle the paperback book she'd brought to read while he was in class.

"You're quiet," he said.

"Am I?"

"Are you trying to come up with something interesting to say? If you are, you don't have to work so hard. I don't mind the quiet." Max put on his signal and changed lanes.

"It's not that. Just thinking about something my dad said."

Emmie didn't say anything more, so after a while, Max started to worry too. Had she changed her mind about him? *Again.* Had he said something to piss her off? It would be just like him, but that couldn't be it. He'd barely said two words to her since they got in the jeep, and she'd seemed all right when they left school.

It wasn't him then. It was something with her. Something was wrong. Had there been another visit from one of her old…He didn't even know what to call them. *Friends* just didn't seem right.

"I have to tell you some things," Emmie said. Max exhaled. She was talking. This was good.

"You do," he said, reaching over and tweaking her nose with the side of his finger. He was trying to keep things light, but it felt forced. He wondered if she could tell.

"That's your response?" she asked.

Max looked over at her, then quickly back at the highway. "What more do you want me to say to you? That you're cute? That you're amazing? That sometimes you scare the shit out of me? That I've been waiting for you to trust me for a long time now?"

"I'm not opposed to any of those things." Emmie burrowed her chin into her chunky knit scarf, but even though Max waited patiently, she didn't say anything more. It had been a dramatic introduction to a whole lot of nothing.

Max exited the highway and a minute later pulled into the parking lot behind Cardigan John's building. He unbuckled and turned his body toward Emmie. "What do you want to tell me?"

"Everything." Then she added, "I think."

Max slid across the bench seat toward her. "Then tell me. You won't enjoy dinner if you're worrying about something all night."

The corners of Emmie's mouth turned up slightly.

"And talk slowly," Max said, trying once more to add a little levity to the tension that was now palpable between them. "I'm just a douchebag Neanderthal, remember?"

Emmie wrinkled her nose at him. "That's true."

"A douchebag Neanderthal who wants to be with you."

Emmie rolled her eyes, then looked out the side window. "You may change your mind about that."

Max shook his head in exasperation. Did she really give him so little credit? Apparently yes, because a few more seconds dragged on in silence. Eventually, Max gave Emmie a nudge, and she nodded with resignation.

"My mom is an addict." She turned and looked up into Max's eyes, but he didn't flinch.

Was that it? Max felt terrible for Emmie if that was true, but it was hardly reason for her to think he'd cut and run.

"I didn't know about it when I was begging my dad to let me go live with her. But when I realized how bad off she was, I couldn't leave. She needed someone to make sure she was eating, and someone to give her a ride home when she couldn't make it herself."

"Why didn't you just tell your dad?"

"Because I really, *really* didn't want him to know I'd made a mistake about going to live with her. I thought I could take care of things. I *did* take care of things. We did okay, I guess."

"Emmie…" How could she feel bad about taking care of her mom? Why would this be difficult to tell him? If anything, it only made him love her more.

The word stuttered across Max's mind. *Love?* He wasn't in love with her, was he? But when she pulled in close and laid her hand against his chest, it didn't take more than a breath for the answer to come roaring back at him. *Christ. I'm in love with her.*

"It's okay," Emmie said quickly, as if his expression had scared her. "She's in rehab now."

"That's it?" Max asked. "That's what you've been struggling to tell me?"

Emmie shook her head. "Not exactly. Last year, Mom and I got kicked out of our apartment, and my mom owed her dealer a lot of money..."

And that's when the pieces started to move into place. Max could see where the tension in Emmie's face was coming from, and he wanted to find the guy and kick the ever-living shit out of him. "Nick," he said.

Emmie nodded. "My mom said that if he gave us a place to stay and set her up when she needed it, I'd work for him for free. He agreed, so after that I was his carrier. Nick called me 'Pigeon.' You know...like a carrier pigeon? Because I always came back. He could depend on me."

Emmie swallowed hard, and Max held her hand between their chests. He could feel the pulse in her thumb, and it was racing.

"Later...later I was more to him than just a pigeon. I was like...*his*." She hazarded another look at Max's face. "If you know what I mean."

Max felt his expression darken, and it made him feel like crap when he saw the flicker of pain in Emmie's eyes before she looked away. His hands trembled as they always did before he lost control, but this time he had the tools to fight it back. He was going to have to thank Cardigan John for that later.

"I mean..." Emmie still wouldn't look at him. "It was kind of a good thing because no one else messed with me since they knew I was Nick's, and he would kill them if they tried anything, but it was bad too because...well...just because."

Max nearly growled. "That bastard hurt you."

Emmie bowed her head, but Max put his fingers under her chin and turned her face toward his.

"I never got involved in the drugs though," she said a little too brightly, "Nick wouldn't let me, so I guess I can thank him for that."

"But you ended up in court," Max said softly, redirecting the conversation to where he wanted it to go. He'd been curious for too long. What had she done?

"It wasn't because of the drugs, actually."

"Then what?"

"One night, Nick got this wild hair about robbing the Taco Bell. He told me to drive for him, and the whole thing went so well that we hit a couple more places the next night.

"Later, he planned to rob the SuperAmerica on Hiawatha Avenue, near where he lived. He picked it because he knew the overnight cashier. His friend was supposed to be in on it. I guess you'd call it an inside job, except that the guy panicked. He called in sick to work that night and didn't tell us, so there was some other guy working when we got there.

"Nick got the money in the register, but the cashier pulled the alarm before Nick knocked him seven ways from Sunday with a bat. The police caught up to us before I'd driven even five miles away. So I guess I should have driven faster…"

"Shit," Max said softly under his breath. He drew an arcing curve with his finger over Emmie's hand, like a pendulum swinging. "What happened to the cashier?'

"Bad. *Really* bad," she said, her voice dropping to a nearly inaudible tone. "Afterward, Nick and I were both charged. I went to live with my aunt Bridget, and my dad got his friend to represent me. She worked out a plea bargain with the prosecutor, who agreed to drop the felony charges against me if I pleaded to aiding and abetting assault as a juvenile. And if I testified against Nick. That included testifying about criminal sexual conduct on account of I was only sixteen and he was twenty-six."

The icy fury was still building in Max at the thought of that monster getting anywhere near her, touching her soft skin, poisoning her lips, but he didn't want to scare Emmie with how he was feeling. He didn't want her to be scared ever again. He kept his voice flat. "He's why you don't like people to touch you."

Emmie wove her fingers through Max's. "I'm starting to get used to it again."

Max fell silent as he processed all that she had told him. She must have been so scared. How bad had it been for her mom that Emmie would sacrifice herself like that? And why—*goddammit*—why hadn't she asked her dad for help? Max had never met Nick, never even seen him, and yet the image of him was very clear in his mind. The idea of him touching Emmie... And what about her mom? What kind of woman set up her own kid like that?

"What are you thinking, Max?"

"That I probably shouldn't meet your mom until I graduate from my anger management classes. Right now, after I finish that asshole, I'd like to have a few words with her about what she did to you."

"*Mom*...? She didn't do anything to me. I made my own choices."

"That's bullshit, Emmie. A mother doesn't sit by and watch her kid basically serve herself up on a silver platter just so she can get high for free."

"Max, she's—"

Max pulled his hand from hers and took the keys from the ignition, shoving them in the pocket of his letter jacket. "Sick. Yeah. I know. Whatever. But you can't expect me to like anyone who'd ever want to hurt you."

Emmie didn't like to think of it like that. Her mom hadn't served her up. Emmie had been a willing participant. At least at the beginning. It wasn't like she told her mom about everything that was going on with Nick, and her mom wasn't exactly the rock-the-boat type. A part of Emmie worried that her father had been right about her mom telling Jimmy and Frankie how to find her. They were another boat that didn't like rocking.

Max and Emmie climbed out of the jeep. Max grabbed her hand and held it tightly in his own. His expression was serious, but it wasn't judgmental. At least not of Emmie, and she was grateful for that. They'd work through the rest of her shit later.

They entered the office building together, right behind a short kid in an American Eagle jersey. "Is this your *girllll*friend?" the kid asked Max in a suggestive, singsong way.

"Shut it, Jesse. And quit acting like you're in junior high," Max said.

"I *am* in junior high," Jesse said. "So is she your girlfriend?"

"Yes," Emmie said, shifting her book from her right hand to her left. "I am."

Emmie's answer made Max's heart do that little flip-flop trick it had done when she'd asked him to go skating, and several more times since then.

"Lucky dude," Jesse said, letting his eyes glance all over her.

"Damn straight," Max said, insinuating his body between Jesse's and Emmie's. "And that's just about enough of that."

"I'll just read out here until you're done," Emmie said, indicating the lobby.

Max glanced over his shoulder at her as she gestured toward the chair by the window. Then he planted a kiss on top of her head, which elicited some catcalls from Jesse. But Max didn't mind at all. He couldn't blame anyone for taking notice of Emmie. As little as she was, she commanded attention. And she had all of his. For always.

The lobby of the little office building where Max took his classes wasn't much of a lobby. It was one hard-cushioned chair with a ficus plant. Emmie thought it would need back issues of *People* magazine to rightfully be called a lobby. But it *did* have a big front window with lots of light, and even though it was freezing outside, the sun coming through the window made Emmie believe that spring was right around the corner.

Which was true. They really only had to get through February, and then it would be spring. Emmie didn't care that March was Minnesota's snowiest month. To her, it still counted as spring. March, April, May. That was spring regardless of the hanger-on blizzards. And it really was right around the corner. The light at the end of the proverbial winter tunnel.

She collapsed into the chair with a hard bounce and tried to get comfortable. She was on page two hundred of her book. The main character had finally infiltrated the government's central command, and she'd found her hot guy unconscious on the floor.

Emmie was turning the pages quickly. She was starting to lose track of time, so she checked her phone. Four twenty-five.

Only another half hour or so, and Max would be coming back down the hallway, his hair tousled, his hoodie bunched under his letter jacket, his jeans riding low. She imagined his face, the grin that she knew would be spreading across his face like the Cheshire cat's. Their first real date, not counting the dance. It still seemed so unreal.

The sun went behind a cloud, casting a shadow across her page. It took her eyes a second to adjust. The shadow shifted, and she realized the cloud was head-shaped. With shoulders. The shadow moved, and the door to the office building opened.

"Hello, Pigeon."

Emmie jumped to her feet, and her book slid to the floor. "Nick? How? What are you doing here?"

"Didn't Daddy tell you?" he asked. "There's been a change of plans."

Emmie's heart turned stony because she saw her error in Nick's narrowed eyes. Nick didn't forgive her for testifying. She'd been completely wrong about Angie's text, about Nick. About everything. But she wasn't the only one who was wrong. If Nick thought she was leaving with him, he was sadly mistaken.

But then Jimmy and Frankie entered behind him, and Emmie knew she was in trouble. For a second, she thought about running down the hall toward Max's classroom, but Nick saw the thought in her eyes and blocked her path. From behind her, Frankie and Jimmy laughed.

"Touch me, Nick, and I swear to you I will scream so—"

A hand slapped over her mouth, a meaty thumb aligned with her nose. The skin smelled like hamburger grease and gasoline. Frankie wrapped his other arm around Emmie, pinning her arms. She thrashed and kicked, but it was without effect. Frankie was a junkie, but he was still strong, strong enough to lift her off her feet. Her legs circled, as if she were riding a bike, trying to strike out at anything whether it was in front of her or behind.

They spun, and Emmie made contact.

"Ow!" Jimmy cried. Emmie struggled to breathe. Her chest burned. Nick got in her face and whispered. She didn't know why, but whispers were always more frightening to her than shouts.

"Listen, sweetness." His gaze glanced over her face and down her neck, resting on her chest. "I don't want to make a scene. We're going to walk out of here calmly. Like old friends."

Emmie bit down on Frankie's pale fingers, hard. He let go, and she screamed.

Nick slapped her across the face, and she shut up. White light flashed in her eyes. Emmie tried to focus on regaining her vision. That was something she could do, and right now she needed to know that there *was* something she could do. Something she could control. If she couldn't, she would panic, and if she panicked, she was as good as done.

"Let's go, Ems." Nick opened his coat and flashed a steely blade. "Nice and easy. C'mon."

Emmie tried to bust past them, but Frankie and Jimmy flanked her, their hands wrapped around her coat sleeves, leading her out of the building and onto the sidewalk. Nick was behind her. So close Emmie could feel him against her back.

She would find a way out of this.

They took her across the street and down an alley where she could see Angie's car parked behind a dumpster. Nick opened the front passenger door and pushed Emmie down and inside. Frankie and Jimmy got in the back seat, next to someone who'd been left waiting in the car.

"Dan?" Emmie asked, trying to make sense of why her probation officer should be sitting in Angie's car. "Wh...what are you doing here?"

Dan McDonald looked up at her, and his expression was pained. He glanced quickly out the window, apparently unable to look Emmie in the eye. "Sorry," he said.

Emmie didn't curse, but she could feel the word, round and salty, in her mouth. It wasn't her mom who'd told them where to find her, how to get in touch. It had been Dan all along.

"Why?" she asked, but Dan refused to look at her. A line of muscle tensed in his jaw. She turned toward Frankie. "Was Angie's text a lie too?"

"Some girls are good little girls and do what they're told," Frankie said.

Nick got behind the wheel and started the engine. "Time to go home, Pigeon."

CHAPTER THIRTY-TWO

UNEXPECTED

"Great work today, guys. Great work. But it's time to wrap up," Cardigan John said, while shuffling his stack of papers into a neat, trim pile.

"Why so early?" Jesse asked.

"I've got a meeting today at five. Didn't I mention this last week?" John glanced around the room. Max tended to space out from time to time when John was talking. Maybe he'd told them, and he'd missed it. But by the looks on everyone else's faces, this was coming as news to everyone.

"Sorry," John said. "I meant to tell you. If you're getting picked up by a parent, call them now."

John walked to his desk and grabbed his sweater off the back of his chair. The guys started pulling phones out of their back pockets. "So we're good?" Max asked. "I can go?"

"Yeah, you can go. See you next week, Max."

And Max was out the door. It was like getting an unexpected gift, and it wasn't even his birthday! He couldn't wait to see the look on

Emmie's face when he came out twenty minutes early. The hallway was long, but it was a straight shot. He expected to see her in the chair at the end of it, but she wasn't there.

Max walked briskly toward the door. Maybe she'd stepped into the bathroom. Her book was on the floor by the chair, lying in a way that bent several of the pages back. It gave him an unsettled feeling in his stomach. He looked up and through the big picture window just as a car pulled out of the alleyway across the street. Max didn't notice who was driving, but he noticed the junker car. Mainly because it was loud. The muffler was broken. But also because he recognized it from before. The last time he'd seen it was at the ice rink. That Angie girl had driven it away after he'd practically attacked her.

Max checked his phone, but there was no text from Emmie, and he had barely any battery life left. A prickly feeling ran the length of Max's neck, leaving a cold little shiver in his arms. He fought back his instincts and ignored the tremble in his little finger. John had taught him a few things, and Max did not find it difficult to piece together a plausible reason why Emmie would have left.

Maybe Angie had called Emmie. Maybe she'd wanted to talk. Emmie would have been obliging, as always. She knew he wouldn't be out of class for another half hour. They'd gone to talk privately in the girl's car, then Emmie would be back. But why would they need to drive away, and why didn't she let him know she was leaving? Maybe they were going to get a Coke at the Burger King down the street. She'd be right back. That was it. That was all.

Max's fingers twitched, and every instinct in him coiled into a tight spiral, ready to spring. But he was getting better at loosening the tension, recognizing the trigger and calming himself. John, it turned out, knew his stuff. The classes were actually making a difference. Max took two deep cleansing breaths and settled into the chair to wait. He smoothed out the pages in Emmie's book and checked out what she was reading.

He was a little shocked by how steamy it was. Is this what girls read?

The other guys started to file out of John's office and come down the hall. A few of them already had rides waiting, and they left. A few of them hung out in the lobby, watching through the window for their rides to show up.

"What are you still doing here?" Jesse asked.

"Waiting for my girlfriend to get back so we can go out to dinner."

Jesse glanced behind him at the bathroom, then back at Max. "Has she been in there a long time? Maybe she snuck out the window. If I had to go out with you, that's what I'd do."

"You're hilarious."

"I know. Hey, there's my ride. Smell you later, man."

"Uh-huh." Max opened the book again and tried to concentrate on the words on the page, but his gut was turning. He tried Emmie's number, but her phone was turned off. Yeah, that made sense. She'd give Angie her full attention, then she'd be back.

But when five o'clock hit, then five-o-five...Max was losing confidence in his hypothesis.

His phone buzzed in his pocket, and he gave a sigh of relief. But when he pulled it out, it wasn't a number he recognized. "Hello?"

"Max?" It was a man's voice and only vaguely familiar.

"Yeah?" Max's phone beeped. He had less than five percent battery left.

"Max, it's Mr. O'Brien. Emmie's dad."

"Is she okay?" Max asked.

There was a pause on the other end. Then. "Isn't she with you?"

"No. I mean, yeah. But she took off with a girlfriend while I was in...class. I thought she'd be back by now because we have dinner reservations."

The silence on the other end made Max's stomach turn.

"I'd hoped she was with you," Mr. O'Brien said. "It took a while for Marissa to track down your number for me. Emmie's not picking up, and I need you to bring her home. Right away."

"What's wrong?"

There was silence on the line, and Max had to repeat his question, this time more insistently. Mr. O'Brien answered with "What do you know about Nick Peters?"

Max felt his heart stutter. "Enough."

"His attorney brought a motion for a new trial Monday morning. The judge granted it today. Nick's been released on bail, which someone has posted."

"What? Why?" Max's head began to whirl. He knew that girl's car had something to do with what Mr. O'Brien was telling him, but he couldn't get the pieces to fit together quickly enough.

"Emmie's mother...at least I think...I don't have time to get into it right now," Mr. O'Brien said. "I need to find my daughter."

"She's with another girl who used to hang out with Nick."

"Angie?"

Max spun around, one hand in his hair. "Yeah. Yeah. She's driving an old junker. Black, I think. Or dark blue? Rusty. No muffler. They went west on Lake Street about"—Max checked the time on his phone—"a half hour ago. I had no idea. Where do you think she is?"

Max punished himself mentally. He should have trusted his instincts. He'd wasted thirty minutes. What kind of trouble was Emmie in?

"I'll alert the police. You go home. Let me know if she calls you." Mr. O'Brien hung up abruptly without saying anything more.

Max glanced down at his screen. It had gone black, and his phone was powering down, the battery dead. Emmie wouldn't be calling him. But there was no way he was going home. He'd had the chance to fix things, and he'd let it drive away. Max slipped his phone into his pocket and ran for his jeep. He'd made a lot of mistakes in his life, but one thing was for sure: Max Shepherd never made the same one twice.

CHAPTER THIRTY-THREE

OLD BUSINESS

Nick zigzagged through town, taking lefts, then rights down one-way streets. Emmie didn't have to ask where they were going. Nick's apartment over the Gold Pedal Bike Shop wasn't that far from the office building where Max still sat, probably watching the clock, waiting to take her to dinner.

Emmie wrapped her fingers around the door latch and jerked. *Locked.* She glanced at Nick, and the corners of his mouth twitched. She couldn't understand what he meant by taking her like this, but she was having a harder time thinking about why Dan was here. What did Nick have on him? Did Dan owe him money? It wasn't like she could turn around and ask him. But if Dan had been the one to give her up, that meant her mom hadn't. It was enough to keep Emmie's mind steady as she watched Nick and tried to figure out what to do.

He looked the same as she remembered. Tall, tightly muscled. He'd aged, seeming older now than his twenty-seven years. She tried to read his mood. She tried to judge how afraid she should be. Did he only mean to scare her? Or was it something worse? His face gave nothing away, and Emmie wondered how she was going to get herself back to Max. She was struck by the sudden, irrational fear that she was never going to get the chance to try Thai food.

Once again, Emmie tested the door latch. She had no qualms about throwing herself out of a moving car. Still locked.

After a few minutes, they passed the site where the TV repair shop burned down the year before. It was under construction now with several shovels leaning up against a chain-link fence. Emmie braced herself against the dash as she prepared for Nick to make a quick right-hand turn. She caught sight of the familiar Gold Pedal logo in the storefront as he pulled into the driveway between it and the Somali grocery store next door. Its blue awning snapped in the wind, distorting its advertisements for phone cards, ATM, fresh meats.

Frankie and Jimmy got out while Nick dug in his pocket for something. The sunlight hit Frankie's closely shorn blond hair, making him look practically bald. Jimmy's dark eyebrows lowered under the flat bill of his cap as he glanced warily up and down the sidewalk.

Emmie stayed in her seat. She couldn't make a run for it. They'd catch her. Nothing good was going to come from getting out of this car. She looked behind her toward Dan. Neither of them spoke, her plea for help in her eyes, and his apology in his.

Nick tossed a plastic bag filled with crystal meth onto the back seat and exited the car.

Dan looked at it lying there on the seat beside him, his lip curled in disgust. For a second, Emmie thought he meant to refuse it, but then he shoved it into his coat pocket, flung open the car door, and made a hasty retreat across the street.

"Judas!" she yelled after him. "You bastard!"

Frankie wrenched open Emmie's car door, and she felt Nick's hand on her shoulder. She turned to face them and braced one foot on either side of the doorframe, refusing to be moved. It didn't matter in the end. She was no physical match for Nick.

"Nick. Look at me," she said. "It's me. *Emmie.* You *know* me."

Nick grabbed Emmie around the waist and slung her over his shoulder, carrying her up the metal fire escape that was mounted to the outside of the building. He acted as if she was nothing more than this week's groceries. She screamed and beat on his back, but she didn't really expect anyone to come to her rescue. Not in this neighborhood.

The metal stairs pulled and strained against the bolts that held them to the brick wall, and the world seemed to wobble as Emmie stared down at the ground that was pulling farther and farther away from her.

When they got to the top, Nick opened the door, and the familiar odor of stale beer, cigarette smoke, and burned chemicals assaulted her senses. Nick set Emmie on her feet and shoved her inside the apartment she used to call home. She staggered backward with the momentum and threw her hands out in front of her as if that would provide her some defense. "Nick. Just listen."

Nick smiled and locked the door after Jimmy and Frankie came in behind him.

"What's going on?" Angie asked as she walked into the living room from the adjacent bedroom. Her hair fell across her face. Her army jacket hung limply off her shoulders, almost as if she didn't have any shoulders at all.

When she and Emmie looked at each other, their faces mirrored the same terror. Angie's face was already swollen, and there was a cut at the corner of her mouth, slightly scabbed over.

"Emmie?" she said. "What happened?" Then to Nick, "Why is she here?"

"Don't be such an idiot," Frankie said, walking farther into the room, toward the kitchen at the back.

Nick stepped between Emmie and Angie, interfering with their eye contact. He faced Emmie but spoke to Angie. "Pigeon's here because she's a narc."

His hand pulled back, then released, slapping Emmie across the cheek and eye. Emmie winced as her head spun sideways. She felt as though her eye was going to explode. Why did he always have to hit her like that?

"You were *my* girl," Nick said. Did Emmie detect a hint of sadness in his voice?

"I was. I *am*," she said.

Nick shoved her, and Emmie's heel caught on the steamer-trunk coffee table. She nearly toppled over, but Nick caught her by the coat sleeve and kept her on her feet.

"You know what happens when someone turns on me?" Nick landed another slap across Emmie's face. The stinging burn sent shock waves through her body, and she dropped to her hands and knees. Blindly, she started crawling for the door. She had to get out. She had to get away from here.

Emmie didn't cry, but Angie did. "What are you going to do to her? Let her go!" Angie demanded, but both girls knew they were useless words. "Please!"

Nick grabbed Emmie by her hair and pulled her to standing. She felt her hair rip from the roots, but she bit down on her tongue. She wouldn't beg, and he wouldn't have the satisfaction of knowing how much he hurt her.

"I'm sitting in prison, and you're running around high school like some brainless cheerleader. Going to parties, hanging out with a bunch of hockey assholes. That's not you, Pigeon." His voice was calm. Almost bored.

Emmie forgot her resolution to stay quiet. "How...?" Then she remembered Dan. He'd told Nick about Max. Would they go after Max now too? Was Dan so far gone that he'd put his job at risk?

Nick yanked Emmie's coat off her shoulders, and his gaze descended again. "You've grown up some since the last time I saw you." He palmed her breast. Frankie and Jimmy laughed. Bile crawled up Emmie's throat, and she swallowed it back down.

"How can you tell under that sweater?" Jimmy asked. Emmie bit her tongue to keep from screaming. More laughter, this time from Frankie, who raked his dirty fingernails over his stubbly head.

"Stop it!" Angie yelled. "Just stop!"

She started toward Emmie, but Frankie grabbed Angie and threw her up against the wall. "Mind your own business, Ang."

Emmie turned her head as Nick came in closer, stroking the side of her neck with the backs of his fingers, his mouth hovering near the corner of hers. Emmie could see Angie, still pressed against the wall, Frankie's hands around her throat.

Angie twisted, trying to break free, but Frankie grabbed her by the hair. "Emmie!" she cried out.

"Keep your bitch in line," Nick said quietly. Then he grabbed Emmie by the shoulders and walked her backward across the living room. He was moving her so fast that she struggled to keep her feet under her. Then Nick gave her a quick shove, and she was airborne. *No. No. Not again.*

A second later, Emmie landed on her back on the dingy blue mattress in the corner of the room. She crawled backward until she was pressed into the corner like a trapped animal. Her arms splayed wide, palms pressed back against the walls. Beyond Nick, Frankie was dragging Angie into another room. Emmie's skin crawled with the sound of Angie's screams.

"Nick," Emmie said. She kept her voice calm and low. "Nick, you don't want to do this." She didn't want him to touch her. She didn't want Jimmy watching as Nick touched her.

When Nick crawled over the top of Emmie, she remembered how deceptively heavy he was. He was crushing her, and his breath was hot on the side of her face. If he'd been drunk, maybe she could get away, but he wasn't. He was very much in control of his body, and she felt every inch of it along her comparatively tiny frame.

She put her hands on his shoulders and tried to push him off, but it was no use. He was kissing her neck now, and she thought she was going to throw up. Maybe he'd get off if she vomited on him.

Nick shifted his weight, unpinning one of Emmie's legs. And that was when the switch flipped. *Never again.* She didn't care whatever else he did to her; she was not going to let this bastard use her body again. Not while there was an ounce of fight left in her. She took her opportunity, jerking her knee up and making contact with exactly the right spot. Nick bent at the waist and rolled off her.

Emmie threw one leg over the edge of the mattress and tried to get off completely, but Jimmy was there in a second, pinning Emmie's arms to her sides. Emmie thrashed and bit his shoulder.

"She's stronger than she looks," Jimmy said with a laugh. "I like a girl with fight."

Nick had gathered himself by then. "You like to fight?" he asked her.

"Nick," Emmie said. There were tears in her eyes, and her heart was pounding in her chest, but her voice was firm. "We're not doing this. It's not going to make anything better. I don't know why you're out, but this isn't going to help your situation. Whatever it is, we can work something out."

Nick stood up. Emmie was now sandwiched between Jimmy and Nick. Her clothes absorbed the sweat from their bodies.

"You're not testifying against me again, Ems." Nick signaled to

Jimmy with a nod of his chin. Jimmy suddenly released her and went into the kitchen.

Even though no one was touching her now, Emmie felt just as bound, just as trapped. "I won't. I won't. I'll say that I don't remember anything." She'd promise him anything right now. She would survive.

Nick smiled knowingly, then smashed his lips against hers. He pushed his tongue into her mouth. He tasted like onions and cigarettes. When he pulled back, Emmie wiped her mouth with the back of her hand.

"That's right," he said. "You won't remember anything."

There was a loud thud from the other bedroom, and Angie screamed. Emmie turned her head toward the sound, but Nick took her by the chin and yanked her face back toward his.

Jimmy came back from the kitchen with a metal spoon that he held level to the floor. He walked gingerly as he carried it to the small table beside the blue mattress. Then he pulled out a syringe from the drawer and sucked up the clear liquid, drawing it slowly into the needle through a small ball of cotton he had dropped in the bowl of the spoon. He then laid it on the table.

Emmie had seen people slam meth on a pretty regular basis. Her mom could shoot a half ounce over the course of a week when she was binging hard. But since they always mixed the meth with water, and because everyone did it differently, Emmie had no way of knowing exactly what Nick had put in the rig. Whatever it was, the barrel was full, and the look in Nick's eyes said he wasn't merely interested in getting her high.

"Maybe you should step out for a while," Nick said. He didn't look at Jimmy while he spoke. "Go get Frankie a pizza. He's going to be hungry."

"Sounds good," Jimmy said, as if he was happy not to be implicated in whatever was going down next. He picked up his jacket off the floor and headed toward the door.

Behind her, Emmie heard the sound of Jimmy turning the lock, then opening the door and closing it behind him. Angie yelled out again from the back bedroom. But after the sound faded, the apartment felt eerily quiet.

Nick pushed up Emmie's sleeve. "I think we've kept our little girl clean long enough, don't you?"

"Nick. No." Emmie twisted away, but Nick held her arm like a vise. "Think, Nick. Think about what you're doing. Why mess this up for yourself? You're out. You don't want to go back in."

"I won't be," Nick said. "No one's going to talk about what went down here, sweetheart. Least of all you. I'm going to make sure of that this time."

"Nick. Remember that time? That time we went to the State Fair? And when the Ferris wheel stopped, we were at the very top. Do you remember that? We could see for miles, and everything was so pretty. Do you remember what you said? You said—"

"I said I'd never felt that free, and I wished I could feel like that forever." Nick's voice sounded sad and very far away. For a second there was a flicker of recognition in his eyes, as if he was seeing her for the first time. Seeing *her*. But then his face hardened again. "And that's exactly how I'm going to be."

Emmie's temperature dropped as terror ran through her veins. She didn't have a lot of time left. Nick pushed Emmie backward, down onto the mattress. She scrambled into the corner.

He stood beside the bed, syringe in hand, and faced her. He didn't look handsome. He didn't look the same as she remembered at all. There was a darkness in his eyes that was foreign and strange. God. How had she ever felt guilty about testifying against him? What a waste of energy. He was nothing more than a thug.

"Our perfect little princess," Nick said with a sneer. "Takes care of her mommy. Daddy's little angel. Thought she could take care of everything. Guess you were wrong about that."

Emmie didn't reply. All she could focus on was one thought: Get out, get out, get out.

She sensed Nick start to move, and she dove for the foot of the bed. Nick caught her by the ankle, and Emmie heard the lightweight *theh-wep* of the syringe dropping onto the linoleum. Nick yanked her ankle, but she kicked free and found herself standing on the floor. She threw her arms out in front of her again.

When Nick took the two quick steps around the foot of the bed, Emmie found her center of gravity. She dropped her shoulder and plowed into Nick with her hip and shoulder.

The move caught him by surprise, but not nearly enough. He spun Emmie around and wrapped his arms around her shoulders, clasping his hands to his wrists to hold her tight.

One second, Emmie's feet were firmly on the ground. The next, they were circling in the air. *Plan B*, she heard Max say in her head. *Play dirty.*

Emmie tucked her chin and bit down hard on Nick's forearm. When he yelled, Emmie latched down harder. Harder. He let go of her, and she turned quickly. She struck the side of his knee with the sole of her boot. Nick folded, just like Max said he would.

What she hadn't counted on was Nick's head hitting the corner of the table. He crumpled to the floor, and he didn't move.

Emmie gasped, her hand at her mouth. Nick was down, but that was all the thought she gave it. A half second later, she was sprinting for the door, leaving her coat behind.

CHAPTER THIRTY-FOUR

PENDULUM

Max didn't know any gym, bar, restaurant, or anything called the Gold Medal, but there was no way he was going home. He would drive every street and alleyway, if that was what it took to find her. He wished himself luck without any real sense of hope. Everything he'd worked so hard to suppress was rushing back toward the surface.

Why was he still so surprised that he could not control life? The world was going to do what the world was going to do, and there was nothing he could do to stop bad things from happening to the people he loved. It all felt like a cruel joke, but in this moment of helplessness, he let go.

What happened to Jade might not be his fault. What was happening to Emmie might not be his fault. He could let go of any imagined part that he might have in the world's cruel twists. But he'd be damned if he was going to stand by and watch it happen. This pendulum was going to swing, goddammit.

Max searched the streets for the rusted-out sedan. He rolled down his windows and listened for the roar of its engine. His head turned left and right as he coasted through intersections, not bothering to slow when lights turned from green to gold.

Max wished he could call Dan. Dan was familiar with that Jimmy guy. He might know where to find this Nick Peters. All Max had to go on was a vague reference Emmie had made to a convenience store on Hiawatha Avenue, near where Nick lived. *Near where Nick lived.* It was something at least, but Hiawatha stretched for at least five miles.

Max left the downtown and followed the long avenue to its end, then checked his rearview mirror. When he saw that the road was clear, he cranked the wheel into a U-turn that left his tires skidding sideways toward a snowbank. He drove the whole length of Hiawatha again, crossing Washington, then Park.

He was going fast. Too fast, given the number of cars out on the streets now that people were getting out of work. Max took a right-hand turn and sped down an empty street past a construction site. The blur of a chain-link fence was crossing his periphery when suddenly a small shape hurled itself out from behind a dumpster and into the road.

Max cursed, and his body lurched backward against the seat. He cranked the wheel to miss the figure and skidded sideways. Max shielded his face with his arm as his car crashed into the chain-link fence. He fumbled with his seat belt, then flung open his door to find himself standing in a dream. Or rather, a nightmare.

Emmie lay in the snow, alongside a shovel caked with dirt. Her face was turned up toward the sky, but her eyes were closed. She was completely still, with her dark curls spread out against the snow. Max's heart stuttered. *Not again. Not again.*

Max dropped to his knees. "Emmie! Oh my God, Emmie!"

Her eyes opened, and she blinked twice. Max exhaled, but his relief was short-lived. There was a welt on her cheekbone with the distinct shape of two fingers.

"What happened?" he asked, gingerly touching her face. "Who hit you?" It was taking everything in him not to go nuclear.

"Max? Oh my God, Max. I can't believe it's you." She was already starting to get to her feet.

"Careful. Don't move too fast," Max said as he worried about her neck. Her back. He checked for blood. Finding none, he lifted her shoulders out of the slush. Where was her coat? "I could have killed you! Let me get you into the car." He glanced up to check for cars, but it wasn't a main street and there was only cross-traffic.

"You didn't hit me. I slipped. I'm f-fine."

She didn't look fine to Max. *How could this be happening? Again?* He wrapped an arm around her back as if she wasn't capable of standing on her own. "What happened? How did you get here?"

Emmie pushed at his chest and glanced over her shoulder at the two-story building. "We have to get Angie out of there."

Max followed her line of sight, then redirected her away from the building and back toward his car. "No way. *We're* leaving." She must have hit her head on the ground. She wasn't thinking clearly. He was going to have to take better control. He needed to get her somewhere safe.

"Max," she said, stopping him. "I need your help."

Max hesitated. For Emmie to suggest she couldn't do something on her own said more than those four words ever could. And for her to ask him to help her…It was something he could not refuse. Against his better judgment, he would help her. He would help her, and he would hope for the best.

CHAPTER THIRTY-FIVE

THERE YOU ARE

Emmie picked up the dirty shovel and led Max across the street toward a storefront, which was when he finally saw the Gold Pedal logo that he'd been looking for before. She pulled him down a driveway that cut between the bike shop and a grocery store.

Max followed behind her, scraping the back of his hand along the brick wall as they trailed it. She was alive, and he'd go anywhere she led him. He cringed at all the horrible places his imagination had taken him. To be standing now in the snow—so white in the sunlight that he was nearly blinded—was like a miracle.

"Remember how you said I calmed you down?" Emmie asked, still walking ahead of him.

"Yeah," Max said, though he wasn't so sure her magic was working on him right now. The welt on her left cheekbone still had his muscles tight and bunchy in his arms.

"Well, forget that," she said. "I don't want to see it. I want to see you in all your badass glory."

Max stopped in his tracks and yanked back on her arm. "We need to get help."

"Then call someone." She glanced up and over her shoulder at the second floor of the bike shop as if she expected someone to be coming down the stairs.

Max groaned. "My phone's dead."

Emmie barely reacted. "Doesn't matter."

"But I did talk to your dad."

"Good," she said, surprising him. He thought she'd be mad that he'd told her dad anything. If she was coming around on him, then maybe Max could convince her to go back to his car. They could wait there for help. But one look at her face told Max that they weren't going to wait.

"My dad'll have an idea about where we are, but please, Max. We can't wait for him. We have to get Angie out of there." She glanced up at the fire escape.

"How many people are up there?" Max asked.

"Two, not counting Angie. Frankie and Nick. Jimmy left, but he'll be back if he isn't already."

"I don't like those numbers." Max needed Chris. Jordy too. He probably wouldn't stand a chance three-on-one. And if he was looking out for Emmie, too, it would never work.

"I'm not sure...Nick may be unconscious," Emmie said. "And Frankie's about a hundred and forty pounds soaking wet."

Max clenched his teeth at the sound of his name. *Nick.* The bastard who'd dragged Emmie into this in the first place. "Why is he maybe unconscious?" He braced himself, in anticipation of her answer.

"Remember plan B?"

Max clenched his teeth. He hated the idea of Emmie having to fight her way out of trouble. He didn't like the thought of this Nick putting his hands on her again.

"I think Nick hit his head."

Max felt the anger stirring again inside him. Still, Max did everything he could to keep calm. He needed a cool head if he was going to get them out of here. Mentally, he started John's counting exercises. *One... two...three...*

"How'd you get out here, Emmie?" a guy's voice said behind Max, and Emmie's face paled. Max spun around, his body naturally falling into a hockey stance. It was the guy he'd seen before when they were shoveling, same flat-billed cap. Same puffy jacket. But this time he was standing on the sidewalk, holding a pizza box.

Emmie stepped in front of Max, like she was going to defend him or something. She could be an idiot, but God, he loved her for it.

"We're getting Angie," she said. She stood with her feet wide, her shoulders squared. Though Max was behind her, he could picture her face set with determination.

"Like hell you are," Jimmy said, dropping the pizza box.

Emmie took a half step toward him, with the shovel half-cocked like a batter getting ready to bunt. When Max realized that Emmie had planned to bust into the apartment—alone—armed with only a shovel, the turmoil inside him started to rumble. Still, he held back. If they could talk their way out of this, they would.

But then the guy made one critical mistake. He grabbed the front of Emmie's coat. Max's face went red-hot, but his vision didn't go to black.

And then Max leveled him. Emmie looked down at Jimmy, who lay prone in the snow.

"There you are," she said with a sigh of relief. "I was wondering when the real Max Shepherd was going to show up." She grabbed Max's hand and started running again.

"Emmie—" Max glanced behind him. Jimmy was out cold.

"Our odds just got better. Let's get Ang out of there."

Max followed her up the fire escape, looking down occasionally to

275

judge their distance from the ground. When she whipped open the door, the smell of sweat and stale beer flooded over Max's face. The room was dark, and it took his eyes a while to adjust.

The first thing he noticed was a metal trunk covered in crushed beer cans and a half-empty bottle of brown-colored liquor. The second thing he noticed was a dingy blue mattress in the back right corner and, on the floor beside it, a man lying facedown on the cracked linoleum.

Emmie didn't pay the guy on the floor any mind, instead turning toward the closed door to their left. Behind it, a girl moaned in pain. The sound shot through Max's chest as cleanly as a bullet. Emmie reached the door and shook the locked doorknob in her hand. "Angie!" she screamed.

There was scraping sound on the other side of the door, and a loud thud that shook the wall. A male voice from inside the room exploded in a string of epithets.

Fear spiked Max's gut as Emmie dropped the shovel and pulled up her knee, punching the heel of her foot to the door, right under the doorknob. It was only a hollow-core door, but she couldn't weigh a buck twenty. Did she seriously think she was going to kick it down?

Max lurched forward, his hand on her shoulder, and pulled her back. He slammed his shoulder into the door, as if facing an opponent on the ice. The door bent inward, but not enough. He reared back and rammed his foot under the doorknob where Emmie had tried it. The lock snapped, and the splintered door swung open.

Inside, a picture of a mountain landscape and a small lamp lay shattered on the floor. Among the broken glass, Angie struggled with a guy who held her by her hair.

"Frankie!" Emmie cried. "Let go of her."

A swollen lump bulged under Angie's eye. That could have been Emmie, Max thought. Or worse—because Frankie was holding a knife in his other hand.

Rage shot through Max. It was a familiar feeling—one that he felt on the ice when someone took a cheap shot—and it was one that he would not suppress. Not this time. His response was quick. He shot forward, grabbing Frankie's shoulder and checking him against the wall. Frankie spun but still managed to lift the knife, his hand swinging backward over his head. Before he could bring it down, all of Max's athletic instincts kicked in. He bowed at the waist, avoiding Frankie's sweeping stab toward his shoulder.

While both of them were at their most vulnerable position, Emmie kicked the back of Frankie's knee and brought him down just like Chris had gone down on the ice. Max couldn't believe how well she executed it, and it made his chest overflow with pride.

The knife dropped to the floor and spun like the dial of a compass as it skittered across the floor. Max snatched it with one swipe of his hand, then raised it high in the air so there was no chance of Frankie getting it again. Not that it looked like he was getting up anytime soon.

Emmie grabbed Angie by the arm, yanking her off the floor. "Let's go!" she yelled. But just then, the door that led to the fire escape burst open, sending a wide path of light across the main room.

"Jimmy!" Emmie gasped, and Max spun around, brandishing the knife at chest level. But it wasn't Jimmy.

"Police!" a voice yelled. Then another, "Drop the knife. Hands on the wall."

And that's when Max saw his whole life get checked against the boards.

He had no history with the police. No reason to think the worst, except that that's what he expected from life. And he knew how this scene must look. He was standing there with a knife slipping from his fingers. It clattered against the floor. He was going to be arrested for assault with a deadly weapon. Associating with drug dealers. He'd be off the team. Out of school. No tournament. No scholarship.

He hadn't planned for this day to turn out like this. Hell, they were supposed to be going out for dinner. He was supposed to be wolfing down pad thai.

Emmie looked at Max with the same calm she always showed. Max had no more inkling of what was going on in her head than he'd had the first time he met her, but one look at her told him that everything was going to be all right.

CHAPTER THIRTY-SIX

NOT GOING ANYWHERE

THREE DAYS LATER

Nick, Frankie, and Jimmy were still in custody and would be for a long time. Nick Peters had been scheduled for the new trial he wanted, but now with added charges for kidnapping, drug manufacturing, drug possession, assault, and attempted murder—though Emmie knew that last one would never stick.

Jordy, Lindsey, Chris, and Marissa were in Jordy's basement, playing *Call of Duty* and sitting on the two couches that were huddled around the TV. Max and Emmie sat together on a third couch in the back corner of the room.

Outside, the wind howled and sprayed an icy sleet against the walkout patio door. Inside, Marissa shrieked every time she dodged a bullet, and Chris was laughing his ass off, calling her a "newb."

Emmie couldn't believe she and Max were both here. Together. Unhurt. Hopeful. "You're still here," she said. She tried to fix his hair with her fingers, but then decided she liked it messy and rumpled it up again. "I keep waiting for you to come to your senses."

"Not likely. Not with you."

A whole bunch of sarcastic comments came to Emmie's mind, but they were overridden by a head full of romantic mush. Max might have been surprised to learn she was even capable of it.

Across the room, Chris yelled, "Duck! That guy's got a grenade launcher pointed right at you." And Marissa yelled back, "I can't figure out the right button." Max and Emmie glanced over at Chris and Marissa, then raised their eyebrows at each other. Something was going on between those two.

"You should play sometime," Max said, his fingers tracing the lines of her collarbone. "After your badassery the other day, you could totally manage a little *COD*."

"Yeah," Emmie said, and then she went quiet.

"*Now* what are you thinking?" Max asked. By this time, his hands had moved to her back, and he ran his fingertips up and down her spine. Her arms turned to gooseflesh.

"Dan," Emmie said with a shake of her head. Her father had talked to one of the arresting officers. Seemed Dan had been too ambitious with the amount of work he'd been taking on—supervising several juvenile day crews, plus an overnight work crew with adults. He'd been taking on more and more responsibility because he was up against someone else for department head when the current guy retired. Basically, Dan was looking for ways to stay alert.

Emmie's heart hurt. She'd seen drugs screw up too many lives, and she hoped that Dan would somehow find his way.

Max cursed under his breath. "If I wasn't so comfortable right now—not to mention a recovering maniac, who'd like to graduate from his program—I might track Dan down and beat him senseless."

"Probably not a good idea," Emmie said with a little smile.

"I wonder if Cardigan John knows yet."

They both fell silent after that, listening to their friends bicker and the sounds of grenades. The wind and sleet beat against the glass patio door. The light from the TV flickered across the darkened room, and Emmie let herself sink into the couch cushions, weighed down by the warm heat of Max's arms.

"I love you," he said, and his dark lashes lifted to reveal the honesty behind those words.

Emmie's breath caught in her chest. She wanted to say it back, but instead it came out as "I don't mind that."

"Me neither," he said, and it didn't seem to bother him that she hadn't said it back.

Max touched Emmie's chin with his fingers and tipped her head up toward his. Their eyes met for one long moment, and then he tipped his head, his mouth slanting against hers, taking the kiss to a whole new level. The taste of him drove Emmie a little insane, and so did the low growl he made at the back of his throat when she nipped at his lower lip.

Max reached to the back of the couch and pulled an afghan down over their bodies. They could have gone on forever. Emmie almost wished that they would. But then Jordy yelled, "Hey, get a room, you two. You're making it hard to concentrate on the game."

"Yeah?" Max said, turning his head toward his friends. "Well, it's only going to get harder from here."

There was a beat of silence, and then Chris, Jody, and Lindsey yelled out together, "That's what she said!"

Max pressed his forehead to Emmie's, and his whole body shook with silent laughter that went right through her, warming her from the inside out.

CHAPTER THIRTY-SEVEN

FOR THE LOVE OF THE GAME

THE NEXT AFTERNOON

"Hello?"

Emmie's head jerked up when she heard her mother's voice over the speakerphone. She'd wondered why her father insisted she sit with him in the kitchen while he made a phone call. Just to hear her mother's voice was a violation of the no-contact order, so she was surprised her lawyer father was allowing it. She mouthed the words *thank you.*

Her father blinked and cleared his throat. "Renee, it's Tom. Listen, I'm calling because I owe you an apology."

"I doubt that," her mother said, and Emmie was relieved to hear how good her voice sounded. Stronger. Healthier than she'd sounded in quite some time.

"Tom," her mother said, sounding startled, "do you have me on…?" She stopped talking then.

Emmie covered her mouth with her hand to tell her father she knew to stay quiet, even if her mom now guessed they were breaking the rules. Her father sat down in a chair next to Emmie.

Her mother carried on. "Tom, it's me who should be apologizing."

Emmie's father bowed his head. "I thought you had given our address out to some bad people. I was wrong about that. I shouldn't have blamed you."

Her mother didn't respond.

Emmie leaned forward and whispered in her father's ear. "Tell her I miss her. Tell her to get better."

Emmie thought she heard a whimper come through the phone. Despite Emmie's silent protest, her father filled her mother in on all that had gone down.

Emmie'd heard her mother cry before—usually when she was strung out or begging Nick for a fix—but never for anyone else. The sound made Emmie grip the table just to keep her body still and her voice quiet.

When it was over, Emmie sucked in a breath when she heard the words she so desperately needed: "I'm sorry. Will you tell her that for me, Tom? Please? Tell her...I love you, baby."

Emmie and her father locked eyes. "I can tell her that," he said, his voice softer than Emmie'd ever heard it before.

"I know I've still got a lot of work to do. On me. On us. I've done too much damage to just be...forgiven." The last word came out in broken syllables, as if she was ashamed of even suggesting the possibility. "But, Emmie?"

Emmie's head jerked up at the sound of her name.

"My baby?" The word sounded like a plea. "She needs to know I'm working on it."

"Yeah." Emmie's father's eyes were brimming. "I'll tell her, Renee. Take care of yourself. Goodbye."

Emmie sat back against her chair. It would be months before they'd be allowed to meet in person, and then only under supervision, but her mother's words left Emmie hopeful they'd put their relationship back together.

That hopefulness led to a happy afternoon, and that happy afternoon lent itself to an exciting two weeks as the White Prairie Jack Rabbits worked their way through the state hockey tournament, ultimately finding themselves in the championship game once again.

Emmie waited at the corner of the rink as the players did their warm-up laps around the oval. By now, she didn't even have to look for Max's jersey number. She could pick him out just by his posture, his gait, and the way he held his stick. Of course...there was also the way he slowed each time he passed her corner, turning his head in her direction.

Marissa found Emmie right before the teams took to their respective benches and the announcer called out the captains. "Should we get a seat? It's getting pretty crowded."

Emmie followed Marissa up into the stands and settled herself in between Marissa and Sarah. Olivia was there, too, plus another thousand more.

Olivia had a sign that said Kiss Me, I'm a Rabbit, which—Emmie guessed—had something to do with tonight being Valentine's Day. Sarah had a sign too. Hers said We're Quick as a Bunny, and she held it up over her head when John Tackenberg lifted his stick in the air to salute the crowd.

Marissa linked her arm through Emmie's, causing a sudden rush of warmth to flood Emmie's previously cynical heart. She belonged here. These were her people. And tonight she would be with Max. He'd asked her to go with him after the game to do something. Something important. Whatever it was, she was honored that he would choose to bring her along.

When the puck finally dropped, the crowd shot to its collective feet. Emmie had to stand on tiptoes to see over the heads in front of her. She searched the ice until she found Max, his head down, his body focused. Good. He looked good. He looked controlled.

The crowd roared in Emmie's ears. Sticks slapped at the ice. Bodies crashed against the boards. Men's voices shouted. Words meant for the players, the refs, and the coaches bounced off the plexiglass and back at the crowd.

The first period ended 0-0. So did the second. The teams were evenly matched, and Emmie wondered who'd be the first to break.

* * *

As the clock ticked down on the third period, Chris and Max were on the bench. "This shit is not coming down to a shootout," Chris said. Max nodded. The lines changed.

Chris sent Max a pass, and he curled the puck into himself, faking out a defenseman. He was heading down center ice, his blades cutting in with powerful strokes. He crossed the blue line and the rest of the team followed, finding their zones.

Chris found Max, who banged his stick against the ice with two sharp taps. Tack crossed in front of the goal, and Max blinked the sweat out of his eyes. A North High School defenseman followed Max along the edge of the boards, and then Max cut toward center.

His stomach clenched in anticipation because he saw his shot. If he didn't hesitate, it was his. His legs tightened, and his shoulders swung. Without really looking, he knew that Chris was reading him right. He blocked out his guy and positioned himself for the rebound, but Max knew he wouldn't need it.

With one powerful swing, his stick made contact with the puck and sent it flying. The goalie snagged it out of the air and tossed it aside for his Number Twelve, who took the puck back down toward White Prairie ice.

Max cursed under his breath, then gathered himself. There was still time.

Brody came in, battling Number Twelve along the boards. Chris poked the puck away from Number Twelve, but North's Number Three picked up the loose puck again and slid it along to his forward.

They were all down in the White Prairie zone now, but North's forward dropped the puck and Max picked it up. He brought it behind White Prairie's net and tried to deflect it out of the zone, but he was checked—hard—from behind by Twelve. Max's neck snapped back, and he hit the ice like he'd been dropped from a two-story building, so hard that it knocked his helmet off.

Number Twelve should have had a penalty, but there was no whistle. The crowd held its collective breath as Max was slow to his feet. Get up, he thought. Get up.

It took a second for Max to get his bearings. His head was spinning, and dark spots blossomed in front of his eyes. He got to his knees. When his vision cleared, he saw the puck, still in White Prairie's zone, held up in the corner by Twelve, with Brody on him like a tick.

Max had an existential moment, as if he was connected to everyone in the arena and could read their minds. They expected him to enter the fray. They expected him to explode on Twelve. But he held his position.

Number Twelve passed it off to Three in the center, but Jordy, who'd just got off the bench with fresh legs, stole the puck and passed it to Max who was coming up the center strong. Max snagged the puck and was moving fast on the breakaway back toward North's net, elbows out, legs pumping, the puck moving left, right, left, right, totally in control, in the sweet spot right in front of him. Max crossed North's blue line as the clock hit :05.

:04

Without his helmet, he felt weightless and fast.

:03

North's goalie found his stance, wide and imposing. He seemed to consume the entire net.

Max pulled back his stick and passed the puck to Jordy.

:02.

Jordy's blade made contact with the puck, sending it sailing and catching the only piece of net left uncovered. The goalie's head turned. His glove came up a second too late. The puck found the net, and the clock hit :00 just as the red flashing light started to swirl over the net.

Keller with the goaaallllll! The crowd went ballistic. Feet stomping on the metal bleachers, the band blasting out the school song, until the decibel level was so high in the arena that many had to cover their ears.

Jordy raced toward Max, and they fell together onto the ice, their teammates piling on top. Their weight above and the solid ice below made it hard for Max to force the air in and out of his lungs. But he decided it was the good kind of breathlessness, the kind that could make him feel crushed and yet weightless and so glad to be alive.

When the team finally let him up, the crowd was still going crazy. Max raised his fist in the air and found Emmie in the crowd. Her bright-pink cap was a beacon for him. And he couldn't help but notice that this time…this time she was on her feet, and for all the right reasons.

Max pointed to the corner of the rink where there was the break in the plexiglass. He hoped she'd understand.

It didn't take more than a second. Emmie nodded and shimmied past her friends, heading for the stairs. Max skated slowly away from his still-celebrating teammates, throwing off his gloves. He got to the corner first and watched with anticipation as the color pink bobbed through the crowd gathered along the edge of the rink.

When she made it to him, her cheeks were flushed and her eyes were bright. "Congratulations, champ," she said breathily. Her bare fingers clutched at the black netting that spanned the break in the glass.

"Damn straight," he said, then leaned against the boards, his face coming up against the net. Emmie did too. When their mouths met in one of the spaces, the net trapped between their foreheads and chins, Max kissed Emmie with everything he had, and she gave the same right back to him. It was both soft and frantic, and said everything they wanted to say but still never had. It could have gone on all night, but they broke apart when the band started to play.

Max glanced over his shoulder at North High School accepting their second-place medals. When he turned back toward Emmie, he had to laugh.

"Are you laughing at *me?*" she asked.

He nodded. "You've got crisscross marks all over your face. You look like a tic-tac-toe board."

"And now..." the announcer said.

"So do you," Emmie said. "Best put your helmet back on. I think you're going to be on camera."

"Nah," he said. "Let them see me."

"Give it up," the announcer said, "for the returning champions, *your* White Prairie Jackrabbits!"

Before Max skated back to center rink, he gripped Emmie's fingers through the net. "And then after this," he said, "you're still going with me?"

"Yes," Emmie said. "Anywhere."

CHAPTER THIRTY-EIGHT

GOODBYES

Large, wet snowflakes began to fall as Max and Emmie left the hockey rink, waving goodbye to Chris and Marissa, who were heading toward Chris's Subaru. Marissa still hadn't said anything to Emmie about what was going on with the two of them. Emmie glanced at Max, but he only shrugged.

By now, it was late in the evening, and the heater in Max's jeep was only doing a half-assed job. Emmie shivered, and Max reached out and wrapped his fingers around hers as he drove on in silence.

Emmie glanced over at him, and her heart did a neat little trick in her chest. He looked ruggedly handsome, particularly with his cheekbone bruised from when his helmet had been knocked off. But more than how beautiful he looked, what really took her breath away was the certainty that he loved her. He was *in* love with her. And she was nearly sure she could say it back if he ever said it again.

Worry crinkled at the corners of his eyes, leaving several thin lines that fanned away toward his temples. Emmie squeezed his hand and smiled reassuringly when he glanced over.

Fifteen minutes earlier, Max had emerged from the locker room, hair freshly shampooed under his knit cap, and told her he wanted to visit Jade's grave. She was surprised. But at the same time, she was happy he was ready to make this big step. And happy he wanted her to come with him. It was just one of the ways he told her he loved her.

"How you doing?" she asked.

He took his hands off the wheel, cupped them, and blew warm air into the hollow. "Okay. I think. I feel shitty that I haven't done this before, and it's making me nervous. I feel like she's going to chew me out when I get there. Is that weird?"

"No," she said. "I'd chew you out if you ignored me for a year."

"Not helpful," Max said with an eye roll.

"Just keeping it real," Emmie said, but she laughed too. "I *am* proud of you though."

A small smile touched the corners of his lips before disappearing. Emmie squeezed his hand again in reassurance.

By the time they arrived at the cemetery, the snow was beginning to accumulate. Max pulled a piece of paper out of his coat pocket and flattened it against the steering wheel. It appeared to be a hand-drawn map with some notations. Following the directions, he drove toward the back of the cemetery and took a left at a gnarled cedar tree, then around a curve to where the pavement ended.

Jade's grave was under a grove of three small pines that gave it enough protection from the falling snow so that her stone was still clear and her name was legible. Max parked on the shoulder, but he left the engine running. He didn't unbuckle his seat belt. Maybe it was enough to come this far. Maybe this was all he could do. The wind picked up and scattered a spray of tiny ice pellets against the windshield. A knot formed in Emmie's chest.

"You don't have to get out," she said. "Whatever you came to say, you

290

can say it from here, and you don't even have to say it out loud."

"No," Max said. "I need to do this right."

She understood. This whole year, Max had convinced himself that it was his fault, that it was because of his selfishness that a life was snuffed out. All this time, he'd been trying to right injustice, as he perceived it, wherever he found it, but it hadn't made any difference. It couldn't bring Jade back, and he'd had to learn to accept that. Life wasn't about what was fair. Sometimes, it just…was.

Emmie'd always understood that not everything in life could be controlled. Max said that was why he was attracted to her. It was why he wanted to be near her.

Several minutes passed and then, as if getting a signal that Emmie couldn't see or hear, Max opened the door. A blast of arctic air rushed into the cab, and Emmie pulled her hat down around her ears. Max slammed his door, then opened the back, taking out a sparkly plastic heart about the size of a dinner plate, mounted on a long stake. Emmie watched as Max walked to Jade's grave. He pushed the stake into the crusty snow, the red heart just breaking the crest.

He bowed his head and crossed himself. Emmie could see his lips moving. She could only imagine what Max was saying. Probably a lot of everything, lamenting how life could be cut so short. So wastefully. She'd thought for a second that she should have gotten out of the truck with Max, but now she was glad she hadn't. He needed this private moment to make his apology. To say goodbye.

After a bit, Max glanced over at Emmie. The questions and vulnerability in his expression were too much for her to bear. It broke her heart to see him in such obvious pain, and she quickly turned her head so he wouldn't see her cry.

When Max came back to the jeep, Emmie kept her head bowed, but she reached out her hand to hold his. Max drew in a deep, shattering breath, but didn't say a word. Emmie wondered if that was because he was still having his silent conversation with his girlfriend.

"I love you," Emmie whispered, not looking at him, until his silence caused her to finally turn her head. "And that's the cold, hard truth."

A small smile spread across his face. "I don't mind that," he said. "Not one bit." Then Max leaned over and kissed Emmie, and neither of them was cold anymore.

ACKNOWLEDGMENTS

This novel arose from my years as a juvenile public defender in Minnesota, so I must thank all the kids who shared so much of their lives with me (the good, the bad, and sometimes the very, very ugly). I hope you are all out there—somewhere—living beautifully triumphant lives now. Thank you for the inspiration. Thanks must also go to my literary agent (and favorite hockey mom), Jacquie Flynn of Joelle Delbourgo Associates, and to my editor, Wendy McClure, who led and prompted me through several rounds of edits and reimaginings. And finally, to my son, who didn't freak when catching me transcribing his gaming commentaries (seriously, my imagination has its limits). To the readers: thank you for reading my books and thereby letting me keep doing this weird thing that I love. It means the world.

FIRST SHE
WENT VIRAL.

THEN SHE
WENT MISSING.

GIRL
LAST
SEEN

HEATHER ANASTASIU
ANNE GREENWOOD BROWN

HC 978-0-8075-8140-7 • PB 978-0-8075-8141-4

READ *GIRL LAST SEEN* BY HEATHER ANASTASIU AND ANNE GREENWOOD BROWN

Kadence Mulligan's star was rising. She and her best friend, Lauren DeSanto, watched their songs go viral on YouTube, then she launched a solo career when a nasty throat infection paralyzed Lauren's vocal chords. Everyone knows Lauren and Kadence had a major falling-out over Kady's boyfriend. But Lauren knows how deceptive Kadence could be sometimes. And nobody believes Lauren when she claims she had nothing to do with the disappearance. Or the blood evidence… As the town and local media condemns Lauren, she realizes the only way to clear her name is to discover the truth herself. Lauren slowly unravels the twisted life of Kadence Mulligan and sees that there was more to her than she ever knew. But will she realize she's unknowingly playing a part in an elaborate game to cover up a crime before it's too late?

PRAISE

"Endlessly twisty, this deliberate head trip will keep readers guessing until the very end. The kind of dark, wild ride that begs to read in a single sitting."—*Kirkus Reviews*

"Intriguing from the start…A sexy, fascinating, fast-paced, and darkly dynamic mystery for teens."—*School Library Journal*

"Exhilarating and filled with twists and turns, the mystery lasts until the final page."—*Booklist*

"Bold, intriguing, and full of surprises. It's the kind of book that haunts you long after you put it down."—Kristen Simmons, author of Article 5 series and *The Glass Arrow*

"Everyone has a secret and no one can be trusted. Don't even think about starting *Girl Last Seen* unless you've got a few hours to spare: it'll keep you flipping pages into the wee hours of the night. Dark, fun, captivating."—Paula Stokes, author of *Liars, Inc.* and *This Is How It Happened*

ABOUT THE AUTHOR

Anne Greenwood Brown has written several novels for young adults, including the Lies Beneath trilogy and *Girl Last Seen*, which she cowrote with Heather Anastasiu. As an attorney, Anne worked as a juvenile public defender. She is a graduate of St. Olaf College and lives in Minnesota with her family. Visit her online at annegreenwoodbrown.com.